Johnny No Luck

Peter Harrison

ISBN No: 978.1.906542.30.6

Publishers: Barny Books
                Hough on the Hill
                Grantham
                Lincolnshire
                NG32 2BB

                Tel: 01400 250246
                www.barnybooks.biz

Other books written by Peter Harrison:

Hovis Brown   978.1.903172.91.9
The Hillbillies   978.1.903172.89.6
Street Life   978.1.906542.05.4

See page 278 for synopsis of these books

PROLOGUE

Sandy Baxter was top dog at Medomsley Young Offenders Prison. His real name was Simon Baxter. No one dared call him Simon. He was nothing special to look at; average height, average weight, carrot-topped, only it was shaved to the bone but even then the dull copper sheen covered his head. One of the youngest inmates at the Centre, Baxter was eighteen years old with severe mental problems. He loved films and was an avid collector of Hollywood trivia and autobiographies. On the surface he appeared controlled and ordered, his room was spick-and-span with everything in its allotted place. Sandy Baxter couldn't settle or sleep if a book had been moved minutely out of sync. Texts had to be placed in alphabetical order with identical authors in strict order of release date. Pride of place was the blown-up photograph of his sister above his bed. Simon Baxter adored her. One month into his sentence he had tried to choke someone who had poked fun at the photograph. He had a touch-paper temper and woe betide anyone who struck the wrong match.

Some of the less sympathetic inmates, said the youth lived in a world of fantasy because of his awful, abusive childhood. Rumours abounded that he came from a pig-sty of a home in Wolsingham, a small village west of Durham. It was said that his parents had systematically abused both Baxter and his older sister, Dottie. His father was a career criminal and a heroin addict, his mother a violent alcoholic. Both siblings tasted Council Care-Homes and protection-orders. Gossip hinted that Dottie escaped from the hovel when she was sixteen, took off with some criminal who lived near the coast, pulled herself out of the gutter and made something of herself.

Sandy Baxter had remained at home, perhaps too fearful of change, without the gumption and the guile of his sister. The youth stayed close to his home town and followed the usual apprenticeship of petty crime, progressed to stealing cars and moving drugs. He terrorized his village from the age of sixteen.

Sandy Baxter was a homosexual and didn't hide the fact. The first time Baxter saw John Briggs he wanted him. He always got his own way.

Both boys were on kitchen duty when the initial approaches were made. Clever too, Sandy talking to the small newcomer, asking all the right questions and making him feel wanted and part of the crowd. Then momentum shifted as Sandy told the youth he was lonely and needed a friend. The naïve John Briggs fell for the spiel, even showed him some deft moves with a football when they were in the gymnasium. Shared secrets with the young criminal too. '*York City approached first,*' he told Baxter. '*Hartlepool was another club, but I wanted to play for Sunderland. Only club in the world for me. Dad used to take me sometimes, used to talk about Colin Todd. Rated him as one of the best, said he ran the team like a general. Who is the best player in the world, who do you think, Sandy? Pele, Charlton, George Best? Disagree there, Sandy. Jimmy Greaves. Jimmy Greaves was a God. If he'd played in the world-cup there wouldn't have been extra time! He was injured! Same man could run circles around Geoff Hurst.*'

The initial flirtations were obscure, harmless but leading inevitably to an obvious conclusion as the Durham youth boasted of his knowledge of irreverent and fatuous cinematic gossip. '*You must have heard of Navarro?*' cited the ecstatic Simon Baxter. '*He was as big a star as Valentino.*' John Briggs had never heard of either silent legends but pretended otherwise. *'Ramon Navarro was the star of Ben Hur,'* said Baxter. John vaguely remembered the film, could have kicked himself when he mentioned the movie star, Charlton Heston, especially when he saw the tide of anger rise over his companion's sullen features. *'I'm talking about silent movies, Johnny!'* He continued spouting irrelevancies. *'Navarro was killed in the sixties by burglars who rammed a lead dildo down his throat.'* Baxter smiled at the image. *'The dildo was a present from Valentino.'* Then the punch-line was thrown to gauge John's reaction. *'I'd rather have the real thing, wouldn't you, John?'*

When the flirting became obvious, John retreated from the younger lad, careful not to offend him. He had heard all about his hysterical, uncontrollable temper. Hovered around other lads, played pool or table-tennis but even then the atmosphere was becoming uncomfortable as most of the inmates knew about Baxter's fixation. John withdrew to his room but the obsession ran unabated. Sandy was always calling, eager to talk, pushing and persuading. The older youth tried diplomacy, told him ever so gently that he preferred the company of females which led to the first assault. It was over in seconds. John Briggs was savagely beaten. It was the first time he had been knocked unconscious. Days later, further threats came from the bully.

In desperation, the young inmate spoke in confidence to one of the guards. He was laughed at; told it was rough justice. Spoke to another jailer who was more sympathetic to his plight. The guard listened but offered nothing positive. *'Johnny,'* he said, *'if I approach Baxter and warn him off, what's going to be the outcome? He'll find a way of damaging you, won't he? Use your head; you seem like a clever lad. Think of a way of persuading Baxter to find another bed-fellow.'*

John felt totally isolated. He had tried to find help and failed. He decided to meet fire with fire. John griped for days before naively telling inmates and guards how he intended stopping the harassment. Trouble was, John was not a violent man and had rarely brawled. He'd had the odd bloody nose from his father but that was all the ring-craft he knew.

The day before the incident, John Briggs reported sick and, after whining to the medic, was given tranquilizers. The same evening he was assaulted again. The humiliation was worse than the battering. John knew he had to do something. The next day he swallowed a mouthful of pills and began work in the kitchens. By 10.30am he'd finished washing-up. Close by were two other inmates mopping the floor; Sandy Baxter was one, Stan Beckett the other. John's head was fogged and fiery, he'd stolen whiskey from his cell-mate, Jason Ridley. The medication and the alcohol did little to lift his mood. He told himself it was time to act but lacked the courage to begin. He was too frightened, too fearful at challenging the psychopath so he stood, steel frying-pan in his hand, rooted to the spot.

'Hello, lover,' whispered Sandy Baxter. He had sneaked up close to the quaking youth who almost fainted when he felt the open palm caressing his rump. 'Changed your mind?' Baxter continued the harassment with a permanent smile over his hungry features. Suddenly, impulsively, John Briggs swung the frying-pan at the leering face and caught Baxter flush on the open mouth. Blood and teeth flew in all directions as the aggressor careered across the room then collapsed in a heap. John should have finished the task, it would have been easy for him to deal the finishing blows to end the battle but it was not his way, he was too placid, too caring by nature. He did the worst possible thing. Flinging the frying-pan across the room, John grabbed a wet cloth and went to the aid of the fallen youth.

Moments later Sandy Baxter recovered enough to struggle to his trembling feet, grab a heavy steel urn and battered the wailing victim to the floor. John Briggs was knocked out. The other inmate, Stan Beckett, who had watched the whole incident with unmitigated joy, suddenly realized that the tables were being turned and poor John was about to be seriously injured. He ran screaming from the kitchen.

Moments later two burly guards ran into view. They saw Baxter battering the victim's legs unmercifully with the metal frying-pan. Used like a truncheon, the weapon hammered at the unprotected knees, *'You'll never play football again, Johnny!'* screamed Baxter. *'Never walk again!'* Suddenly aware of the guards storming at him, Simon Baxter left the unconscious figure and ran at the jailers. He was lightning fast and wielded the weapon like an expert. One guard was felled immediately with a severely dislocated jaw; the other, with a broken arm dangling useless at his side, ran for his life.

Ten minutes later the mayhem was over. Tough as he was, Baxter was no match for half a dozen baton-wielding officers. Battered into defeat, he was handcuffed and frog-marched out of the kitchen. Defiant to the end, Simon Baxter lunged at the lead jailer and clamped his teeth on his unprotected arm. He was like a human pit-bull in his ferocity and determination and it took several powerful head blows to weaken his grip. He was still howling with rage when he was driven out of the ground for medical treatment.

Baxter was badly hurt in the attack. His skull was fractured, his cheek-bone crushed and, thanks to John Briggs, his teeth were bloodied stumps. He never returned to the young-offenders institution in Medomsley but was moved instead to Kirklevington, south of Middlesborough.

Because of his savage assault on the prison guards, Simon Baxter was given an extension to his sentence of eight months. For being instrumental in starting the fracas, John Briggs had his stay in Medomsley increased by an additional twelve months.

Outwardly it appeared that Briggs made a full recovery from the beating. He could walk, run and exercise but the aches and pains never left his knees. The teenager developed arthritis. His plans to pursue a career in professional football were abandoned; his dreams to play for his beloved Sunderland were at an end.

CHAPTER ONE

Frank Briggs squatted uncomfortable on the kitchen chair in the council semi in Moore Terrace, Shotton Colliery. He looked at his pendulous belly and sighed loudly. Promised himself he would definitely start the diet tomorrow. Expelling air like some giant bellows he began struggling with his shoe-laces. It was ten in the morning and the man had decided to spend a pleasant hour in the small allotment before returning home for dinner. Then it would be a quick change of clothing and an afternoon session at *The Comrades*. It was a daily ritual for the ex-miner. He liked routine.

Frank used to work at the coastal colliery of Dawdon, Seaham, three miles north-east of Shotton. That was a long time ago. The fellow was forty-eight, overweight and on long-term sick-benefit. There was nothing ailing Frank Briggs, he simply couldn't take the daily grind of employment. Told folk he had spinal trouble. Said it long enough and loud enough until he had fooled every naive doctor and specialist that ever treated him. Granted there were some days he could hardly get out of bed, but usually it was Saturday mornings when he'd had a skin-full of liquor the night before. Frank didn't grumble, he managed well enough on the weekly invalidity benefits from the Potto Street Post Office. Wasn't only the State Benefits that made him smile. There were the miscellaneous kick-backs from the state coffers - free prescriptions, free dental treatment and a boatload of tablets every few weeks that he sold to the local riff-raff for cash - that allowed him to enjoy the good life. Same daft Government even helped him buy a new motor every few years so naturally he believed in the Welfare State and the good old Labour Party. It was a double whammy for the

Government because his skiving wife, Elsie, also claimed Sickness Benefit. For the last ten years the woman had collected her sick-note proclaiming she suffered from depression. Frank and Elsie Briggs deserved Oscars for their roles as life-long fakers.

The man had sired two very different offspring. Robert, the oldest, was hard-working, mature and happily married. Staid and dull, and apart from a strong work ethic, he was a virtual clone of his father. John was something else; he was a feisty, irrational lad and lived life in the fast lane and, according to his father, had more in common with his wife's side of the family.

Elsie Briggs, short and solidly-built, wandered in from the living-room, "I'm worried about John," she said.

Frank, wheezing like a consumptive, lifted his sweating head and glowered at his wife. Didn't wait for an answer, 'Must cut down on the grub.'

"John's been through hell and high water," she repeated, "He's never been the same since Medomsley."

"Self inflicted woman!"

"He's your son," said Elsie grumpily, "all said and done!"

Frank stood, his jowly features blotched crimson. "He's a grown man," he answered, subconsciously pushing fingers through his thick oily locks. "Let him look after himself!"

"He's only a bairn, Frank."

The man was adamant, "Lead a horse to water, Elsie!"

"How can you talk about your own flesh and blood like that?" admonished the woman.

The man glowered at his wife, his head shaking with annoyance, "It's a pity he doesn't take after me."

"What are you saying, Frank?"

"You know fine well what I'm saying woman," said the man petulantly. "The little beggar takes after your side of the family!"

Elsie stood proud, arms over chest, pouted defiantly, "What's wrong with the Motsons?"

"You want me to talk about your brother!" mocked Frank. "There's not the hours in the day!"

"Leave Micky out of this, Frank," said Elsie, raising her voice. "He's had some bad luck is all!"

"Bad luck, you say," he whined sarcastically, "bad luck!"

"Yes, rotten luck!"

"How many times in prison, eh?" said Frank haughtily.

"Ran with the wrong crowd," said Elsie. "Micky has a heart of gold!"

"Just as well it's not made of gold," spat the man, "because he'd have weighed it in at the scrap-yard!"

"Shut up, Frank!"

"Same man would steal off everyone!"

"You wouldn't say it to his face," replied the woman defiantly. She pondered for a moment, "He's done you some good turns."

"All I'm saying is that John is as daft as!"

"He's nineteen, Frank!"

"Almost twenty!" derided the man. "And already father to three kids! Two of the brats to different women … and both of them under-aged when he made his mark! Married three years and two of those years locked up!"

Elsie grimaced but didn't retaliate.

"You'd think he had a hard paper-round!" commented Frank Briggs. He pulled on an ancient coat and strode towards the door. "He's the double of his Uncle Micky now that he's started to lose his hair!" Frank pondered before adding,

11

"Should take a leaf out of his brother's books! Robert's twenty-five and not a bit of bother!"

"John called in this morning for a cuppa. He's determined to get a job..."

Frank interrupted, "There's no chance of that!" A big fat smirk filled his bull-dog face, "Not after all the trouble he's caused!"

"He was always a good worker," replied Elsie proudly. "John was well-liked at Suncrest!"

"He's an ex-jailbird, woman!"

"Don't say that!"

Frank's reply was to open the back-door and break wind. "Back in about an hour, Elsie," he said. "Try and have dinner ready. I'll try one plate today, must cut down!"

Elsie Briggs walked into the living-room, grasped the copy of *Woman's Own* and moved towards the stairs. She glanced at the clock above the fireplace, it read 10.15am. She'd intended going to the Co-op first but then her stomach began to rumble in earnest. Elsie ponderously climbed the steep staircase, her head filled with thoughts about her youngest son, wondered if she should write any more letters to those football people, wondered if it was too late now for her son to be famous and rich. She sighed. It was too late, a year too late.

She pictured her brother, Micky Buff Motson, scourge of Wingate, once. Elsie's favourite, a few years younger and a character if ever there was one. He was full of life, bursting with energy and fun. Errol Flynn, her Dad had called him, Robin Hood of the colliery. He was a dashing, lovable lothario. Captain Blood himself, a brigand and a pirate, always in bother, always in scrapes, wild at school and ever wilder when he tried to find work.

Elsie reached the top of the steep staircase and gasped for breath. She wondered if she should join her husband and start dieting. The idea was pushed aside as she moved into the main bedroom and looked out of the window. With elbows resting on the window-sill she gazed across the garden and the street and thought about her brother. Visits went down the plug-hole once he attached himself to the Middlesbrough girl. He drifted apart then and started running with the wrong crowd. She whispered his name and agonized. The years in prison had changed Micky so much.

*

John Briggs couldn't return to his old job at the factory once he had been released from prison, he didn't want the flack from his former work-mates so he applied for a job at Easington Colliery. At the interview he omitted to mention his time in detention at Medomsley Young-Offenders' Institution. Told them he wanted to leave Suncrest Fire Surrounds because he had a young family and needed a bigger wage packet. *'Don't mind working a shift system,'* he'd told the overweight, lecherous-looking, training officer. *'And weekend work will be a piece of cake.'* He stood humble, his stomach on fire with nervous apprehension as he watched Gilbert Pawden, the colliery recruitment-officer, solemnly scan his glowing, fraudulent, reference from Suncrest.

Alice Drinkwater, almost nineteen, had been employed at the same firm as John Briggs. She worked in the office complex and John laboured on the factory-floor. It was Alice who had supplied the letter-headed paper and written the fake testimonial. The pair had known each other for years, attended the same school, same class too, and had been friends for ages. Before his incarceration, John could sense that Alice wanted him and had taken advantage of her good nature. The pair enjoyed a passionate ten minutes in the larger-than-normal invalidity lavatory on the ground floor of the factory. Their shift was over, and apart from the cleaners who were at the far end of the complex, they were alone. *'I'll do anything for you,'* she promised. He remembered Alice saying that as she stared wide-eyed in amazement as John unzipped his pants. *'God,'* she'd gasped with incredulity, *'it's right what they say about you, Johnny!'* So naturally, months later and free from jail, young John Briggs had reminded Alice Drinkwater of her promise. She was straddled over his car at the time, gasping with pleasure, *'Yes! Yes!'* she cried and John didn't know if she was talking business or pleasure at the time. However, the very next day she fulfilled her oath and a well-written, up-to-date reference was handed to the smiling youth. He gave his solemn vow to meet up with her the very next week.

Gilbert Pawden, N.C.B. Recruitment Officer, was in his early forties. He eased his ample frame on to the office desk and looked again at the young man. Saw the bulge in his trousers and gasped with pleasure. He was swayed, especially when the youngster smiled innocently at him and looked too long into his eyes. Gilbert asked if the newcomer was literate and handed him a standard file full of miscellaneous safety and warning signs relevant to the colliery. He listened patiently as the recruit whizzed confidently through the miscellaneous lists.

"Fine, fine," said Gilbert, "you can read!"

"I really need the work, Mr. Pawden," begged John Briggs, using a little psychology to oil the cogs.

The teenager was on his best behaviour. He smiled constantly at the man and was attentive and charming; he fawned and grovelled as if his future depended on it. The mind games worked because the colliery official decided to hire the lad. Pawden looked at the wall clock and realised he would have to act quickly. An hour ago a dozen newcomers' had started their initial five days training at the pit. He knew if he didn't allow the youngster an immediate start there would be a three month delay before the next recruitment.

He waltzed out of the dusty office and into the enormous acreage of the colliery grounds and gestured for the lad to follow.

"Have I got the job, Mr. Pawden?" John asked.

"Start today, if you want," said the recruitment officer. "You're only an hour late."

Gilbert Pawden was right of course. Moses Harris was still in the canteen with the youngsters, drinking tea and telling tall tales. He'd taken the recruits on a slow circuit around the main areas of the colliery: the lamp-cabin, timber-yard, pit-showers and the like. After refreshments the old man would show the kids the stores where they would be decked-out with heavy boots and overalls. After a few minutes of harmless banter he would take the newcomers to the belts and let them see first-hand a bit of grafting. Had the spiel all ready, *'Only way to separate the shite from the coal!'* he'd spout. Might let a few of the bigger kids stand next to the moving conveyor-belt and grapple with the huge chunks of slag that was mixed with the coal. Always good for a laugh seeing smart-arse younguns pissing their pants as they heaved and strained to remove the stone. Half an hour of make-believe and then it was back to the canteen sharpish and a slap-up lunch. Moses Harris, understandably, liked his job.

At 4.40pm John Briggs walked into the terraced house in Victoria Street, Shotton. It was late afternoon. He had left the house at 9.30am that morning having told Iris, his young wife, he needed to find work. The television was blasting away to an empty room so he walked towards the kitchen. His two boys were sitting at the kitchen-table with their mother watching the second television. The canary-yellow portable, volume full-on and showing cartoons, was positioned precariously on top of the microwave. John pushed his head into the smaller room and forced a smile at the sombre face of his annoyed wife.

"I'm back," he said.

The boys ignored their father and sat mesmerized watching the television. Iris shrugged her shoulders, folded her arms over her prodigious chest and stared icily at her husband.

John sighed, backtracked into the living-room and switched off the television. He slumped on to the sofa and closed his eyes. His head was pounding like a jungle-drum. Iris, a seventeen year old seductress, followed him and stood next to the settee. She was still wearing her dressing-gown, slippers too; pink and fluffy, like Iris. Loved John Briggs to death but didn't trust him. She had reason enough.

"Where the hell have you been?" she snapped. Didn't draw breath, "You've been out all day! You know I have shopping to do at Peterlee!"

John opened his eyes and nodded grudgingly. "Missed you too!" he spat.

"Well?"

Pushing aside the migraine he said, "I got a job at the pit."

"A colliery!" replied Iris incomprehensibly. "Which pit is that? Shotton Colliery has been closed donkey's years?"

"Easington," he said wearily. "I've worked all day!"

Iris took the news like a pinch of salt. "Hang on," she mocked, "I'll get you a medal!'

"Hell of a greeting, Iris!"

16

Wily Iris didn't rise to the bait. She took off her dressing-gown revealing a black bra with contrasting white knickers and reached for the dress draped across the back of the settee. It took her seconds to dress.

"Be an hour," she said, 'Ma's taking me." Added firmly, "The bairns need a bath, okay?"

Iris grabbed her coat and was out of the door before he could think of an answer.

John shook his head dejectedly. His life was a mess and it was all his own doing. A few short years ago he had imagined his life was going to change, thought he was going to be a star, the next George Best but the enforced holiday at Medomsley Young Offender's Institution changed everything.

Eddie, three years old and a chip off the old block, interrupted his thoughts. "Dad, Frank has thrown his fish-finger sandwich on the floor!"

John trudged into the kitchen and turned down the volume of the portable. The young tike followed his father.

"Can't hear!" shrieked Eddie.

Little Frank screamed in agreement.

John grimaced. He cranked up the volume, picked up the discarded sandwich, found a biscuit for his youngest and retreated back to the living-room. The food was delicious, still hot and soaked with butter. Three mouthfuls and it was gone. He stretched out on the sofa and closed his weary eyes. In the background he heard the kids arguing. He cared less; he was drifting and thinking of the prison again. Didn't know how he survived. Subconsciously he touched his balding pate and winced with the pain of hair-loss. He was touching twenty and almost bald. Blamed the lock-up, the abuse, blamed everyone, especially the young babysitter, Julie Brooks, whose accusations had sent him to prison. Julie was a tease and had made it known she wanted him. *'Let me baby-sit, Johnny.*

We'll think of something, eh? Iris likes me, she has no idea about us!' And she was certainly no virgin, the young temptress was proud of her prowess. Shameless too. *'Swear to God, Johnny, you're only the third!'* The trial judge, out of touch with reality and out of time with colliery mischief, had smugly labelled him a pervert and a lecherous destroyer of young lives. *'Thirteen years of age!'* he had pronounced grimly. *'You are nothing but an animal!'* A long stretch inside Medomsley Prison followed which turned out to be a nightmare for John Briggs. Medomsley, with its lack of discipline and gung-ho attitude from the guards, was hell on earth for the teenage tear-away. *'And what do you want me to do, Briggs?'* barked one insensitive warder when the youth confessed his fears. *'Shall I guard your arse all night?'* He blamed himself of course, lived for the thrill of the chase, been that way since he was eleven years old when hormones first kicked his head into overdrive and led him a fine dance ….

"Dad!" screamed the youngest of the boys, shaking at the spread-eagled figure on the sofa.

It was Frank, his precocious two years old and with a tan impervious to seasons. John used to call him his little *Paki* friend until ructions and recriminations with Iris made him bite his tongue. Young Frank was naked and dripping-wet.

John struggled out of the stupor and observed the soaked carpet.

"Daddy, Eddie peed on me!"

Still groggy, the young father stumbled to his feet and followed the distressed child up the staircase.

"Eddie pushed me!" said the child, glancing back at his father. "Hurt me, Daddy!"

"The little bugger!" grunter John.

"Peed in the bath, Daddy!" wailed the child. "On me!"

Johnny Briggs shook his head, "I'll knock his head off!" he said loudly.

The infant started to cry. He stopped and put his hands over his face, "Want Mom!" he cried. "Want Mom now!"

Father and son stood poised halfway up the stairs when the offender appeared on the landing. Eddie had his arms clamped on skinny hips. He was defiant and ready with the denials.

"Not true Dad!" shrieked Eddie. "He peed on me first! Stood up in the bath and aimed at me!"

The front-door suddenly cranked open and Iris struggled in with bags of groceries. Cries of protest erupted from the boys.

"It was him, Ma!" shrieked Eddy and started jumping on the spot.

"No! No!" cried Frank, tears falling like rain, closest to his Mother and possible punishment. "It was him, Ma!"

"What the hell is going on, Johnny?" shouted Iris. She stood at the bottom of the stairs and stared incredulously. Her eyes darted from a naked, dripping Frank to the nude, foam-covered Eddie. "Can't I leave you for a minute?" she bellowed at her husband.

John Briggs could take no more. His temper broken, the youth charged down the steps and ran out through the open door. It was raining cats and dogs and he had no coat. He cared less.

Only then did Iris place the bags on the floor. Shook her head, resigned to the fact that marriage was mayhem and her mother had been right all along.

"What the hell happened, you two?" she bellowed.

The screaming and accusations started again.

**

CHAPTER TWO

Edwin Butler, twenty-eight years old and office manager for Suncrest Fire Surrounds based in Peterlee's North-West Industrial Estate, stomped back to his office. He had spent an unsuccessful morning accusing nine office workers of providing ex-employer, John Briggs, with forged references. Over the top when he sidelined a fuming Alice Drinkwater and asked her the same question and received the same frosty reply. The office girls were unanimous with their denials.

Butler was adamant he would find the guilty party. No joy from his investigations in the office so he turned his attention to the factory floor. Three cleaners had access to the complex so he escorted the trio to the office complex, stood them next to the photo-copier and started the interrogation. The psychology did not work. After ten minutes of barracking and accusations the young manager threw in the towel and stormed back to his small office.

Nothing, not even a hint, mused a fuming Edwin Butler, standing like a sergeant major, arms behind his back, glowering at his staff. *Briggs must have stolen letter-headed paper last year before he was locked up for raping that child.* Butler had never warmed to the gregarious, popular labourer from nearby Shotton, and if truth be told, his feelings were tempered with a heavy cloak of jealousy. Everyone liked the testosterone-charged Briggs and it irritated the young manager to the point of distraction. After all, the fellow was a common labourer without a single qualification to his name. Edwin Butler had heard all the office gossip about the pint-sized lothario. Briggs was liked by everyone; he was witty, honest and with a heart as big as a diamond. *There's no accounting for taste,* he thought. Before the debacle of the court case,

Edwin had tried every way to dishearten the factory worker. He'd altered the shift system periodically so as to dishearten the man. Asked him to start early and finish late, even ordered him to work outside in all weathers. His efforts to oust Briggs failed. The youth took it all with a smile on his angelic face. When the gory details of Briggs' indiscretions made headlines, Edwin Butler was ecstatic. Didn't need to sack him, left it to the police instead. '*Good riddance to bad rubbish,*' he told his staff but instead of agreeing with him they sympathized with the pedophile who was rightly imprisoned for his heinous deeds.

He sat at his desk and gazed around the room, looked lovingly at his framed qualification: Birmingham University. *B.A. (Hons.) Accounts and Financial Management.* The award made him smile with pride; after all, he did possess the only degree in the factory. He thought again about the phone-call from Easington. Some chap in charge of recruitment at the local coal mine had queried the reference held by a certain J. Briggs. Edwin Butler had almost choked at the news. Didn't mince his words when he informed the fellow that the glowing testimony was a blatant forgery. The despicable Mr. Briggs had lasted precisely one day at the colliery and it made Edwin Butler smile.

He thought about Alice Drinkwater, so young and beautiful, a truly wonderful creature who confessed her love for him. Loved him truly, madly, deeply. Said she didn't care if he had thinning hair and thick spectacles, and wasn't the least bothered about his *Audi* or his detached house in Peterlee. Told Edwin he was her soul mate. Meant it too. He was so fortunate finding someone as special; a virgin still, nineteen years old and still untouched! He stole a glance through the glass-door and saw Alice stooping over the photo-copier. He gasped at the perfection, at the exquisite shape of her rump. Edwin closed his eyes and imagined what it would be like, *I love you Alice Drinkwater,* he mused, *truly, madly, deeply!*

*

"You've really messed-up this time, Johnny!" said Iris. She stood next to the window of the terraced property in Victoria Street, "You need to find work!"

John Briggs was livid, couldn't understand his bad luck. Hired Monday and sacked Tuesday, his tenure at the mine dead and buried before he could draw breath. It had to be some kind of record. The girl at the end of the phone had been terse and condescending as she demanded an explanation about his faked testimonial. John spluttered feeble excuses and hung up. His mining career was over before it started.

Grabbing the packet of cigarettes he flipped the lid. The box was as empty as his wife's head. John threw the packet into the blazing grate and inadvertently gave him an excuse to get away from the house.

"John!" Iris took the last cigarette from her painted mouth and offered it to him, "You'll have to do something!"

"I'll go to the Paki's, then I might call in and see Ma. See what the chat is, eh?" He accepted the fag-end.

"What about going to the dole-office," asked Iris. "Try and sort out your benefits?"

"Got no petrol in the Mini," he complained.

She found her purse and handed over coins. She would try anything to goad John into action.

"After I see Ma," he said flippantly, "I'll have a drive to Peterlee. Might be a job waiting for me."

John wouldn't hold his breath. Not many firms hired jailbirds. He knew that for a fact. He'd spent all of the previous Friday, cap in hand, hawking around the industrial estate, escorted by Likely Lads, Delbert Hancock and Timmy Turten. They reached the third factory and struck gold. Fisher-Price was hiring. Two of the youths were successful and one was refused. The only one who wanted a job was quickly shown the exit-door, the firm averse to convicted felons loose on their premises. The management didn't say as much but John could read their thoughts during the embarrassing interview. His two friends, older by one year, had never worked since leaving school. They had accompanied him as a favour. John Briggs was understandably nervous after his long stint at Medomsley and sorely in need of company. Delbert and Timmy almost wet themselves with laughter when they walked away from the toy-factory with the definite offer of employment. *'Work for a living!'* they said. *'Legitimate graft, that'll be the day!'* Between them they owned a clapped-out truck and did the odd bit of scrap, cleaned the occasional garden and all for cash-in-hand. The pair bought and sold, moved stolen property, drugs, drink … any mortal thing, without qualm or conscience.

It was after the embarrassing episode at the Fisher-Price Factory that John formulated his plan for obtaining a dodgy reference. He knew there was no other way to hide his stint in prison, no legitimate excuse to explain his long absence. Conniving Johnny was resolute when he drove the short distance to Suncrest Fire Surrounds and begged Alice Drinkwater for the forged testimonial. The strategy had almost worked.

He thought of Alice Drinkwater and wondered about possible repercussions. John quickly dismissed the thought. Alice had her head screwed on the right way. Same female could talk her way out of a paper-bag. No one would suspect the boss's fiancé of such underhand behaviour.

"Johnny, you won't forget,?" reminded Iris, desperate for her young husband to secure employment, needing the security of a weekly wage-packet.

No one knew more than Iris about surviving without a bread-winner. Iris had gone through hell and high water struggling to make ends meet when John was in prison. It had been a horrendous time for her trying to put bread on the table. She had two hungry kids to feed and clothe and bills to pay. Iris had played the devil's fiddle and danced a wicked jig to keep afloat. If John ever found out what she'd done to keep a roof over her head he would have a coronary. Temper like John's she'd have had to leave the area.

He said determinedly, "I'll get a job, I promise!"

Handing back the remains of the cigarette John left the house. He wanted to go to bed and sleep away the misery but knew he couldn't. The rain slapped and riled him and made him curse. He drove the decrepit motor to Brunton's Garage, bought £2.40 worth of petrol and watched the look of disapproval on the girl's face. He was past caring. About to climb in the Mini when Dean Crumplin's coal motor chugged into the forecourt. An idea hit him.

"Dean," he shouted, watching as the grey-haired man struggled out from the lorry. "Hello!"

"Johnny, you little rascal," said the coalman.

Dean Crumplin looked as if he had the world's problems on his broad shoulders. He limped to the pumps and started filling the tank with diesel. Used to work at Horden Colliery years ago. He was a coal hewer then, a big-money earner until the nasty accident finished his career. It was the end of the road for the collier. Dean took compensation and went self-employed. A decade later the fellow still walked with a definite limp and chewed on tablets all day long to stifle the pain.

"Days like this, Johnny," he muttered as the rain bounced and splattered its presence. "I could pack it all in!" He looked like he sounded, exhausted and weary.

"Dean," said the youth desperately. "I've tried everywhere for a job. Don't suppose you'd be hiring anyone?" He saw the look of surprise filter across the man's features.

"You want a job?" replied the coal-man.

Dean Crumplin had a busy schedule. Every day he visited the nearby collieries of Shotton, Wingate, Wheatley Hill, Thornley and Ludworth. Peterlee if he was lucky. The man worked day and night. Lived on painkillers, a packet a day, some days, two. The previous evening he'd returned to his ex-council house in Salter's Lane in Shotton at 8.45pm, too tired to watch television. He had washed then struggled to his bed. Lived alone since his wife Beatrice ran off with Sammy Bruce, a miner from Blackhall. *Sammy Bruce,* thought the coalman at the time, *another pal!* Beatrice had warned him enough. *'Work, bloody work!'* she'd moaned. *'What about us, you want to be the richest man in the graveyard?'* That was ten years ago. Since then his love life had been erratic to say the least. He knew his health and looks were on the wane, so he took what he could, paid for it too, sometimes in kind ... delivered coal to customers and occasionally didn't charge. Until three weeks ago he was seeing Iris Briggs. Minutes earlier, when the youth had approached him, he'd almost had a heart attack. If he had been fit he would have run. Dean Crumplin was weighed down with guilt.

He felt a little better now, realizing the lad had no idea about his gallivanting. Dean looked at the youth and was touched with remorse. The kid had been dealt a bad set of playing-cards. Nothing had gone right for him. Everybody in the colliery knew about John. He had married way too young, lacked common sense and had little parental guidance. Frank Briggs, the boy's father, was a bottle short of an alcoholic. Any decent father would have warned his son against marriage, Christ, the lad had just left school. Then John's little fling with the schoolgirl proved his downfall. The Lolita, thirteen going on thirty, with her short skirts and come-hither looks had been some baby-sitter. The only time she'd been properly dressed was when she attended court. Fooled no one but the silly old judge. Poor lad lost his job and scuppered his chances of playing professional football when he was locked up. Dean sighed, even he'd taken advantage. He looked at the lad and cringed with remorse.

"I'm not sure," said the coal-merchant.

Dean was soaked to the skin. He pondered, wondered if perhaps he could use the lad, let him do the heavy work, the fetching and carrying. He began to nod agreeably. The thought of sitting in the warm cab of the truck while the youngster grafted tickled his fancy. It would definitely make his days more acceptable.

"How much would you be willing to take, John?" he quizzed. Added cautiously, "I'm not a rich man, you understand?"

Dean Crumplin was probably the richest man in Shotton after Johnny Ridley, the local book-maker.

"I'll take anything, Dean," gasped an incredulous youth. John was desperate and it showed, "If you want, I'll park up the car and start now!"

"If I pay you basic, would you be happy with that?"

"Basic?"

"£100 a week?" said Dean Crumplin meekly. He waited for the protestations but when none came he crumpled. "Try it for a month and if you still like it, I'll increase it?"

John stuck out his hand, "Deal."

26

"Cash in hand for a couple of months, okay" offered the merchant. Cringing at the thought of paying the lad's National Insurance Stamp, he said, "It'll allow you to claim benefits."

"Thanks, Dean, you've saved my life."

A car-horn blared at them; an irate driver needed the pumps.

"I'll follow you back to Victoria Street," said Dean Crumplin. "Number 100, is it?"

"Thanks, Dean," said the naïve youth.

John Briggs climbed into the Mini and roared away, a smile etched across his wet features. Everybody knew where he lived; his prowess at football, his infamous reputation on and off the pitch made him known throughout the area. The smile turned into a wide grin. Things were improving.

The coal-wagon trundled behind the billowing exhaust of the youth's car. The older man cursed to the heavens, shook his wizened head from side to side and prayed that the youngster hadn't realized his error. Until Iris Briggs had approached him and made it obvious what she wanted, Dean Crumplin had never delivered to their door. Iris always bought off George Jones, Dean Crumplin's main rival in the colliery. Everybody liked George and it was easy to see why. The man was laid-back, gave credit when his customers were struggling, and even allowed payment on the never-never. The man, according to Dean Crumplin, was a fool, content to make enough to earn an honest crust. George Jones was without drive or ambition and made life difficult for bona-fide business folk. Dean demanded cash up front or he wouldn't drop as much as a nugget. He'd been stung too many times in the past with false promises and guarantees so he steered away from such dizzy dealings unless it concerned affairs of the heart. Payment by results was Dean's unofficial motto. Iris Briggs was in credit.

Minutes later the coal-wagon was heading for Victoria Street. Dean Crumplin prayed that young Iris could handle the situation.

**

CHAPTER THREE

Iris had left John asleep on the sofa. He had returned home a little before six-o-clock, the stresses and strains of the new job had left him exhausted and after wolfing his supper he collapsed on the sofa. An hour later, with the boys washed, fed and tucked up in bed, she slipped out of the house and headed for her parents' home.

Iris thought of the events of the day. It had been chaotic. John had run into the house bursting with enthusiasm about his new-found job. He had grabbed work clothes then disappeared through the open door. Iris watched him leap into the coal-motor like his backside was on fire. *Men,* she had thought at the time, *either up in the clouds or as flat as farts!* She had to wave him away to keep his spirits up and then that old rascal, Dean Crumplin, joined in the chorus by sounding his horn like some born-again boy-racer.

Before Iris met John Briggs she lived with her parents in Station Road next to the little church opposite the school and close to the recreation grounds. In her opinion it was the nicest part of Shotton, a bit up-market from Victoria Street. Lived there all of her life until she fell pregnant with Eddie. John Briggs' fault. He had plied her with drink and then had his wicked way with her. It was a nightmare. Iris was almost fourteen and pregnant. She had to tell the Social Services that she had been out celebrating with the girls and had succumbed to some stranger's charms. Couldn't say who the father was for obvious reasons. Eddie was John Briggs' son, she was sure of that. There was a nagging doubt about young Frank, however. That was the trouble with falling out with your boy-friend. At the time it felt like the end of the world for Iris, a definite slap in the face when she discovered John with his pants down once again. What a handful he was, had his priorities all wrong; football, his mates, floozies and then Iris. The order was back to front according to her. After one blazing row, fifteen year old Iris rebelled, kicked John into touch and had a fling with Maxi Stubbs. She had reason enough, heard that John was seeing Avril Jennings who was a year older than Iris and with a reputation as big as her bust. Avril's older brother, Jake, trying to win favour with Iris, had spilled the beans on his sister. Iris lost it good and proper, abandoned all plans with the despicable John Briggs and made a bee-line for Maxi Stubbs. The affair lasted months and only stopped because Maxi got cold feet, frightened that John would hear tittle-tattle and do something silly. Iris was livid at being dumped. Not only humiliated but frustrated because Maxi Stubbs was some lover. He was the same age as John but other than that, the two were like chalk and cheese …

Maxi Stubbs and his mother, Winifred, had moved from Peterlee to Shotton a year earlier. Maximilian could have been a model. He was tall and dark and handsome. Only blemish was his permanent tan. His mother was as white as flour so it had to be his father responsible for altering the colour-code. Maxi wouldn't speak about his dad so it fuelled rumours that he was half-caste, more Hindi than Horden, more Sikh than Sacriston. He was always getting into arguments with the local youths because of the wisecracks. 'You from India, Maxi?' the kids would jest. 'Your relations own the self-service shop, Max?' they would quip. Always scrapping was Maxi Stubbs, too sensitive to grin and bear the racist digs … always battling but never successful. That was how they met - Iris watching as Maxi was battered into defeat once again. She walked him home - he lived in nearby Dene Terrace - and they started talking. One thing led to another and the one-night stand lasted weeks until John Briggs came back on the scene.

Later, when John was in custody for having sex with the under-aged Julie Brooks, Iris rekindled her relationship with Maxi. It had been months since she'd had a proper show – her periods were always a hit and miss affair – so Iris imagined it was safe to play. And because Maxi had always been careful first time around she assumed he had taken precautions. Fate, with a little interference from conniving Iris, brought them together for a second time. Maxi Stubbs worked on the checkouts at Safeway, one of the big supermarkets in Peterlee, and Iris and her mother used to shop there. Sometimes Iris, full of wilfulness because of John's wandering ways, would shop alone and search out Maxi. The inevitable happened and the two started seeing each other again. The youth, bolder now that his rival was off the scene, expressed his true feelings to Iris. Told her he loved her, but Iris, with both feet planted firmly on the ground, brushed aside his idiocy and simply enjoyed their time together.

A month after John's imprisonment little Frank was born. Iris struggled through long weeks of melancholy. She rarely left her home and spent dark hours alone in her bedroom. Everyone imagined the young mother was struggling under the weight of depression. Two small boys was an almighty handful for anyone, but add to that a husband languishing in prison! Folks imagined it was all too much for poor Iris! Both families rallied to her aid, fussed and fretted until finally she recovered. There was not a disparaging word about her new baby. All agreed he was a beautiful healthy boy. 'Picture of health,' said her mother, 'double of his father.' Elsie Briggs was in raptures with the infant. 'Gorgeous!' she cried. 'Pretty as a picture, looks as fit as a fiddle.' It was fortunate for Iris that John was locked up. The time alone allowed her to

31

discover an inner resolve. Iris somehow found the courage to face possible recriminations. The expected storm became a minor squall, an incipient shower, when the young mother finally faced her husband. Iris, filled with mettle thanks to the positive reaction from family and friends, found the grit to openly jest about her beautiful, bronzed boy. Months into his sentence John Briggs was joking about Frank's colour and Iris was breathing a sigh of relief.

Iris Briggs was never sure about her youngest. Spin a coin because little Frank could have been either a Briggs or a Stubbs. A whiter shade of pale he definitely wasn't. The colouring, if anything, tended to move goal-posts away from home turfs and more towards foreign fields. Luckily for Iris there was never a hint or suggestion of scandal from those closest to her and she was able to push all fears aside and forget about her recklessness. Maxi Stubbs was like-minded. The teenager thought it prudent to steer his ship to safer shores and, fearful of possible repercussions, he started spending his leisure time in nearby Peterlee. Iris, naturally, was pleased her sweetheart had taken the initiative ……..

Iris reached the phone-box. A few minutes more and she would reach her mother's home in Station Road. The female had a quick look around. The whole place was deserted. Even the Co-op was quiet with no kids loitering about. Iris didn't want anyone telling John they'd seen his wife using the public-phone. She took a deep breath to steady her nerves and dialled the number. It seemed to take an age before the man answered.

"Crumplin's Coals," said the croaky voice.

"It's me."

"Pardon?"

"Iris!" growled the girl. "Who else would phone you, Dean?"

"Iris," he replied, a slight tremor in his tone, "how are you?"

"What are you playing at, Dean?"

There was silence for some moments before the woman spoke.

"Dean," she demanded, "don't play funny buggers!"

"Iris," protested the coal-merchant, "Johnny caught me unawares. Begged for a job. What was I supposed to do?"

"Don't you think it's a little awkward, Dean, you know, you and me?"

"He has no idea about us."

"Obviously not!"

"Well, he'll not find out anything from me."

"What about my coal?" she demanded. "We had an arrangement!"

Dean Crumplin was astonished at the gall of the woman.

"Well, Dean?"

"Can't afford it, Iris," persevered the man, adamant that the free coal was stopping. "I'm paying Johnny a decent wage. Cash too. He'll be able to claim all his benefits." He took a long intake of air. "Be reasonable Iris, I've got a living to make, overheads and the like."

Uneasy moments past before Dean yielded. He sweetened the bitter pill with a little psychology.

"What about a compromise, Iris," soothed the merchant. "I'll let you have it cost?" He was going to offer the discount anyway but kept the gift as a reserve. Always the businessman was Dean Crumplin.

"Suppose so, Dean," she said, relenting. The old man had always been kind to her. She added, "Dean, it is a proper job for John, isn't it?"

"What d'you mean, Iris?"

"You know, Dean," her voice sarcastic and mocking. "It's not your way to keep me in your good books?"

"That's awful!" he said, cut by her accusations. He added apologetically, "Have I once bothered you since Johnny was released?" He'd wanted to phone but knew he was being an old fool, knew for certain the relationship, if one could call it that, was over, "Have I ever troubled you, Iris?"

"Suppose not, Dean."

"I respect you, Iris," he admitted grudgingly. "You know how I feel about you."

"Dean," asked Iris as an afterthought. "Is he any good, I mean, can he graft?"

"Hell of a worker, Iris," said Dean Crumplin and he was not jesting. The lad never took breath all day, worked non-stop, so keen he didn't want to stop for lunch. Best thing he'd ever done was to hire young John Briggs.

"You wouldn't just say that, Dean?"

"If I'd known, I'd have hired him straight from school," said the man. "He's that good."

"Dean," asked Iris, a little curious, "does he talk about me?"

Not a mention, love, mused Dean Crumplin. *It fact, said he was pleased to be out of the house.*

"Dean?" prompted Iris Briggs.

"All he talked about, Iris," said Dean, "you and the boys." Satisfied at the answer, she said, "Right then, I'll be off?"

"Okay, Iris."

Weakness taunted the old man and for a brief moment his heart ached for the girl. He missed her company so much it hurt.

Couldn't stop himself saying, "If you ever want to call, you've got my number?"

There was silence as the girl began coldly calculating the odds. Never knew what the future might throw at her. "Let me think about it, Dean?"

"Okay, Iris," said Dean Crumplin. "Be good, eh?"

"That'll be the day, Dean." Iris chortled. She replaced the phone.

**

CHAPTER FOUR

November roared in mercilessly. Icy winds and continual snow flurries told everyone of the coming winter. Temperatures buckled week after week. So severe was the cold that trees and shrubs glowered with the permanent sheen of frozen snow. Safe indoors, the scene appeared magical and children became excitable and whimsical for Christmas. By early November the main highways, despite the daily spray of gritty salt, were virtual rivers of ice. The side roads resembled polar landscapes and were impossible to traverse. The footpaths became congealed and bubble-wrapped with tiers of grime.

The scant few who braved the elements did so out of necessity. It was a truly dreadful time for those who had to work in such awful conditions. Encased in multiple layers of clothing and cocooned like Eskimos, workmen struggled and laboured through tortuous hours and prayed for the day to end, their thoughts on warm fires, mountainous meals and steaming hot baths.

It was almost noon and the numbing wind had not abated. The inside of the coal-wagon was cocooned in warmth. The owner, sitting relaxed inside the comfortable cab, was reading the newspaper. *Crumplin's Coals* had been delivering in Wingate for almost an hour and were almost finished. The wagon was parked facing the incline of the road and despite half of the axle straddling the footpath the slow moving traffic protested vehemently. Dean Crumplin seemed unfazed, occasionally glanced at the passing motorists and nodded sympathetically as irate drivers gestured and threatened. Twice that morning his wagon had been shunted as cars skated or fishtailed into his motor. The old wagon was barely bruised whilst those responsible cried crocodile tears at their damaged cars. After the initial rebukes, smooth talking Dean always suggested ways out of the mayhem: if the hapless victims stumped up cash he offered to forgo the insurance channel. The ploy worked every time.

The next port of call was Shotton, a mile to the north. The driver folded the newspaper and looked through the side window. The youth toiled effortlessly. Reminded Dean of a youthful, effervescent Norman Wisdom, the lad was all energy and buzz. Despite the liberal assortment of clothing that made him appear to be as wide as he was tall, John Briggs worked non-stop.

"Global warming my arse!" muttered Dean Crumplin. He flung the newspaper to one side and switched on the radio. Jimmy Young's version of *The Wayward Wind* echoed through the cab. "Too bloody true, Jim!" he muttered. "Freeze the balls off a brass monkey!"

John Briggs struggled into the passenger-seat. "It's bleak out there!" he said. Sticking his gloved hands deep inside his coat-pockets, he settled into the seat.

"That's Wingate finished, Johnny," said Dean. He clanked the gear-stick forward and released the handbrake. The lorry inched its way along the frozen road. "Shotton next."

John loved the job. He was always busy and the days flew. Dean had already upped his wage. Tuesday last, with the older man struggling with a cold, the apprentice had persuaded his boss to allow him to drive and deliver on his own. John had worked until 7.00pm. Days later his pay had been increased. There were no hard and fast rules about lunch-times. They tended to vary depending on the district and the number of drops. Usually around noon Dean Crumplin would drive the motor near to Victoria Street and drop John off. Anything over 30 minutes was the normal break. If Dean fell asleep in front of his fire the lunch-break was extended.

John had walked to the rear of Victoria Street, stripped off the outer layers of clothing and his boots, carried them into the kitchen and placed them carefully on the linoleum. He was scrubbing the grime off his hands when Iris appeared. Feigning a smile she mentioned the visitors.

"Your Robert and Dorothy are here," said Iris.

Iris disliked Robert and his obnoxious wife Dorothy. Years earlier the couple blamed her for trapping John into an early and scandalous marriage. The pair had made it obvious at the time that they cared little for her. Iris, understandably, disliked her in-laws and didn't hide the fact.

Still drying his hands, John walked through into the living-room. He was greeted with a beefy grin from his older brother and a blank stare from his dowdy, overweight spouse.

"Johnny," said Robert. "We were just passing. Saw you climbing out of that coal-wagon ... Dorothy saw you actually."

John nodded an acknowledgement and glanced at the glum face of Dorothy.

Dorothy Briggs raised an eyebrow. She looked at Iris standing close to the fire. Iris was holding Frank in her arms whilst Eddie pressed against his mother's thighs. The trio looking decidedly uncomfortable. Not many people liked Dorothy. Her aloofness and self-love was the reason for the loathing. Some didn't enjoy her company because of the job she had. Understandable. Dorothy worked full-time for the D.H.S.S. Couldn't trust someone like that.

"I was talking to Mother," said Robert. "She said you'd got a job?"

"Very lucky, I'd say," said Dorothy. She gave a brief nod and smiled like an undertaker viewing an expensive corpse. "Very lucky."

"Work for Dean Crumplin," John said. "Good money too."

"I saw the wagon," said Robert proudly. "It's about time you had a bit of luck, eh?"

Dorothy interjected. "You be careful, young man," she said harshly. "There's some nasty people about."

John eyeballed her, shrugged his shoulders and waited for an explanation.

"Dorothy was telling me," said Robert, his voice faltering. "Someone wrote a letter to her office last week. It was about you having a full-time job. It was anonymous. Dorothy tore it up. Can't act unless someone is prepared to sign."

"Right then," said John, nervously biting on his lip.

"Anonymous," interjected Dorothy. "I don't do anonymous!"

"Thought I'd let you know," said Robert. "Dorothy doesn't want you in any more trouble."

The youth nodded as his young features bristled with annoyance. He did not reply.

"If you're still claiming, John," said Dorothy doggedly, "it's probably best to sort something out before you're caught?"

"Point taken, Dorothy!"

At 1.05pm Dean Crumplin picked up the youth and they headed for Fleming Field. There were two drops at the northern end of the village and then the rest dotted willy-nilly about the village. Half an hour into the afternoon shift and John was still preoccupied, his head aching with a mix of anger and trepidation because of Dorothy's recriminations.

39

Moments after the couple had left Iris erupted in an almighty rage, pointing the finger of blame at Robert's wife. *'Of course it's her, Johnny!* Iris raged. *'She's practically telling you to sign off the dole or she'll report us!'* Couldn't stop her tongue if her life depended on it, *'What a bunch of hypocrites your family are!'* He had tried to calm her, hated leaving her when she was so angry because she was liable to do or say things they'd both regret. *'Steady on, Iris,'* he said, *'hypocrites?'*

The girl didn't stop for breath. *'Yes, bloody hypocrites! Why doesn't Dorothy report your mother? And what about your bloody lazy good-for-nothing father who'll neither work nor want! The pair of them makes more than the Queen every week!'* Iris stormed up the staircase, she couldn't bear to be in the same room as her vacillating husband. *'Hypocrites!'* she bawled. *'Every last one!'*

"Dean," he asked humbly. "I couldn't ask a favour, could I?"

"Of course lad," replied the coal-man. He was enjoying his days now. The driving was easy for him, made him regret the long years struggling alone. "Ask away."

"Dean," took a deep suck of air to steady his nerves, "you wouldn't let me go on the books…legitimate?"

"Thought you'd want all the benefits, lad?"

"I'm frightened, Dean," continued the youth. "Especially with all the trouble I've been in over the last few years?"

Dean chuckled, "It's not like you're bloody anonymous, eh? One of the more colourful characters of Shotton, would you say, Johnny?"

"Suppose," said the youth. He couldn't raise a smile.

The older man calculated. "Tell you what," he said. "I'll put you down for minimum hours. Anyone asks, you're on the books ... say 10 hours a week, eh?"

"Appreciate it, Dean," said a relieved John Briggs.

"That way," said Dean, "you'll only pay a small amount of National Insurance, and you'll be able to claim all the benefits."

The coal-wagon left Salter's Lane and eased into the small private estate of Atkinson Grove. There were four bags to deliver to number 13 and then the rest of the afternoon would be spent amongst the council houses. The motor pulled up outside the big detached house, John clambered from the cab and grabbed the first sack of coal. He didn't notice the figure staring from the house opposite.

Josephine Brooks walked away from the window. She was fuming. The sight of John Briggs made her ill. She squatted at the bureau and tried to think about what to put in the letter. It had been her third attempt in two weeks. Her last two letters, unsigned, had been posted to the Department of Social Security. That was ten days ago. She had camouflaged the letters. One had been printed as if she were near illiterate; the second letter had been flowing and positive. The correspondence both concerned the scoundrel John Briggs. Josephine pondered, she had an idea. Her old neighbour in Grange Terrace, Mildred Clarkson, whom she hated almost as much as the cretin who had seduced her only child, could be used as a pawn. She smiled and started writing the third letter, she would sign it with her neighbour's name. The Social Security needed to know that John Briggs was working full time for that miserable coal-man and was, to all intents and purposes, claiming benefits.

The cries from the infant stopped her. She left the dresser and eased to the large couch. The child, Sheila Josephine

Brooks, eighteen months old and quite stunning with beautiful blonde ringlets and angelic looks, whimpered and wept as she awoke from the dream. The grandmother lifted and cuddled the child, walked to the large bay-window and stared into the street. The coal-delivery was still on-going. Visibly upset at the sight of the young man who had so damaged her status in the place, not to mention the reputation of her daughter, the middle-aged woman crunched her features with distaste and moved towards the massive kitchen. It was the child's lunch-time. The infant was placed and secured into the safety chair and the meal commenced. The daily routine had been that way since the baby was born. Josephine's only daughter, Julie, wanted the child adopted at birth as did Josephine's bus-driver husband, Maurice. They were both over-ruled. What Josephine wanted Josephine got. There was only one master in the Atkinson Grove house and it wasn't Maurice Brooks. Josephine doted on the infant and, if truth be told, the child helped her through the long, lonely days. Maurice worked all the hours under the sun and daughter Julie was still at school in Wingate for another six months. Baby Sheila was her prop.

As she prepared the meal, Josephine thought about the trauma that had so tortured and blighted her life. Until a few years ago, especially since they had moved out of the small terraced house and into the four bed-roomed detached with double-garage, and then in the same glorious year traded in their cheap Peugeot for a luxurious Mercedes, Josephine had been in heaven. More than heaven. Paradise. Imagined she had made it. Had it all, a hard-working husband, a beautiful daughter, an enormous home, and a six month-old Mercedes. Josephine liked to drive ever so slowly around the village. On parade. Once, out of spite, she had called on her old feuding partner, Mildred Clarkson in down-market Grange Terrace, and rubbed her ex-neighbour the wrong way by comparing the two-up, two-down house with her four bed-roomed mansion with en-suite and Jacuzzi. Didn't tell Milly she was up to her neck in debt. It was all about appearances for Josephine Brooks.

And then the bomb fell. The horror of knowing the entire colliery would be talking about her. After a lifelong struggle to better herself and finally achieving her goal in life, a virtual nightmare in the making landed on her doorstep. Her only daughter was pregnant. Her little girl was having a baby! Her mind went into overdrive. She could imagine the snide remarks because it was history repeating itself.

Thirteen years earlier, Josephine had fallen for the charms of a local Romeo. She was fifteen at the time and still at school - her mother made sure of that - shaming her as if she were a common whore. School every day until she was seven months pregnant. Josephine still cringed with pain a lifetime later. Michael Motson was her seducer. The diminutive, fair-haired rascal beguiled the smitten Josephine. Months into the relationship she told him the news of her pregnancy and the Wingate-born Motson suddenly vanished. Rumours abounded. He had enlisted in the Armed Forces. He was on the run from the police. He was in prison. Whatever the truth, Michael Motson had disappeared. Colliery folk, tight as clams, wouldn't talk. Poor abandoned Josephine was left alone to shoulder the shame. Few knew of her predicament.

Josephine had ditched Maurice Brooks when Michael Motson came on the scene. She now imagined her life was over. After all, she was alone, pregnant and single. Then, unexpectedly, Maurice came back on the scene. He wasn't exactly God's Gift but he did come with the begging bowl. Maurice professed his undying love and offered to shoulder the blame for the pregnancy. Josephine played hard to get naturally, didn't want Maurice Brooks thinking wrong thoughts, thoughts above his station, so she told him the Wingate philanderer had been ditched because of his wandering ways. When Josephine allowed Maurice back into her life most folk assumed Maurice was the father. Josephine, naturally, said nothing about her indiscretion with Michael Motson, an awful man with the fatuous name of 'Buff.' He was a scoundrel from a family of scoundrels! A lifetime ago and she still cringed at the memories of the Wingate womaniser.

Josephine hated John Briggs as much as she hated Michael Motson. Mortified twice in a lifetime, the humiliation and indignity almost destroyed her. She couldn't ever settle the score with Michael, there was too much water under the bridge, although if she knew his whereabouts she might reconsider. Briggs, however, was a different matter. Thanks to Josephine's persistence and resolve the youth had been imprisoned, although the sentence was not enough to satisfy the woman. The truth was there for all to see, the horrid youth had despoiled and wrecked her daughter's reputation and Julie would be avenged, in full.

Josephine decided to tell the Inland Revenue about the coal-merchant, Dean Crumplin. She would inform them that the crooked businessman was employing benefit scroungers. She made up her mind, she would crumple Crumplin.

Josephine Brooks decided to make an immediate start on the correspondence. She didn't want anyone else in the house knowing about her nefarious plans. Not Maurice, nor Julie. She walked towards the wide-eyed child, gently pulling the high-chair towards the table. It was lunch time. She had several hours to compile the two letters and she would post them on the way to the surgery. Dr. Todd was so sweet, knew all about her mounting depression. The countless times she had wept in front of the good doctor had worked a treat. The aged doctor knew more than anyone the miserable life she'd had. Josephine had been on medication since she was sixteen years old. Sixteen and with a child, and with everyone talking about her she needed tablets to get her through each day. That's what she said to the doctors. She liked Dr. Todd better than her previous doctor, Emir Abdullah. The coloured doctor had tried for years to direct Josephine away from regular medication. Turned nasty when the Nigerian-born G.P. refused to write further sick-notes after he told her the daily dose of tablets would do her more harm than good. The doctor was a fool, thinking Josephine actually took the medication. She was only trying to keep the job right. It was the final nail in the coffin when Abdullah suggested she might sign off the sick and seek some kind of employment. The fool of a doctor said it would be therapeutic! The threat was enough for Josephine to change surgeries and swap doctors. Sign off the sick? The fellow was an imbecile! Didn't he realize that the weekly benefits were a necessity and part-paid the mortgage. Josephine relied on the regular income and had no qualms about collecting the weekly cash. Half of the village was on some kind of benefit or other. They were work-shy and proud of it. Josephine was a genuine case. She had stress, not all the time, granted, but some of the time, definitely. If other, less authentic cases could claim benefits, then so could she. Josephine ditched Abdullah and grabbed Todd.

She started with the letter.

**

CHAPTER FIVE

Friday night the couple argued. It suited Iris, allowed her to get ready in peace, much to the annoyance of John. They rowed because he had planned a night without her, his first since coming out of Medomsley. John wrongly imagined Iris wouldn't mind. After all, he had taken her out the previous Saturday. They'd had a good session at The Comrades with a belly-full of booze. They had played and won the bingo - single-line for £50 - and watched an excellent group called *The Drifters*. The posters said they were the genuine article but when the couple were in the bar they were joined by John's inebriated father who said the band were definitely frauds. Said there were other bands called *The Drifters* all working the clubs. Arty Millar joined them at the bar-counter. Arty, in his late fifties, had signed photographs of Marty Wilde, Craig Douglas, Tommy Steele and Terry Dene so he knew what he was talking about when he said the band were imposters. John Briggs cared less. The group was brilliant.

"If you're going out," said Iris, "I'm going out."

Arms on hips, Iris started with the accusations "You and drink don't mix!" she said. "You're married, John! You've got the worst track record in the village!"

It was the pot calling the kettle black.

John was too weary to argue. It wasn't that he didn't trust Iris. He believed her when she'd said he was her only love. Believed her totally. It was the thought of Iris full of drink that worried him. Anyone filled with booze worried him. It was more than that. He was troubled because Iris was socializing with Thelma Cruddace and Tammy Bryce. Both girls had dubious reputations. John had first-hand knowledge of the females, he'd had flings with both of them. All it would take was a slip of the tongue when they were drunk to bring the curtain down on his marriage.

He looked at the clock. It was 7.00pm and he hadn't washed. He groaned out loud and began to reminisce about the rumpus. The argument with Iris was his fault of course. With hindsight he should have mentioned the unexpected meeting with his friends hours earlier and of the impromptu get-together that had been suggested. John had been ecstatic. He hadn't seen any of his pals for months. His only fault was not telling Iris. A little diplomacy on his part would have won the day, a little grease on the wheels and everything would have been hunky-dory. He came in from work, freezing outside, red-hot inside, and made the fatal error of sitting down in front of a blazing coal-fire. Hypnotized in minutes, John barely finished his meal before falling asleep. He never heard Iris taking the boys to his mother's house or Iris returning and having a bath. He woke up at 6.00pm and informed Iris he was having a night out. She hit the roof. Naturally. The kids had been fostered out and suddenly the Friday routine of takeaways and drinks was being shelved. Iris lost her temper, grabbed her coat and her purse and stormed out of the house.

John trudged up the stairs and turned on the bath. He was supposed to be meeting his friends at the Fleming pub. He was in a foul mood and wished he'd never made arrangements for the night out. Five minutes later he'd shaved, lowered himself into the steaming-hot bath and started to relax. Thought again of the prison sentence and shivered as pictures filled his head. His eyes focused on his protruding knees that stuck through the rich suds. The bruising and swellings had long gone. Both joints appeared normal but the persistent aches remained, a constant reminder of his time at Medomsley Young Offenders Institution. He closed his eyes and thought of earlier times, buoyant times when everything was so right for him, when optimism ruled. John remembered the Sunderland football coach watching his final performance on the football field, still recalled the name of Dennis Lawson. He was a big star once, almost in the same league as Charlton and Peters. John thought of that last game. Didn't know it was to be his grand finale at the time. With a little prior knowledge he would have run a mile from the game. He began to drift away …..

It was a beautiful autumnal day, the sun a brilliant orb that dazzled and brought false promise that summer was still alive. Skies were clear and blue, birds chattered, called and busied themselves as the leaves sprinkled and spun to the earth like nature's confetti. Sunday morning and the recreational grounds east of the small pit village echoed and reverberated with a growing crescendo, the noise and excitement lifting from the soccer pitch as two local teams battled for honours seemed at odds with the scant few who were present, the lack of numbers more than compensated by the fermenting passion from loyal supporters as they shrieked and bellowed in an incessant show of enthusiasm.

Amongst the crowd one figure stood apart, the fellow neither proud parent nor friend of one of the contestants. Tall, middle-aged and with greying, receding hair and an ever-expanding paunch, Dennis Lawton looked very much a parent mesmerized by the play, a subdued and studious father who held tight his emotions even though the game tantalized and taunted. A dozen years earlier the same man, minus the paunch and the blight of age, would have drawn crowds of loyal fans and admirers. Seemed like yesterday when Dennis signed the autograph-books and handed out the picture-cards. It was all gone, his heyday a distant memory. Dennis Lawton had been a star once. One of the best, played for Leeds, Everton and Newcastle. Ended his career at Newcastle. Lost his teeth at Newcastle. Not playing, clubbing; his downfall, his demise from the beautiful game. Counted himself lucky that he was still working, scouting for Sunderland and drawing a wage every week.

He knew about the youngster. Over the past few years his club had received glowing references about Johnny Briggs; one from the sports teacher at his school and the others from family, friends and the general public. Lawton had watched the youth a year ago in an inter-school match and was impressed at the skill and energy of the lad. Briggs was all bustle and bite, reminded Dennis of a young Jimmy Greaves, maybe a miniature version of Dennis Law. His only flaw was his lack of inches. The lad was undersized and gaunt. Briggs had the look of a fair-haired Macari and the aggression of Bremner, sixteen going on seventeen, and in his final year at school and he was what ... five feet five in his stockings. A definite half-pint. Dennis was back today, checking on the little dynamo, see if he'd improved, see if he'd sprouted some.

The game was a battleground, Peterlee versus Shotton; amateur matches were usually fought without quarter. The match was drawn and time was an issue. The youth, Briggs, had been hammered by bigger, less talented rivals but seemed impervious to the rough treatment from his rivals or the poor skills of the referee, his adrenalin sky-high as he battled on regardless and ran circles around the opposition. Only minutes remained of the game when he was brought down near the rival's goal-mouth and a penalty was given. Someone threw the ball at the youngster and Briggs strutted like a peacock towards the penalty-spot and raised an arm in the air as if the result was a forgone conclusion.

A police-car skidded into the nearby car-park and drew the attention of the spectators. Two uniformed officers hurried from the vehicle and strode across the muddy pitch. It was an amazing sight. The only sound was the twittering of birds and the solitary yapping from a mutt that followed in the path of the policemen. All eyes centred on the direction they travelled. The two giant officers walked straight to the smallest figure on the pitch, dwarfing the diminutive striker. The conversation lasting seconds before the football was placed on the spot and John Briggs reluctantly followed the uniforms across the muddy field. Someone shouted: "Take the bloody penalty, Johnny!" Another spectator bawled, "You can do it, kid!" The youth stopped in his track and spoke to his captors. John Briggs pleaded for a few minutes of time so that he could take the penalty. Both policemen shook their heads solemnly and gestured for the boy to follow. The officers continued on their way believing the youth was following. John Briggs, ignoring the order, turned and jogged back to the goal-mouth and lifted both arms at the goalkeeper. 'You ready?' he mouthed and acknowledged the nod from the keeper. He glanced at the referee, "Okay, ref?" he called. Heard the whistle and walked up to the ball, smiling broadly as if already knew the result. Mentally judging the distance, John whacked the ball straight into the top corner of the net, the strike so fast that the keeper stood transfixed and embarrassed. A final whistle blew and the match was over. The uniformed constables stood a distance away, arms on hips, glowering at the antics of the youth. When John Briggs hurried to their side, he was grabbed, hoisted aloft and carried to the vehicle. The jeers and catcalls began in earnest.

Dennis Lawton sighed; he had seen enough of life to let nothing bother him. 'Win some, lose some,' he thought wistfully. Lawton smiled as he recalled the pub in the centre of the small colliery. He was positive that was called Shotton Comrades. The same pub served a hell of a pint. He walked slowly across the sodden grass and made his way to his car. Dennis was in no hurry, he had all the time in the world. He would have a pint or two, might even find out why the little tike had been arrested.

Four hours later, Sammy McGuiness, chief scout and prize arsehole, was fuming, "Can I smell alcohol, Dennis?" he demanded.

Dennis Lawton wanted to say so much. Would have once, years ago. 'You never had a drink on duty,' mused the man, 'short memory, Sammy!' Dennis still recalled the pair of them, buddies then, Lawton and McGuiness, the Terrible Two, they had played their last match together in Blackpool. They were out together the night before. Never went to bed because two young strippers kept them company all night long. It had been a hell of a night, the kind of night to end your career on. Sammy, full-back at the time, didn't need the wind like Dennis, was still supping at eight that morning and played the whole match pissed. 'Did I say a word, Sammy, did I mention your name when the gaffer bollocked me for smelling the booze on my breath? Conveniently forgotten, Sammy?'

"When the lad was escorted off the pitch I went straight round to his house," replied the scout. "Been there a few times over the last couple of years. Mother's okay, the father is a waster. It was empty, so I called at the Comrades to find out the chat. Thought we needed to know whether or not we could still sign him."

"The Comrades!" bawled Sammy, strutting and pouting like some middle-aged Prima-Donna. "The bloody Comrades!"

Dennis Lawton grimaced. Last thing he wanted was McGuiness acting like Cloughy. He let the jibe go over his

51

head, skin like a rhinoceros. For a miserly £100 a week Sammy McGuiness could stick his job.

"Only place to find the juice, Sammy, the gossip."

"And?" grunted McGuiness sourly.

"Young Johnny is touching eighteen. Married a year already," continued Dennis, unabashed at the manner and petulance of his boss. "He has two kids to his childhood sweetheart...."

"Do I look like Eamonn Andrews," interrupted the chief scout, "do you see the Big Red Book?"

Dennis Lawton was immune to the sarcasm. Shrugging his shoulders he continued regurgitating the colliery chit-chat. "Few months ago, Johnny and Iris, his sixteen-year old wife, went out for a drink. They had a baby-sitter, thirteen year-old. An hour in the club and Briggs makes a lame excuse about forgetting his wallet, nipped back home, spent ten minutes in bed with the young girl and then calmly rejoined his wife at the club. Everything fine and dandy ... until the baby-sitter found out she was pregnant. Apparently she was a virgin before young Romeo wooed her".

"Bloody hell!"

"Statutory rape," said Dennis glumly. "He'll be locked up soon enough."

"Jesus!" gasped Sammy McGuiness. Shook his head, he'd wanted to sign the kid so much. "Up in smoke, what a bloody waste!"

The older man lit a cigarette, looked blankly at his former friend and colleague. "Chat is," continued Dennis Lawton, "the lad can't keep his trousers fastened. Fellas at the Comrades were laughing about young Johnny, apparently he's one for the ladies."

Sammy McGuiness sighed, "Lost him then, Dennis?"

Dennis Lawton shrugged his shoulders, "Well and truly."
He started walking to the door, paused for a moment, turned
to his old pal and said, "Shame really, the lad had class
………

It was the numbing cold of the bath-water that woke him. Shivering uncontrollably, John struggled out of the tub, grabbed a towel and hurried down the stairs. He gasped at the lateness of the hour. It was 10.15pm and he'd slept for hours. The fire was barely alive. He threw more coal from the skuttle and started rubbing frantically at his wrinkled white skin. It was too late to socialize, and he was too weary to make the effort. John Briggs found pyjamas and made himself supper. He switched on the television and flopped on the sofa. Minutes later John was asleep and dreaming again, his body jerking and moving, his mind bouncing with myriad images.

**

CHAPTER SIX

He'd waited until 10am before tramping across the deserted frozen streets of the colliery. It had been three days since he had last driven his car and John was a little agitated. The motor was out of action again and big money was needed for repairs. Front-Street Garage had quoted a farcical fee so he had tramped to Fleming Field Motors only to be told the replacement clutch was going to cost an arm and a leg. He blamed Iris, Iris blamed him. Either way they had no transport, hence his long walk through the snow, cursing all the way to Salter's Lane and Dean Crumplin's home.

Something was wrong with his boss. He was not his usual self, complaining of aches and pains all week. Said it was heartburn or indigestion. Whatever it was, it made him grouchy and he took it out on his only employee. John Briggs, however, took it all in his stride. Never mentioned his own problems and never griped once about his aching knees. Not a word from the teenager who bit his tongue and got on with the job.

John reached the house and knocked until his knuckles hurt. The door was locked which was unusual so he rapped and shouted until the neighbour appeared and informed him that an ambulance had taken his boss to hospital. It took a few minutes to gather his thoughts. He paced up and down the yard in a quandary. Thursday was always a busy day. Suddenly, impulsively, he made up his mind. Knowing Dean Crumplin would agree he took out his bunch of keys and found the right one, pleased he had persuaded his boss to give him the spare. Initially Dean had not been keen, worried that the youngster might lose the key. Then he'd relented, mainly because the previous Tuesday he'd been forced to leave his sick-bed to unlock the door, hand over the key to the wagon so that John could work alone. Now Dean was poorly again and customers were waiting for supplies. Not for the first time John Briggs would have to work on his own. The thought of doubling-up didn't bother John. Dean Crumplin was a decent boss and he would willingly work till the cows came home for him.

At 6.30pm that evening John finally pulled up outside his home. He had worked all day without a break and without food. Locking the coal-motor he entered the warm house, ravenously hungry and aching from exhaustion. All he wanted was to eat and rest but knew he could not. He had to visit Dean Crumplin. Despite protestations from Iris, who always enjoyed a Thursday evening out with her mother, John stuck to his guns. He washed, changed and gulped down a meal, knowing that he needed instruction and direction from his employer. Also he had a mountain of cash from customers and was at a loss about what to do with it. When Iris began whingeing about her night-out he acted decisively. Drove the wagon to his mother's home, collected the willing baby-sitter and deposited her at the Victoria Street address, then, as he was passing Station Road en route to Durham, he ferried his young wife to her mother's house. The task was over in the briefest of time. Everybody was happy, especially Iris, who apologized and pecked him on the cheek before she clambered from the coal-wagon.

He reached the hospital car-park at 8.00pm and hurried into the building. Street-smart John Briggs used his wit, knew being related was the key to the door, a necessity ploy if he wished to see his employer. He told the receptionist he was Dean Crumplin's son and hurried through the warren of corridors until he eventually found the ward. Hurried past bed after bed looking for his boss and walked past Dean - the smart, middle-aged, blonde squatting uncomfortably on the chair blocked Bill's view of the prostrate patient - before a nurse led him back to the bed.

Beatrice Crumplin, still carrying the marriage name from a decade ago, was momentarily confused at the new arrival. Dean, dressed in pyjamas, smiled a nervous welcome. John handed over the cloth money-bag telling his employer he had taken only diesel from the takings. Dean Crumplin placed the package to one side and began spluttering feeble excuses about the dire state of his business.

The female smirked, "Right, Dean," she said. "You'll have business to discuss with the lad. If you want me, phone me and I'll call in tomorrow night, that's providing you'll pay for the taxi again."

Dean Crumplin said weakly, "Sammy doesn't mind then?"

"Sammy does what I say!"

Beatrice Crumplin stood, dusted down her skirt, patted the spread-eagled Dean as if he were a family pet and walked quickly away. The men watched her in silence.

"Never changed," muttered a disgruntled Dean Crumplin.

The old man had foolishly imagined that ten years with Sammy, her balding lover, might have dampened her ardour, that seeing him all forlorn in the hospital bed might have drawn her back to his arms. He was wrong. Beatrice was a law unto herself, and as penny-pinching as ever. When the hospital staff had contacted Beatrice she had demanded a taxi! He thought he was at death's door and she'd asked for the fare! Made up his mind it would be the first and last time he'd contact Beatrice. The reconciliation was definitely no-go.

As John Briggs found a chair, Dean tipped the cloth-bag open across the bed-sheets. When he saw the piles of money Dean smiled like a Cheshire cat.

"How are you, Dean?" asked the youth with a genuine affection.

Dean looked up. He held a wad of notes in his hand and mountain of cash strewn about the duvet. The man became emotional as his rheumy eyes glanced from the cash to the lad. Knew then that John Briggs was a God-send. He could not think of another person who would have struggled alone all day in the awful weather to deliver fuel. Suddenly realised that circumstances had changed forever, knew his health was on the wane - the doctors had informed him he had suffered a mild heart-attack and told he had to change his life-style or suffer the consequences - knew he was in trouble.

"Dean, you okay?"

The old man nodded solemnly. His mind made up. The lad had proved himself time and time again. John Briggs was better than a son. He suddenly knew then what he had to do.

Dean said "Anyone but you would have walked back home this morning. A few more days stuck in a hospital bed and my business would be down the toilet."

Dean Crumplin began counting the money. The exercise took moments. Dean then divided the money into two piles. He scooped one of the heaps into his massive palms and handed it over to the astonished youth.

"Son," said Dean, "what say we form a partnership? Down the middle from now on? Deal, son?"

John was speechless. Tongue-tied.

"I was going to sign out of this place tomorrow," continued Dean. "If you agree I stay another day, maybe have the weekend off. We'll start properly on Monday, you agreed, Johnny?"

"Dean, I don't know what to say."

Dean Crumplin felt better than he had for years. It was as if a weight had been lifted from him. He felt *alive*.

57

"Tell you what else we'll do," said Dean. "We'll change the logo on the lorry: *Crumplin and Briggs: Quality Coal.* We'll do it next week."

"Dean, I'll not let you down."

John Briggs stayed late. Chatted until he was evicted by the smiling nurse. He told Dean he'd return the following night but the older man insisted his new partner have a night at home.

John arrived home minutes after his wife. Iris hadn't won scratch at the bingo, although her mother had scooped £50 and shared the proceeds. John couldn't have cared less; he was on a high, in cloud-cuckoo-land.

"He's made you a partner!" Iris exclaimed, already mentally spending the new-found wealth. She recovered enough to add stoically, "Mind, it's about time. It took him long enough to realise just how good you are."

"Oh, John!" beamed a delighted baby-sitter. Elsie Briggs gushed, "I'm so proud of you! Wait till your dad hears the news."

He drove his mother home in the coal-wagon, persuaded her to do the honours and tell his father the good news. He was never sure how his father would react, especially with booze inside him. Didn't want his day ruined by some drunken remark. He left her standing at the garden gate. Elsie waved her son away. Watched John struggling along the frozen tundra until he was out of sight. She was weeping.

John Briggs had little sleep that night. He tossed and turned, his head in flux. He was a partner, a co-owner in a business. He grinned manically into the dark, his mind a whirl of magical emotion. He didn't care that the windows rattled or that the wind scratched and howled, he was elated. Heard the snow slapping at the house and felt euphoric. It had taken months to achieve monumental success. He couldn't believe his luck.

John listened to the soft melodic wheezing from Iris. In the distance a lone mutt intermittently yelped. Frank, his youngest son, struggling with a cold, moaned out loud as he fought through a troubled sleep. Twice John had gone to his side and found the duvet on the floor. Felt his cool forehead and knew the fever had lifted. He made his son comfortable as he calmed him against the night demons, soothed his hair until the boy eased and relaxed again, covered him with the blanket and stayed by his side until he slept.

John snuggled close to his young wife and smiled at the sounds of slumber. He closed his eyes and tried to sleep. The nagging aches were pushed aside, deemed inconsequential now, part and parcel of the business … his business. His damaged knee twinged alarmingly and he gasped with pain. Stretching and moving John tried to ease the discomfort. The injured limb cranked his thoughts away from the events of the day to another era before fatigue finally swamped him. His slumber was tortured slumber as images from yesteryear collided with the present. Dreamed he was inside the surgery and heard for the first time about his arthritis. Told by the doctor that the daily dose of pain-killers would not halt the deterioration of his health. He was bluntly informed to change his job for something less physical, leave the coal-delivery business or suffer the consequences. The news had shocked him. He was weeks away from this twentieth birthday and riddled with arthritis. His mind spun and weaved as he tried to find solutions.

"John! said Iris. "Wake up, you're having a nightmare!"

He croaked an apology and began to ramble about the dream.

"Go to sleep, John!"

A faint wail echoed from the second bedroom.

"You've woken Frank!" groaned Iris. She turned away from John and pulled the duvet over her head.

John Briggs stumbled from the room and entered the smaller bedroom. His son was thrashing and groaning. John remembered the medicine and hurried down the stairs to the kitchen.

**

CHAPTER SEVEN

Four weeks later, driving through Wingate on the way to a single customer in nearby Station Town, Dean Crumplin had a second heart attack. One moment Dean was talking happily to his new partner then suddenly he turned grey, his eyes rolled and he keeled forward onto the steering column, jerking and quivering as if electric shocks were bombarding his chunky frame. John Briggs was frozen with shock. Dean Crumplin was unconscious, draped over the steering-wheel with his dentures forced from the drooling mouth and the coal-motor out of control! John was stiff with fear and watched helplessly as the vehicle careered along the highway. Frantic drivers sounded their horns as brakes locked and tyres whined and drivers waited for the imminent collision.

Fate intervened on that drab December morning. It was a little after nine-o-clock and the streets were almost as deserted as the roads. John lifted from the stupor, grasped the hand-brake and pulled with all of his might. The wagon rocked, spun and lifted as the big wheels caught the kerb and shuddered to a halt across an empty path. Providence smiled that fateful day. The fickle hand of fortune touched everyone on that bleak frozen morning because not one accident occurred. Despite the place looking like a miniature version of motorway mayhem there was not a bump or blemish as the road filled with half a dozen skewed, protesting vehicles.

People started yelling and shouting. Folks left their cars and went to the aid the stricken man. A passing policeman pushed through the milling throng telling everyone of his knowledge of first aid. He reached the unconscious man and gently eased him from the cab to the road. The constable's overcoat was removed and used as a make-shift blanket. The officer started the resuscitation with John Briggs nervously looking over his shoulder. When the ambulance finally arrived Dean Crumplin was driven the short journey to Hartlepool General Hospital.

A short time later the youth was driving the wagon towards Station Town. He had a full day of work ahead of him and knew the sooner he started the quicker he would finish. John sighed knowing it would be another late night before he reached home and he could imagine the whining from a disgruntled Iris. He sympathized, understood where she was coming from. Dean had taken a full week off work after his initial discharge from hospital leaving John to work late every night. The setup did not suit Iris and so they rowed constantly. His pleas for patience fell on deaf ears. His argument that Dean would soon return as an active partner didn't wash with a disgruntled Iris. She had been proved right. Normalcy had lasted days before the older man collapsed and it now was back to square one for John Briggs.

He should have phoned Iris and told her about Dean's heart attack. Thought about the grief and the griping and decided to wait until that evening.

As he drove through the back streets of Station Town his thoughts focused on Iris. Her behaviour unsettled him. More and more Iris seemed dissatisfied with her lot. Nothing seemed to please her. She complained about the house, the boys, everything. John could recall when the grumpiness had started. Four weeks earlier, the night Iris bolted like a freed canary when he'd mentioned a boys' night out and he had fallen asleep while Iris had partied. Not satisfied with the one-off celebration, Iris had pouted and pleaded for another bite at the apple and twice since had disappeared with the girls for a Friday-night special. Arrogant when she defended her actions, blaming her young husband for putting work before her. Iris was right. Before he was made a partner in the firm, the couple had regularly enjoyed their weekends at the pub. Nowadays John was too weary to make the effort. Whereas he wanted to rest, she wanted to socialise. John wanted to save and plan for their future; Iris wanted to enjoy the new-found wealth. Iris moaned like she'd never moaned before, cursing his new job but grabbing the money. It was if Iris had been cloned from Viv Nicholson in her quest to spend, spend, spend.

Despite the graft, John had zero in the bank and only a paltry few quid in the post-office. Iris had been busy raiding the funds. She had refurbished the entire home with carpets, a three-piece suite and a new television. And when the cash had gone she dipped into credit. John, naturally, was livid. He thought it was so wasteful, thought the money could have been put to better use, could have been used as a deposit for a home. Their Victoria Street home was rented from Cecil Peacock and Peacock was Shotton's answer to Rachman. Rent money, according to John, was dead money. His pleas fell on deaf ears.

He parked the wagon outside the terraced property, took a deep breath, pushed aside his worries and headed towards the rear door. The house was owned by Mary Cunningham. The woman was forty years old and looked and acted like a woman half her age. She had three gorgeous daughters. Tina was the oldest at nineteen, Melissa was a year younger and Denise was still at school. They drove John Briggs to distraction the way they flirted and teased. Dean had warned him about the Cunningham girls, told him never to mix business with pleasure. But then John discovered Dean didn't practice what he preached. Maybe once a week, once a fortnight, Dean became a devious operator. He would never admit to dalliances with the odd willing customer, look you in the eye and lie through his teeth, but he couldn't stop his face cracking into an uncomfortable smile when he offered feeble excuses for his occasional disappearances.

"Morning Mary," he said. Tried to be upbeat, knowing he had a stressful day ahead and guaranteed grief when he got home.

The woman smiled approvingly then disappeared inside to find her purse. As John waited, the eldest daughter appeared at the doorstep. Tina was unmarried with two children and lived three doors from her mother. She practically lived at her parents home. Tina Cunningham had two children and two different men in her life which was not enough for Tina the Tease who fancied John Briggs and didn't hide the fact.

"Hi," said Tina. She was dressed provocatively in a short tight skirt and flimsy blouse that showed her bra. It was the middle of winter and still needed to be noticed. Goose-bumps the size of buttons didn't bother her.

"Tina," he answered. Couldn't help but look, he was only human.

"Time for a cuppa?" she asked. Gave him that *come-on* look and eased open the door to tempt him, "Have a break, why don't you," she said flirtatiously.

He told her about Dean. "Another time, Tina," he said.

"Dean was fine last week," said Tina. She folded her arms under her ample chest so as to accentuate her bosom, "I still couldn't get you inside!" Added dryly, "I'm doing something wrong? Maybe if I offer coffee instead of tea I could tempt you?'

"Iris finds out and I'm dead."

Mary reappeared, oozing charm and sexuality by the bucket-load. According to Dean Crumplin she'd had more men than hot dinners. Dean seemed to know everything there was to know about Mary Cunningham. It was surprising what a few bags of coal could buy. Made John wonder if the woman's fuel bills were wavered periodically for *favours* rendered.

Mary handed over the single £10 note. She had a big smile over her face. "Dean said he'd sort out the money, John," she purred. "Last stuff he delivered was rubbish, more stone than coal. I did phone him earlier in the week, okay?"

The youth felt angry, irritated by the number of free-loaders on his books. Despite his lack of business acumen he knew it was money lost, aware that a business couldn't flourish if stock was given away free or for favours. Suddenly, from somewhere deep in his psyche, John Briggs found the strength to query the customer.

"Dean never said anything to me, Mary," he stammered.

The woman gawked at the youngster.

John smiled apologetically but stood his ground. "In fact, he was just saying how much was due from you when he collapsed." Took a deep intake of breath and asked diplomatically, "Why don't you give me £20 and I'll get Dean to sort it out?"

Mary Cunningham winced. She peered over his shoulders and stared at the coal-motor. When she saw the new logo emblazoned along the side of the lorry Mary grimaced.

"Crumplin and Briggs!" interrupted Tina. "Dean never told us."

"Part-owner," he answered.

Another £10 was reluctantly pulled from the bulging purse. Mary laughed but her eyes stayed cold. She turned and disappeared inside the home leaving the teenager beaming triumphantly at her daughter.

He walked back to the motor accompanied by Tina.

"You never go out now, Johnny," quizzed the female. "Iris got you tied to her apron-strings?"

"Give over, Tina," he said. He was on cloud nine, "You're living with someone."

"And you're married to someone."

"Trying to be good, Tina," he replied. Meant it too, there was too much to lose.

"And you think Iris is worth the trouble?"

Warning bells sounded in his head, "What do you mean?"

"Too soft, John Briggs," she pouted. "Give a woman enough rope and she'll hang herself."

"Spit it out, Tina!"

"If Iris wants to raise the roof in The Fir Tree pub it's not my problem. Iris wants to drink herself legless with the usual morons from Wingate and then disappear to Hartlepool for the rest of the night … whatever!"

He was concerned now; the warnings too close for comfort. Shaking his head, the youth opened the wagon-door and waited for more.

Tina fired another broadside, "Denise was in *42ⁿᵈ Street* last Friday with her best friend. Hartlepool nightclub."

Denise was the youngest of the Cunningham girls, almost sixteen and still attending Wingate School. She was the alley-cat of the family and as wild and wanton as they come.

Tina said, "Did you know Julie Brooks is Denise's best friend?"

The youth grimaced. The anger and the anguish obvious for all to see. His dalliance with the nubile, under-aged Julie Brooks was the reason for his imprisonment. Lost two years of freedom because of the teenage nymph's testimony. Julie had teased and tormented John until he succumbed, and then heaven turned to hell when she announced she was pregnant with his child. A spasm subconsciously rocked through his

66

body as he re-lived the shameful episode. Julie Brooks could have denied everything and saved his skin. Despite pleading and begging, the school-kid named him as father. She was more frightened of her awful mother than anyone else.

"The one and only," John said ruefully. He climbed into the cab.

"You know what Julie thinks of Iris," replied Tina. "She hates her."

"The feeling's mutual."

"If she can nail anything on Iris she will," said a vengeful Tina. "Do you agree?"

John scowled and waited for the news.

"Denise said your precious Iris was dancing and flirting all night. Word is, the boys were round her like a bitch on heat."

"I'll have to go, Tina. I'll sort it out." He turned the key and revved the wagon.

"Friday," teased Tina Cunningham, "I'll be in The Queens until nine. Think about it, Johnny. Iris is not worth it."

"Might see you," he smiled weakly and started driving away.

"One life, John Briggs," she yelled after him. "You can do better than Iris!"

His head hurt and his stomach ached but he knew he had work to do. Had to concentrate on the deliveries and push aside everything else. He was pleased that the work meant he could not run home and confront Iris. Couldn't stop thinking, however, and he had all day to mull over the news. John drove back into Wingate, he had one drop in Coronation Street and one in Queens Street then the journey took him to Thornley. His mind was in overdrive and he kept regurgitating Tina's words. He tried desperately to think rationally and keep a lid on his emotions, knew Iris was headstrong, occasionally dizzy, but other men, he'd never known her even look at another man. Never. Despite his anger, and a gnawing fear, he still believed Iris was a one-man woman. He thought about Tina's sister, Denise. The same girl was the biggest temptress on the planet. Years ago, when Julie Brooks held a torch for him, she had told him all about her best friend, Denise Cunningham.

He began to reminisce. Grimaced at the damage he'd caused to everybody. His actions had shamed his parents. His mother suffered most. She had stayed indoors after an altercation in the Co-op, turned more than a few heads when she overheard the tittle-tattle from gossipmonger, Janice Freeman. Elsie Briggs, on her knees checking out the sell-by date on some bargains, honed in on Janice Freeman telling Bessie Winthrop that John, her son, was acting like his no-good Uncle, Micky Motson. Janice was on a roll as she regurgitated tales about Bessie's infamous brother, Buff Motson. Elsie exploded with anger, lost her temper and attacked the hysterical Janice Freeman. She managed to get Janice Freeman's head half-way into the open freezer before store-manager, Albert Jingles, saved the day. John's mother was hit by a wave of depression after the incident. Imagined everyone was cursing her youngest and became a virtual recluse. She knew her shortcomings, knew there would have been further retaliations, and Elsie didn't need reminding about her roots. The woman had lived with the back-biting and chitchat all her life. She had been a wildcat in her younger days and bred from a family of wild-cats. Elsie fretted and freaked with the supposed slander that swept the village, stayed out of sight and out of trouble because she didn't want to fuel the bonfire with more outbursts. When Frank Briggs first heard the news about his wayward son he lost his temper good and proper. Belted his son black and blue until the shame was out of his system, used him like a punch-bag but at least he calmed after venting his wrath. Called the lad a silly bugger but, after he'd calmed, Frank backtracked and started cursing the girl. Everyone took sides - small village values - but deep down, John blamed himself. He had been weak, then and after. It was like a fire taking hold and he felt powerless to stop. But now, especially after the prison term, with long, lonely months to reflect, he felt different, able to think about the consequences. The flames of temptation still stoked his furnace but he tried, honestly tried, to resist the lure.

By 5.20pm the snow was falling like feathers from the dark skies, soft and gentle as they floated slowly to the earth. The severity of the day had mellowed as blankets of clouds filled the heavens. He had worked tirelessly without a break from early morning. Hungry as the devil, his body hot as hell-fire, John Briggs had eventually calmed. The lad had grown tired after hours of hysterical one-sided rambling, his mind chock-a-bloc with myriad thoughts of Iris.

His mood eased as irrational thoughts were pushed away. He knew the Cunningham clan and their friends despised Iris. Added to that list were a host of others who disliked him as much, especially after the sordid episode with Julie Brooks. There were many who would stop at nothing to hurt him, even if it meant using his wife as a pawn to destroy him or his marriage.

John thought again about Julie Brooks. When she first discovered she was pregnant she was keen to have an abortion. Then suddenly everything changed and out of the blue she decided to have the child. John found out later it was Julie's mother who had bludgeoned her selfish views on to her family. Josephine Brooks was adamant in her determination to punish John Briggs. The youth was hauled to court and, later, imprisoned. Two years later, older and wiser, he was freed. A short time after his release John had called at the house in Grange Terrace. Decided to do the right thing, he would face the bitter Josephine Brooks and ask to see his daughter. His visit was in vain. A neighbour told him that the Brook family had moved. It had taken all of his courage to visit the house. He knew he could not repeat the exercise and found excuses to stay away.

John reached Haswell. Switching off the motor he took a deep draught of cool air and jumped from the cab. Trudging through the falling snow he reached the rear of the wagon, grabbed at one of the remaining sacks of coal and struggled to a nearby rear-yard. Another hour and he would be finished. He weakened when he thought of the long drive to the hospital. He was exhausted. Made up his mind to phone the hospital once his shift was over, thought he'd call and see Dean Crumplin the following evening. He needed to find his head, needed reassurances from Iris.

The long hours on his own had calmed him somewhat. Earlier irrational thoughts had been replaced by more sensible, logical images. He decided to stand tall against the scandal-mongers. Imagined Julie Brooks was determined to destroy him and Julie's friends were in on the wicked game. It was nothing short of revenge on their part and he had to rise above the bile.

**

CHAPTER EIGHT

John slowed the coal-motor opposite the front-door of his home, bumped over the kerb and eased the wagon away from the road and on to council land. Didn't want any neighbours complaining that the street was congested or bottle-necked. Because he was dirt-encrusted, John walked to the back door, placed his grubby boots and overalls in the landing then moved to the kitchen. He nodded appreciatively as warmth enveloped him and the succulent aroma wafted his way. The noise of the television greeted him when he opened the kitchen door. His youngest son, Frank, was squatting at the table with three young friends. Eddie, judging by the racket echoing from the adjoining room, was arguing with his mother. Young Frank smiled briefly at his father before returning to share the trough of snacks with his pals.

John Briggs stared at his boy, his very own piccanny, and something snapped inside his head. Tina Cunninghan's words returned to torture him, Tina taunting and laughing as she spread the poison thick and fast. John was transfixed, his mind spun with hateful thoughts as he focused on his youngest child. Young Frank stood out like a beacon against the pale-skinned, sallow faces of his friends. A rush of images engulfed him. The face of his mother appeared, at first comforting then chiding him when he first confided in her. His child was months old at the time when Elsie took him to task. Sat in the prison's visiting room and castigated him, told him his son was a bronzed, healthy boy and the double of his father. Elsie Briggs eased his worries with illogical comparisons of other village boys. Henry Iveson was mentioned. Henry, who looked more oriental than English, had been ribbed all of his life for his foreign looks. Then his mother referred to Ronnie Jepson who was a virtual giant compared to his diminutive parents. Last but not least was carrot-topped, wan-faced Myra Morrison, whose parents looked more gypsy than mining-stock. At the time, Elsie's no-nonsense approach put his mind at rest and his fears were pushed aside. He never thought such insecurities would ever be resurrected.

For a time his worries had eased, he even found the strength to poke fun at his fears. Used to laugh and call his son Punjab Pete. Other times he'd taunt Iris by referring to his youngest as Farouk. But now, full of nagging doubt, the questions returned to haunt him. Iris was only human and he had been out of circulation a long time. John knew all about temptation, knew the fickle, irresistible magnet of forbidden flesh. He wondered if his imagination was playing awful tricks with him, after all, no one had ever commentated on his son's appearance. Folks made the occasional congratulatory remarks about the healthy look of the child but never once had he endured sly digs or off-the-cuff observations.

John sensed Iris's presence and realised he had been joined in the room. His wife was close, speaking to him, but he couldn't stop staring at his son.

"Is there something wrong, John?" she asked. "What's the matter, has Frank upset you?"

He looked at Iris, glared like never before … at her eyes, at her face. He was numb, dumb with doubt.

"What the hell, John?" she queried, her face draining of colour.

Iris was caught unawares. Too quick to prepare herself, the smudge of guilt cracked over her waxen features. Her mind raced in all directions when she saw the tortured features on her husband's face. She cringed with fear.

He found words at last, talked gibberish, couldn't stop, and cared little about the gawking audience of children. It was the frightened look on Iris's face that sent shivers through his body. He couldn't ever remember her looking so terrified. He told her of his conversation with the Wingate female then foolishly asked if it were true. Felt light-headed with pain, the ache so real he had to grab at the chair to steady himself.

Iris recovered enough to retaliate. Screaming at the top of her voice she attacked, never stopping for breath as she barracked and cursed her floundering husband.

His courage deserted him. Wanted to say so much more but couldn't find the words. All he could see was the guilt radiating like a beacon from Iris's face. He could take no more. Grabbing his coat and boots he stormed from the house.

Despite his mood John drove to the hospital. Dressed to kill in filthy work clothes he was given orders by the nurses, John was allowed a brief moment with his partner. Dean Crumplin was covered in tubes and drips, and delirious with medication. The older man nodded vacantly at his visitor, tried to converse but was unable. A short time later John left the hospital, drove into Hartlepool and parked close to a burger-van. He bought food and wolfed it down. Didn't matter that the pie was stale or that the chips tasted like cardboard, it was hot and welcome and washed down with a big bottle of *Pepsi.* It was his first meal since breakfast.

He started driving, didn't know what else to do. Drove a mile along the coast from Hartlepool and reached Seaton Carew, a picture-postcard holiday resort in the summer but different again in the middle of winter. John parked near to the crashing shore. The place was dark and grim as the forlorn line of lamp-posts that struggled to throw light on the deserted street. The snow flakes, as big as daffodils, swirled, pirouetted and jigged their way earthwards. A couple walked past. They were joined tightly together, a wide jabbering bundle of coat and cloth. The fellow held the long lead that allowed the downcast mutt to meekly follow its masters, the animal not sharing the romance of the night. The animal wanted to be home close to a warm, open fire. The couple was unaware of the voyeur. John Briggs stared enviously at the pair, wrapped like jesters and without a care in the whole world. Made him sad, wanted it to be like that for him and Iris. His head was demented with emotion, bouncing one way then another; full of doubt, then hope, repentance followed grief. One moment he was filled with uncertainty, the next, buoyed with confidence, optimistic then pessimistic, on the see-saw of life.

John awoke. He was in shock. An earsplitting din enveloped the entire motor; the noise of explosions peppered the outside armour of the vehicle and forced him to take cover. Then, as suddenly as it started, the thunderous racket ceased. With his heart racing he peered through snow-covered windows and glimpsed the Council gritting-wagon disappearing into the swirling gloom of the night.

John Briggs checked his watch and gasped. It was 12.45am. It was the middle of the night. His entire body ached with long hours cramped in the small cab. Rubbing his eyes, he switched on the engine and started the slow and perilous journey home. The time alone had mellowed him. He felt crestfallen and ashamed of his actions.

Minutes later the wagon was crawling along Church Street in Hartlepool. Either side of the road, the pubs and wine-bars were boarded-up, shuttered and deserted. A lone tramp, covered head to feet in thick cladding, stood at the roadside and watched him pass, the vagabond tapping an uneven tune in oversized Wellingtons as he sucked greedily on a jerking cigarette. John neared the round-about and saw two policemen, side by side, kicking the same surreal tune at the icy ground.

Iris had not locked the door, had not barred him. He crept into the house. Iris was asleep on the sofa. Her head was skewed one way, her eyes were closed and lines of eye-shadow and mascara had run with her tears. She looked like a sad clown. He spoke to her and touched her shoulder. John begged for forgiveness. Iris opened her eyes and tears fell. The couple came together, caressed one another, frantic in their passion, both weeping, both apologizing, blaming one another as they kissed and touched. The madness of suspicion and jealousy was forgotten as they held each other.

Outside the wind shrieked and hail rattled windows. It was hellish outside, and heaven inside.

The morning was blissful. Iris and John were both repentant, fearful of destroying a relationship over a senseless argument. It had been a spat, a terrible but temporary cloud that had blackened their hearts. The couple overslept. When they finally awoke and saw the dark heavens and the falling snow they entwined and caressed and made love silently and passionately. They touched heaven, whispered their true feelings for one another. Slowly, carefully, John repeated the spiteful gossip, told Iris of his fears, mentioned those who wanted to hurt him and wound their relationship. She listened quietly and attentively, hanging on to his every word, frequently interrupting and giving explanations and answers, kissing and caressing and silencing his worries. She calmed him, explained subtly that others - enemies, rivals - were exaggerating and spinning webs of intrigue and slander. Over and over Iris repeated her oaths, telling him how she would never hurt him. Told him she loved him and that she couldn't look at another man. There was only one man for her, Johnny Briggs.

A little after nine they finally left the warmth of their bed and breakfasted. A flask and sandwiches were prepared to see him through the long day. Iris didn't question the time he would be away, told him only she was regretful about her immature ways and whims. Admitted she had been selfish but vowed to change. They were a team, the two of them facing the big bad world, John and Iris and their beautiful boys, their sons who had been created because of their union. They cuddled like newlyweds, hungry for one another. They were a family once again. United.

John opened the door. The howling wind made him shiver. Driving snow sprayed his face and clothes and still he smiled as if he did not have a care in the world. He kissed Iris, regret etched over his face. Told her he was sorry. She comforted him, blamed herself and said she had learned her lesson. They kissed and then kissed again. John left the house.

The house was so quiet. Iris sat alone without the howl from radio or television. She needed to think and find a way out of the mess. The living-room was hot but she sat close to the fire and shivered with fear. She prayed for an escape. Closed her eyes and imagined the uproar and bedlam if the truth came out. Her head was bowed with anguish and her body cried with utter despair. The enormity of her idiotic, immature behaviour suddenly hit her. The realization tortured Iris. She covered her face with her hands and began to pray. Begged God for another chance.

"Please give me a chance, one more chance and I'll never hurt him again," she wailed softly. 'Please! Please, and I'll never stray again." Iris started to weep, 'I love him, God, don't let me lose him!

"Ma!" cried Eddie, suddenly next to her, distraught at the sight of his mother crying. "What's the matter?"

Iris Briggs grabbed and held her oldest son. She cried bitter tears.

Young Frank heard the commotion and hurried down the stairs. Saw the picture in front of him and stopped mid-way. He watched wide-eyed as his big brother wept and his mother howled. He put his hands up to his drooling mouth and began to cry.

Iris gestured to her youngest. Opened her arms and watched as he sprinted towards her. She knew she had to be strong, not only for her own sake but for her children, most of all for her husband. Iris wanted one more chance to redeem herself. One more chance and she would never hurt Johnny again.

**

CHAPTER NINE

Dean Crumplin spent two weeks in hospital followed by two long months convalescing before he accepted his working days were at an end. He was worn-out, mentally and physically. His crippled leg, his damaged heart and his depression all contributed to his thoughts for retirement. Behind closed doors he had attempted to lift his spirits and tried to instil commitment and perseverance. He had managed in the past to battle adversity, he had successfully overcome life's trials, but not this time, not now. This time it was different.

His conscience scratched weals over him, bothered him as much as throwing in the towel. It was the young John Briggs who had saved his business from ruination. The lad was as honest as the day was long. Too honest if truth be told … a better person than he, up front about everything, wasn't frightened to graft until he dropped, wasn't too scared to speak his mind. Told Dean Crumplin uncomfortable truths when he mentioned that the so-called discounting - the freebies and the give-a-way stuff - should end. Straight to the point, said it like it was, Dean spouting tall-tales about his cash-only business when in reality he gave credit to selected customers. The deal was better than never-never because the favoured few either part-paid or had an *arrangement* with the proprietor. The lad was right of course. He might have been a youngster but he had the makings of a businessman. It was he who informed the ailing coal-merchant that he could put things right, put the business on an even keel. Dean was apprehensive and rightly so. After all, he'd been lax for years, and such changes could lose valuable customers. The youth was adamant, stood his ground and presented the figures showing the monies lost weekly. And if that wasn't enough, John Briggs offered something new. Told his partner about printing a business-card with the logo of daily deliveries, and an emergency phone number covering weekends. He wanted Dean's permission to print thousands, promising to drop a card through every house in the area with a smoking chimney. Concluded with a statement of fact; since being made a partner the sales had doubled. He was right of course, cocky but correct. Dean had never seen so much cash.

The business had been deteriorating, gently hemorrhaging so slowly that Dean had not realised that sales were dipping week in, week out. It had needed the gumption of the lad to realize the problem and start revitalizing the coal-business. After two horrendous weeks of working alone, the youth finally hired a local lad, Kenny Wilkinson. John Briggs had taken charge of recruitment, interviewed five youths and picked the only one who was working full-time. He offered basic pay plus time-and-a half for Saturday morning and double-time for Sundays. Two months had past since he'd hired and young Kenny was still as keen as mustard. The business was making more money despite one extra employee and one absentee boss. For weeks Dean had struggled with his conscience, taking his cut every week and not lifting a finger to help. And John Briggs had never complained.

John and Iris were killing with kindness. While John was building the business, Iris was calling daily with parcels of food still piping-hot, usually home-made, occasionally from the fish shop. The girl was so different now, more mature, the brashness long gone. Dean confided in her - John and the two boys waited in the wagon out-side while Iris carried in the home-made cooking - told her how much she had changed. He felt foolish, a right old codger, saying kind words to the embarrassed girl. Iris took it in her stride, feigning confusion, patting his tousled head before hurrying away. He watched them a few times, from behind curtains naturally and got a little upset, envious even, wishing Beatrice would come to her senses, aching for family life again.

Dean Crumplin had made up his mind. He'd done all the leg-work yesterday, he was transferring the business to the youngster. The letter was on the mantle-piece next to a second containing the log-book. Both ready to hand over to John Briggs. Didn't need to tell fancy accountants or the tax-man about the business transfer, there was no need, he'd never paid tax. The business was worth a fair penny; the value of the lorry was a couple of grand, give or take the odd shekel. The matter would be done and dusted. His conscience would be clear at long last. He checked the clock, it was almost noon. It was Sunday and the sun was shining. He couldn't wait to see the look on his face. Dean closed his eyes and waited for his young friend. John Briggs was more than just a business partner; he was a good friend, a Christian who put others before himself, a juvenile Good-Samaritan.

His head started filling with other images. He thought of yesteryear and Beatrice. It was always Beatrice who dominated his thoughts. Not a day past when didn't think of his beautiful, absent wife. Missed her so much it hurt. Dean wondered if she had any feelings for him. He'd always hoped there was a smattering of love buried somewhere deep inside her cold heart. Beatrice kept him guessing, never asking for a divorce or even a formal separation even though they'd been apart ten years and more. On paper they were an item, in the eyes of the law they were still married. Maybe it was true; perhaps she held a candle for him. There was no other logical explanation for her inaction. The first thing on the agenda when a couple parted was to put the necessary paper-work in order … separation and then the divorce. It was the only course of action for a woman starting afresh to sever the knot from the past. Beatrice didn't do a thing. She never demanded weekly maintenance. Gave him free reign to act like a lot of spurned husbands and make her haggle for money. It wasn't in Dean's nature to act in such a way. He could never humiliate Beatrice even though she had been the guilty party. No, there had to be some logical reason for her reluctance to formally end the marriage. He imagined that pride had been a factor. Beatrice, truth be told, oozed conceit. It took Dean moments to discount the idea. His ex-spouse had skin as thick as a rhinoceros. There had to be something else. It certainly wasn't religion, Beatrice was a lapsed Methodist, Dean a Catholic. When they married, on Beatrice's insistence, the ceremony was held in the Methodist Chapel in Peterlee even though Dean had hinted towards another haunt. Religion therefore held no barrier to annulment. He wondered if his estranged spouse was hedging her bets. When he first took ill before Christmas it took one phone call to persuade Beatrice to visit the hospital. One phone call and she came running. Dean smiled, convinced Beatrice, in some unfathomable way, loved him still.

He struggled from the big settee and wandered to the window. It was a glorious day. Dean felt good; convinced he was on the slow road to recovery. He had started exercising. Twice a day for the past week Dean had walked to Haswell and back, early morning and evening, three miles either way. Only thing that bothered him was his bloody limp, made him look so foolish, hence the early hike when the road was deserted, and again in the early evenings when dusk was settling. Walked like Walter Brennan in *Rio Bravo,* couldn't recall the cripple's name in the film. *Stumpy* was it? Felt like *Stumpy,* definitely walked like *Stumpy.* He'd tried a few sit-ups yesterday and was fine. An hour ago he'd done the same but felt a twinge of discomfort and stopped immediately. The last thing he wanted was another spell in a hospital bed. He yawned again and raised his arms above his head. The sun made him smile. Summer was on the way. It was good to be alive.

A searing pain tore over his chest, an indescribable stabbing as if his chest was being smashed open with an axe. His breath stopped and his eyes rolled. Colours and shapes, anguish and images all thrashed him simultaneously, a surreal nightmare of torture bombarded him. His body convulsed and racked as the tremors smashed on him. He tried to call out but the excruciating pain stopped him. Bright strobes bore down on Dean, powerful, shimmering, lights so bright his eyes were forced shut and he could sense someone or something hovering close but he couldn't talk, couldn't think. Awash with misery his torso thrashed and his body convulsed in agonizing spasms, a kaleidoscope of colours enveloped him and forced his protesting body to stumble round the room. Suddenly Beatrice appeared at his side, next to him, holding and caressing him. He screamed out her name and watched as she eased him to the floor, draped blankets over his protesting body and offer words of comfort.

"Stop the pain, Beatrice!" he cried. Dean stumbled into an abyss of blackness, careered and thrashed into a raging ocean of darkness. "Beatrice," he pleaded, "I'm frightened!"

For the briefest of moments the hallucinating Dean Crumplin felt the warmth and reassurance from the only person he had every loved. He saw the smiling face of his wife close to him, kissing him on the lips. Couldn't stop the tears falling. Beatrice had come back, everything would be all right. He smiled contentedly.

Eight minutes after Dean Crumplin died, John Briggs tried his partner's door. It was locked. The youth shielded his eyes and stared into the small kitchen. It was empty. He hurried to the front of the house and peered through the big window. The sun shimmered against the pane and panned into the living-room like some giant torch. Dean was spread-eagled across the floor, his upper-body part-draped with curtains wrenched from mountings and looking like some garish shroud. John did not panic, it had happened too often for him to be shocked. The front-door was locked but the design of the door, with its four small sculptured panes across the upper section, allowed access. Using his elbow he side-swiped the window nearest to the latch. It shattered and allowed him to prize away the broken sections. Naomi Bates, the neighbour sharing the same yard as Dean Crumplin, heard the racket, opened her door and began firing accusations.

The youth interrupted her ranting. He told her to be quiet and to call an ambulance. Naomi hesitated momentarily before disappearing back into her home.

Once inside John hurried to the living-room. Taking a deep breath he kneeled next to the silent figure. And touched Dean's face. He was warm still. John carefully pulled aside the curtains that covered him. Dean Crumplin looked peaceful, as if he were sleeping. John didn't panic, remembered the last attack, when the policeman aided the stricken Dean. He concentrated, recalled Dean Crumplin being pulled from the motor and laid face-up on the ground, the constable resolute with the procedure: forehead pulled back, nose nipped, mouth to mouth, blow, count to three, blow, palms together and bump the chest, one and two and three. John wasn't frightened anymore, he cared too much for old Dean. Taking a deep breath, he said a prayer and started the resuscitation.

It was late afternoon when John Briggs dropped off
Kenny Wilkinson in Hopper Terrace, a stone's throw from the
Crumplin home. Kenny was a good lad. Seventeen, six feet
six and maybe ten stone, wet through, a walking beanpole, but
he could graft all day without rest. John had picked the best of
the bunch when he hired Ken Wilkinson.

"With Dean out of the picture," queried Kenny, "is my
job safe?"

"Safe as houses, why?"

The lad shrugged his shoulders, "Just asking," said
Kenny. He turned and strode away, steel toe-cap boots clip-
clopping along the street.

John watched him disappear into the semi-detached, a
deep frown etched over his features. Kenny's inquiry had
bothered him. Why should their futures be in jeopardy? His
job was safe, Kenny's job was safe, after all he owned the
firm. John drove the coal-wagon towards the Salters Lane
house and parked outside the Crumplin house. It was a little
after five-o-clock and the house was curtained and closed as a
sign of respect. He stared long at the home, at a loss as to
what to do. He'd passed earlier in the day en-route to South
Hetton and seen the solitary car pull up and the couple
walking to the house. Recognized Dean Crumplin's ex-wife
and recalled Dean's whining explanation months earlier, *'She
not my ex-wife, Johnny, we're still married!'* Adamant too, as
if he was proud about the fact. Even when his young partner
had protested, *'Ten years, Dean, that's a hell of a temporary
arrangement. If you ask me, it's divorce without the
paperwork!'* Dean had become agitated so the subject was
dropped. John now wondered what would happen to Dean's
home. Would it be sold or would his estranged wife move in.

Knew for a fact that he would be sharing the business with a woman, a stranger. Beatrice Crumplin, like it or lump it, would be his new partner.

*

The coal-face was cleared and Jonty Myers, the shot-firer, was busy preparing for the blasting. The Deputy, Robert Briggs, approached, checking that everything was okay. Jonty had completed his first week as an official and was understandably nervous. Satisfied with the work, the Deputy then joined the group of miners' out-bye. The colliers squatted on the ground, on the stationery conveyor-belt, anywhere and everywhere, taking a break from the work, talking quietly, guzzling from water-bottles, grateful for a few minutes rest before the continuation of the shift.

Peter Caine, six feet three, and built like *Big Daddy* with girth to match, was yards away urinating. His vest and shorts were drenched with perspiration. His massive body stooped as he relieved himself; a decade of cracked helmets conditioning him. Peter Caine - known as P C or Copper to his friends - lived opposite Robert Briggs' old home. He had attended the same school as Frank, Robert's father. Thought the world about John Briggs.

The collier shouted at the nearing official, "Robert, what cheer?"

"Copper," said Robert Briggs, "how's tricks?"

"Your little brother," asked the miner, "how is he?"

"Doing okay, Copper," shouted the Deputy. "He's turned himself around. Got himself a partnership with old Dean Crumplin."

"Poor Dean, eh?"

Robert answered with a brother's pride, "John tried to save him, Copper. Gave him mouth to mouth!"

"Fella had nowt but bad luck all his life."

"The accident down Second-North," agreed Robert Briggs. "Almost amputated his bloody leg! Then he goes and has a heart-attack!"

"Some people will do anything to get away from their wives!" interrupted a chortling Ricky Keith. He had shared his school-days with Dean's estranged wife and knew her better than most. "Beatrice was some girl!"

Peter Caine shook himself, adjusted his baggy shorts and crept towards the crew. He squatted between Robert Briggs and Ricky Keith.

"Robert," said Peter Caine, "do you think John's job is okay?"

"Can't see why not. They were a partnership, even had John's name on the coal-wagon."

Ricky Keith intervened with the bombshell news, "Did you know that Dean was still married to Beatrice?"

"That's shite!" snapped Peter Caine.

Ricky Keith was adamant. "Beatrice was shacked up with Sammy Bruce from Blackhall! They might have had ten years together but they never wed!"

"Load of rubbish!" said Peter.

"Put your money where your mouth is!" demanded Ricky. He stuck out his hand. "Name the bet!"

Robert interrupted, "Makes no difference, surely?"

"Put your head on straight," said Ricky Keith. "Beatrice is still Dean's wife. She's entitled to everything."

Peter Caine shook his head, a grim look on his face. He started talking. "The missus and me used to socialise with Dean and Beatrice before she ran away with Sammy. Tell you for nowt, Robert, she's one hard bastard. If you see your John

86

give him the news. Beatrice won't be happy until she has it all." He paused then added, "She'll not be happy with a partnership, mark my words."

Jonty Myers, the shot-firer, appeared. He spoke to the Deputy. "Safety-lamp is showing a bit of gas, Robert. I thought we'd wait a while longer. Take a pew, eh?"

Robert Briggs shouted loudly, "Half an hour break, lads! Have a bite to eat. We'll let the ventilation do it's job!"

Peter Caine opened his metal bait-tin. "Corned-dog again!" he muttered. Spat a wad of phlegm on to the floor and groaned, "That bloody missus of mine! Swap anyone?"

Someone shouted, "Corned-beef or your missus, Copper?"

"I'm game," replied Peter Cain.

"Think I'll pass, Copper," came the sarcastic reply.

Peter turned to Ricky Keith, grinning widely, "Can't say I blame him, the missus is some size!"

Ricky inspected his sandwiches, "Cheese and onion, Copper?" and offered the bait-tin to the huge collier.

"Why not," replied the collier. He added, "What's it like?'

"Dog food!"

"Thanks a lot!" said Peter Caine. He grabbed the sandwich and pushed it into his mouth.

Robert Briggs sat quietly. Reflective. His stomach churned with a gnawing worry about his young brother. He mulled over the gossip about Beatrice Crumplin and wondered if he should call John and put him in the picture. He pondered a while then changed his mind. Thought he would have a word with Dorothy first. One thing guaranteed from his wife; she would give him a straight, no-nonsense answer.

CHAPTER TEN

Michael Motson, John Briggs' infamous uncle, was down on his luck and had been for some time. His unemployment benefit was always blown within days; and he was driving a decrepit Hillman Imp that coughed more muck out of its rear end than I.C.I. on a bad day.

A few weeks earlier Micky's luck had lifted. He had won a wad on the horses and was celebrating. Twenty minutes easy driving from Stockton and he only stopped once to stick oil into the leaking engine before they reached the seaside. Redcar was the chosen venue with long-suffering girl-friend Eileen McCufferty. Peace and tranquility however had lasted as long as the car journey. Things had gone belly-up when his girl started going at it hammer and tongs outside the fish restaurant; Eileen wanted a sit-down meal but Micky, always thinking about the pennies, wanted a take-out. Would have saved a fortune but no, Eileen, *up-her-arse Eileen*, wouldn't budge. Even when he explained about the lack of funds and the petrol money home she retaliated, stuck it in his face good and proper about his constant dalliances with illegal substances. Like a record on repeat was Eileen as she regurgitated the long line of muck that coursed through Micky's veins. He fired back with his ready excuse when he told her that the only reason he took the occasional tablet was because it helped him relax and, more importantly, to eased the pain.

Like talking to a hornet's nest after you've trodden on it.

Micky lost it. He'd had enough of her bad-mouthing so he went walkabout. Head down and cursing venomously Micky collided into Alex Heslop. The bouncer was as broad as he was tall, five feet four or thereabouts and solid as a concrete bunker. The diminutive, scowling doorman unceremoniously elbowed Motson to one side and glowered at the smiling stranger.

"Alex," Micky Motson exclaimed excitedly, "it's your old pal, Buff! Recognize me or what?"

Michael Motson never forgot a face, he knew Alex from way back when. They had shared duties as heavies at a nightclub in Stockon before misfortune turned into disaster for Micky and took him first to hospital and then to a long spell behind bars. Alex Heslop cursed again and tried to push past. Then he stopped and looked again at the bedraggled, balding, pig-tailed figure. Nothing registered.

"I know you?" Heslop asked aggressively.

"It's Buff!" said Micky Motson. "We were on the doors at the Fiesta nightclub years ago, man! Bouncers, the two of us, Friday and Saturday nights, you gotta remember!"

The penny dropped, the comical features of the stranger unrecognizable but the whining tones twirled cogs inside Alex Heslop's head.

"Buff Motson!" Heslop muttered grudgingly. "It's been years!"

"How's things, Alex," shouted an ecstatic Micky. "You haven't changed, man, still as ugly as ever!"

When a curious Eileen McCufferty waltzed over, Micky shooed her away so anxious to hear all the latest from his old crony. The female, her features knotted with fury, stormed away to the nearby line of shops and left the two men talking.

Alex Heslop was still working the nightclubs, mainly week-ends but not in Stockton. Told Motson he helped run the doors in nearby Middlesbrough.

"Bongo's Nightclub and Wicker's World," said Alex Heslop, his cherub face full of smiles. 'Good money and very little trouble.'

Motson asked, "You still selling shit to the punters?"

Alex Heslop was adamant with his denials, "Not worth it," he said matter of fact. "The boss is on my back all the time,"

According to Heslop, his employer had his greedy fingers in all the pies. Wicked he was, owned a few pubs, couple of slot-shops in the centre, and in charge of security at most of the clubs. Alex Heslop had to answer directly to Sugar Ray.

"Proper gangster he is," spouted squat Alex Heslop, "one evil piece of shit is Raymond Robinson."

Alex Heslop didn't know the history between Michael Motson and Ray Robinson. With hindsight he would have kept quiet about his employer. Motson smiled manically as if he were snorting a line. He had searched for Sugar Ray Robinson since his release from jail, searched high and low around the old haunts of Stockton and drawn a blank. He thought that his old boss had left the district for good, imagined Robinson might have left the country after turning Queen's Evidence.

"Put in a good word for me, Alex." Micky Motson kept hold of his emotions. "I need the bread, man."

"Sure, I'll do that, Buff," answered Heslop, faking sincerity. "First chance I get."

Motson could not believe his luck. A few short miles away was the man who had ruined his life.

Alex Heslop smiled, said he would talk to Sugar. Would have said black was white, anything to get rid of the whining, festering low-life that was Michael Motson. Imagined his old crony was living rough judging by the state of him, either on the streets or a genuine paid-up member of Alcoholics Anonymous. Heslop promised the world, anxious to put distance between himself and the wino.

Motson quizzed, "You live here, Alex?"

"Redcar is okay in the summer!" said Heslop, gesturing at the leaden skies. Added dryly, "Another month and we'll see the sun."

"And Sugar Ray," pushed Micky Motson, a steely glint suddenly filled his eyes, "he like playing with sand-castles too?"

"Lives in Grangetown, Middlesbrough."

Heslop stepped back a pace, suddenly uneasy in the presence of the wild-eyed hobo. He vaguely remembered stories about the volatile, violent Buff Motson.

"You got his address, Alex?"

Alex Heslop gulped apprehensively. The man was giving off all the wrong vibes; he was a clown one minute, a psycho the next. His head spun as he tried to recall the old gossip about the one-time hard-man. Prison rang a bell. He would have to check the facts. Heslop stared at the damaged features of the man, at the scar-tissue, the lumps and bumps. Motson's face looked as if it had been used as a punch-bag.

"Sure Buff," replied Alex Heslop, "It's a council house. Low key is Ray Robinson." He tried to jest, "You gonna give Robinson your C.V. or what?"

"Something like that." Michael Motson smiled coldly.

The shorter figure rattled off the address, made his excuses and disappeared into the crowds of meandering shoppers, ignorant about the history and the animosity between Robinson and Motson. Alex Heslop was a novice when he first met Motson and knew nothing about the festering feud.

"Keep in touch, Alex," shouted a delighted Michael Motson.

He found Eileen and kissed arse until she relented. They had a sit-down meal in the fish restaurant; he even bought two large cokes to wash down the food topped up with a little brandy from his flask. Eileen, fooled by the ploy, said she didn't mind the detour around the outskirts of Middlesbrough. Believed the ex-con when he said he was looking for his old mate.

"So he was a friend as well as a boss?' quizzed Eileen. Smiled sweetly as she pictured the man who owned clubs and drinking-dens, wondered if she could wangle a meeting with the millionaire. "You'll have to introduce me."

"Sure Eileen," replied a cheerful Micky Motson.

"So why the dumb name of Sugar Ray?" asked Eileen.

"The middleweight champion of the world was Ray Robinson. The fifties I'm talking about, Eileen. He was as sweet as sugar in the ring. Cassius Clay said Robinson was the best pound-for-pound fighter in the world!"

"So the man who owns the nightclubs was a boxer?"

"No, he was as soft as butter, Eileen!"

"I don't understand?"

"Wore the coat, honey but he couldn't fasten the buttons!"

Michael Motson was in exuberant mood. He smiled and nodded lamely as he drove the banger expertly through the back-streets of Middlesbrough. One hand was on the steering-wheel, the other up Eileen's dress. He felt better than he'd felt for years … five years in fact.

*

Beatrice Crumplin stood stiff-legged next to the hearth, her features twisted with suppressed anger seemingly impervious to the heat and the ricocheting dust from the roaring fire. The woman gripped the log-book and the crumpled letter, her fingers taut like talons as she balled and bent the evidence. Cursed her dead husband for being an old fool.

Sammy Bruce shifted his stance away from the television screen and looked at the woman. He feigned a smile and smoothed a hand over his shining pate, knew from bitter experience not to speak when Beatrice was in one of her moods.

Beatrice shook her head in disgust and glanced at the letter again. She turned and stared at her disinterested partner then looked momentarily at the television. Sighing loudly she squatted on the arm-chair next to the open fire, took another look at the correspondence and then hurled it into the flames. Noticed Sammy was staring nervously at her.

"What?" snapped Beatrice.

"Nothing, love," he answered softly. "Suppose you'll know what you're doing."

"Why give the business away for free when I can sell it to the lad?" She studied the log-book, "I'll sell the wagon too. It'll be worth a penny or two."

"What if Dean had told the lad, you know, about transferring the business, Beatrice?" Studied her reaction; poker-faced with anger as she glowered back at him, "There's no need to look at me like that, Beatrice," he reasoned placidly, "it's a sensible question."

"The lad doesn't know!" Beatrice grasped her bag and placed the log-book inside. "Or I'd have heard by now!"

Sammy nodded. He glanced at the clock on the mantle-piece. It was six-o-clock, another half an hour and he'd be safely in the club, out of harm's way.

The woman had the power to read minds. "And don't you have too much ale tonight, Sammy Bruce! Tomorrow we are going through that house with a fine tooth-comb, right?"

Beatrice grimaced as her spineless partner nodded subserviently. She pictured Dean and smiled self-righteously. Knew all of Dean's hiding-holes and he was a creature of

93

habit. Beatrice thought about the bundles of cash waiting to be found. Pictured the youth and wondered if there would be problems. The lorry was one hiccup especially with two names on the logo. Dean was such an idiot, always digging holes for Beatrice to fill. She would have to think of something.

"Right then," said a subdued Sammy. He eased his frame from the sofa. "If it's all sorted, might as well have a wash and shave."

He slunk past Beatrice as if he was on the way to the Dunce's Corner.

"Bloody men!" muttered the woman.

Sammy Bruce stopped and raised both hands in protest, "What do you want me to do, woman?" he said nervously.

"That's all you're good for!" she whined. "Gossiping with your stupid boys!"

"There's no point in me offering advice when you've made your mind up anyway!"

"Go on, bugger off!"

"Beatrice there's no need to be so abusive!"

"Get out of my sight!"

Sammy Bruce shook his head wearily. There were times when he could have run a hundred miles from Beatrice. Days like this he could have gladly strangled her. Taking a deep breath he stormed out of the room.

"Bloody miners!"

Beatrice walked to the door and slammed it shut. It was at times like this she needed to be on her own. Needed time to plot and plan.

*

94

John Briggs and Kenny Wilkinson worked all week with neither sight nor sound from Dean Crumplin's estranged wife. Initial trepidation slowly disappeared as the weekend blossomed and the youthful entrepreneur began to fill with a buoyant optimism. Day after day John had waited for Beatrice Crumplin to make contact and when none came, the foreboding was pushed aside. Dean's prophetic confession about his matrimonial status was ignored. John said nothing to his co-worker. Even when the subject was mentioned by young Kenny it was dismissed with a dispassionate shrug and a casual response. The small voice of reason, however, continued to scratch at him, warning him of impending trouble. He lay awake at night deeply troubled, one minute thinking the business would not change much, with Beatrice putting on Dean's shoes and essentially taking a back-seat, or being persuaded to sell her share to him. The next minute he was down in the dumps imagining the worst possible scenario with Dean's ex demanding everything. John tossed and turned night after night with his thoughts in turmoil, knowing that if only Dean Crumplin had put something in writing his future would be a little more secure.

Saturday arrived and John Briggs imagined good times ahead. He returned to his home to collect the pay-packet for Kenny Wilkinson and was met by a stumped, bewildered Iris. The news wasn't good. He and Kenny had been dutifully summoned to the house on Salters' Lane. Beatrice Crumplin wanted to see both lads personally and demanded the business takings. It was crunch-time.

Beatrice Crumplin was standing sour-faced by the open door. She invited them in and then casually dropped the bombshell. Saturday lunchtime John Briggs' world fell apart. He was bluntly informed he was no longer a part-owner of Crumplin's Coals.

95

Kenny Wilkinson was handed cash and ordered to leave with a curt reminder that she expected to see him, bright and early, eight-o-clock Monday morning.

"See you where, Missus?" asked Kenny

The youth was informed that the coal-wagon was to remain parked outside of the Salters's Lane home every evening. When the lanky youth reminded her that John collected and dropped him daily Beatrice stamped her foot belligerently and said some unpalatable truths. The lad walked away, his tail between his legs.

John stood livid with anger. He had been offered a wage-packet by the woman and had refused to take it.

"You are definitely not a partner," insisted Beatrice Crumplin.

The wages were once again offered to the youth and again refused.

"I'm telling you, Missus!" muttered John Briggs. "I'm a partner! Me and Dean split the profit down the middle!"

"I've found no documents anywhere in the house," she whined, "apart from a will."

"A will?"

"Dean has left everything to me! The house, the belongings, the business *and* the wagon! There is not one mention of a partnership on any document or letter! Nothing!"

"Missus," said the irritated youth, gesticulating towards the lorry, "there are two names on the wagon!"

"Dean told me about that," replied the ballsy Beatrice. "He said it was to keep the peace. Said you were very pushy. It was Dean's way of keeping you quiet. Said you wanted everybody thinking you were part-owner. It was his way of keeping the peace!"

"Missus, that's not true!" John started to tremble with tension.

"Listen," said a condescending Beatrice. "I've seen a solicitor and he agrees with me totally, the logo has no bearing in law."

The woman saw the resignation wash over the young face and knew she had beaten him. Beatrice knew the bait had been swallowed and she could pull gently on the fishing-line.

"We were a partnership," whispered John Briggs. He stared blankly at the floor.

"Dean thought you were a decent worker," said Beatrice. She waited patiently, allowing moments to pass before offering the prize. "John, there might be a way out of this. A solution."

He looked at her, his eyes widening, "Right!" he said.

"George Jones has been to see me twice this week," she said casually. The mistruth was a necessary evil for the female. She had thought about the rival coal-merchant the night before and realised immediately she had found a way to silence the lad. "George offered excellent money for the Goodwill of the business."

"Goodwill, Missus?" John was nineteen years old and naïve to business jargon. He stood perplexed and pensive, "Don't understand?"

Beatrice Crumplin smiled, thought it was so easy to manipulate men.

"You don't just buy the business, love," said Beatrice, her voice softening. "You buy the name. You buy the name and hopefully get to keep the customers. *Crumplin's Coals* have regular customers, John."

"*Crumplin and Briggs*," he corrected her, "and I've doubled the business!"

"Forget that foolishness, son! I've told you I've taken advice from a solicitor and you haven't a leg to stand on!"

97

Beatrice paused, folded her arms defiantly. "You want to hear my suggestion or not?"

"I'm all ears," he said grudgingly.

"£10,000 and that's a bargain."

John felt sick. The amount was out of his league. Beg, steal or borrow he might be lucky enough to raise £100.

"George Jones has offered a lot more than that, son," said Beatrice, lying through her teeth. "I'm trying to be fair."

"How much has he offered?"

"£15, 000," she answered firmly. "In cash."

The youth's head slumped in despair.

Beatrice said, "Between you and me, love, how much was Dean making every week?" she didn't wait for a reply. "I was married to the man and all he did was plead poverty." The woman laughed contemptuously.

"The business does all right."

She continued, "The first time I saw you, in the hospital, remember?"

John nodded, "Dean's first attack."

"You waltzed in carrying the money-bag, put it on his lap, and how did Dean react?" A big smile filled Beatrice craggy features. "He looked at it, remember? Wouldn't open it, well not in front of me. He waited until I was long gone before he started counting."

The lad nodded grudgingly.

"I was married to Dean for years. I know him inside and out. The business is a gold mine!"

"Gives you a living."

"Add up what the business will give you," she said bluntly. "Then work out the time it will take to make £10,000." Beatrice smirked, "It won't take long!" she added.

Resigned to defeat, the youth could only shrug his shoulders.

"Well?" asked the woman impatiently.

John asked, "How much time will you give me to raise the money?"

"One week," she answered firmly. "And remember you're getting the wagon as well."

"One week, Missus, that's not long!"

"Seven days"

John Briggs shrugged his shoulders. Looked like he felt. Defeated.

"You'll be wanting your pay." A triumphant Beatrice handed over the packet. She added dryly, "I'll see you Monday morning."

"Thanks," he said.

Crestfallen, the youth turned and walked away.

**

CHAPTER ELEVEN

John Briggs persuaded Kenny to work late Monday and Tuesday evening because of the heavy schedule on Wednesday. It was interview-day for the young entrepreneur and he had appointments with three big banks.

By early afternoon he had visited Lloyds and Barclays. Both interviews had been unmitigated disasters. Both assistant-managers were respectful, asked almost identical questions before politely refusing his request for a loan. At three-o-clock a despondent John trudged wearily to the upstairs room of the Yorkshire Bank and was greeted warmly by a tall, stout young lady called Laura Tweddle, the Deputy-Manageress of the branch.

"Sit down," said the tall, stout female, ushering the youth to the nearest chair in the poky room. A big smile oozed from the young woman, the large identification-badge stuck between her huge cleavages announced her name. Laura Tweddle was bursting out of her protesting blouse. "How can I help you, Mr. Briggs?"

John Briggs rattled through the brief history, all the while smiling and attempting to create a good impression. Called her by her name more than once, trying every way to charm and persuade.

Miss Tweddle asked, "So the business makes substantial income every week?"

"Substantial!" agreed the youth. He liked the sound of the word. Added quickly, "And growing, I've almost doubled the takings in the last few months, the leaflet-drop worked really well."

"Your late partner, Mr. Crumplin," Laura Tweddle smiled, hoping she could persuade the young entrepreneur to transfer the young entrepreneur's business to her branch. "Where did he bank?"

The silence in the room was telling. Both looked at one another, one waiting patiently for a response, the other without valid answers.

John Briggs spluttered, "The other banks didn't ask about that." He grinned haplessly at the foolishness of his answer.

The assistant-manageress smiled at the anxious young man, shrugged her ample shoulders and waited for an explanation.

"I think he kept all his money at home," said John. He coughed nervously.

"And your bank, Mr. Briggs?"

The youth could only shake his head.

"Right," continued the pessimistic assistant-manageress. "We'll move on, shall we? If I could have a brief look at your business-books for, say, the last five years?"

"Miss," said John, oozing despair. "All I want is £10,000. I'll pay it back in two, three years, honest. I'll pay it back with interest."

The manageress shook her head despairingly, "No proof of earnings, no collateral and no business books, Mr. Briggs." Laura Tweddle closed her file, sighed and shook her head. "I'm sorry," she said, "I don't think the bank can help you."

"Don't know what else to do," said John glumly. He rose slowly from his chair and reached reluctantly for the door.

"A suggestion, Mr. Briggs?"

"Anything, Miss," said John. His eyes lit up as he whiffed a resolution, "Tell me what I have to do and I'll do it!"

"Mr. Crumplin's wife?" The woman offered a crumb of hope. "Might she be persuaded to take a weekly amount from the profits?"

"I've asked," he said. "She won't."

101

John paused at the door. It was too soon to throw in the towel. Might have lost the battle but he hadn't lost the war. He was adamant he would try every avenue in order to stay self-employed. The few months working with Dean had instilled him with a new-found belief in his own abilities. He knew what he had achieved by his own efforts. Knew it more than anything. The last thing he wanted was to work for someone else. Hell and high water would not change his mind. All he needed was a little guidance and help.

"Miss," said John, "can you explain what goodwill means, in words I can understand?"

"Goodwill is an intangible asset," spouted the banker. She saw the look of incomprehension on the youth's face and realised she would have to re-jig the elucidation. Gesturing for the youth to return to his seat she began the elementary lesson. "Imagine the town-centre has two pizza shops, and one for sale at £60,000 … a lot of money for a small leasehold shop which might posses a few pizza ovens and related equipment: a fryer, micro-wave, and maybe a potato chipping-machine. Probable cost for the lot could be as little as £15,000. Laura Tweddle paused, smiled condescendingly then continued. "The difference between the sale price, the transfer of the lease, and the expenditure of the equipment is, roughly, the cost of the goodwill. The shop for sale might have regular clientele, sorry, customers, who buy on a daily or weekly basis. These are regular customers, Mr. Briggs, who would rather spend their money at that pizza shop than the other pizza shop in the town-centre. The shop is sold at such a high price because the new owners hope the customers will stay loyal."

Perplexed, John Briggs asked, "What if the customers don't like the new owners?"

"There's nothing stopping the customers from switching to the other pizza shop, Mr. Briggs."

"Goodwill is a gamble then?"

"Biggest gamble in the world, but keep the recipe the same, keep the staff behind the counter happy and the customers usually stay."

"Thanks, Missus," said a grateful John Briggs. He felt optimistic once again, his head bouncing with ideas as he grabbed at the lifeline of an idea. He shook her hand and walked confidently to the door. John glanced back at the manageress and smiled.

"Miss," he said, toying with the door-handle. "Leasehold. What does it mean exactly?"

Half an hour later John was sitting in the kitchen of his parent's home in Moore Terrace, confiding to the only person he felt able.

"Trouble is we can't put too much money in the Post Office," said Elsie Briggs. "It might mess with our benefits."

"Ma, that's perfect," said John. "It's cash I need."

"That's the problem, John," replied Elsie, pausing as she filled the kettle. "Any cash in the house and your father grabs it. Promises not to, but it burns a hole in his pocket." The woman smirked, thinking of her husband's two favourite watering-holes: *The Comrades* and *Johnny Ridley*. "Weren't for that," reflected Elsie Briggs, "I'd have a fortune."

"Beer and horses," John said resignedly. Took a deep breath before asking, "How much can you lend me, Ma?"

"Everything I've got, love," said Elsie.

The woman left the room and climbed the stairs. Returned minutes later holding a large cloth purse. She smiled as she handed over the prize.

While Elsie finished making the tea John started counting the notes. Two steaming mugs of coffee stood close to the small piles of money that festooned the table-top. The bleak look on her son's face told Elsie it was insufficient. She sipped silently at the beverage and watched him finished the tally.

John groaned, "£725," he said.

"Obviously not enough?" said the woman.

"That's messed my plans good and proper!"

"Your dad doesn't know about the money," said Elsie. "It's yours, son, if it'll help. I don't want it back."

John Briggs leaned over the table and kissed his mother, fussed her hair then walked to the window. "You're an angel, Ma," he said. Tears filled his eyes, couldn't stop the frustration seeping out, "Shit!" he moaned. "Shit!"

"Is there no one else to ask, son?"

"No one."

"What about Robert. He's never away from the pit?" Elsie smiled hopefully. "He thinks a lot about you, John."

"I think the world of my brother, but his wife is something else."

"She is a stuck-up cow," agreed Elsie. Pondered a few seconds then added, "But blood is thicker than water."

"Robert can't fart unless she lets him."

"Ask him, John," insisted Elsie Briggs, ignoring the sarcasm. "Squeaking doors get oiled."

The youth returned to the table and sat opposite his mother.   Minutes passed as both struggled for solutions.

"Our Micky would do anything for me," mused Elsie. "He'd made loads of money in his time."

"Uncle Buff," replicd an enthused John Briggs. "I never knew he had money?"

"Blown a fortune in his time has Micky," uttered a reminiscing Elsie. "Has a heart of gold, my brother."

The youth sat mesmerized, wondered if his luck was about to change.

Elsie said, "John, did I ever tell you how Buff got his name?

Micky Motson earned his nick-name a lifetime ago when he fought and won Wingate hard-man Scrapper Allan. Scrapper, a two fisted dynamo of a collier, ruled the colliery. Could have been a professional boxer only his size did not equate with his height. Five feet five and sixteen stone of solid muscle, the street fighter was a formidable advisory and lightning fast for one so heavy. Scrapper Allan Pugh could punch holes in people. He had never lost a fight in his life.

A dozen miners were relaxing in the lounge of the Fir-Tree pub. It was a Sunday afternoon and the men were drinking and playing poker. Everything was fine and dandy until Scrapper suddenly up-ended the table and grabbed at young Motson. Accused Micky of cheating, shook him like a bean-bag and threatened to kill him. The bar-man, Vince Todd, pleaded to the mob to take their dispute outside. The pub car-park had only one solitary car - Vince's Citroen, worth its weight in scrap - and was no hindrance to the developing quarrel. The crowd quickly left the pub.

Initially the fight followed the usual route with the diminutive Allan pounding Micky Motson to the ground. Micky, however was unlike all of Scrapper's other opponents and refused to stay down. Time after time the younger man struggled to his feet and continued with the epic battle. 'What's Micky shouting?' said one of the onlookers. The colliery gladiators fought toe to toe, young Micky Motson up

*and down like a yoyo, bloodied but fearless as he persevered
with the bulldog collier.*

*Every time Micky Motson swung a punch he grunted:
'Buff!' Another haymaker: 'Buff!' Ten agonizing minutes
later and Scrapper Allan fell to his knees, bruised and
battered, stood again on unsteady feet, wiped blood from a
deep gash above his eye then suddenly bundled into Micky.
The colliery pugilist changed tactics, stooped low, wrapped
powerful arms around the younger man and clamped his teeth
in to the stomach of Motson.*

*Micky would not be beaten. Ignoring the pain, he
pounded at the kidneys and lower back of Scrapper, shouting
like a madman, and every time his fist smashed into his
opponent the same words were howled. Exhausted and
beaten, Scrapper Allan slumped to the ground with a jubilant
Micky on him like a man possessed, his fists like pistons as he
destroyed the champion, his voice ceaseless as he battered at
the stricken man. Micky Motson was pulled to his feet by the
spectators, the youngster crowned champion by the spirited,
vociferous mob. 'Hell of a fight, Buff!' they cheered. 'Good
old Buff Motson.'*

"Uncle Buff didn't tell anyone," said a mischievous
Elsie Briggs. "Well, apart from me!"

"What's that, Ma?"

"Buff *was* cheating at the cards," laughed the woman.
"He was a right character, always had to win, no matter the
consequences."

They finished their tea but stayed at the table. Elsie
looked at her watch. It was five-o-clock and husband Frank
would be in from the pub soon, tended to play snooker in the
afternoon session and be home between five and five thirty.
He was a creature of habit. She stood, bundled the money
back into her purse and moved to the stairs.

"I'll hide it before your Father gets back," she said. "It's there if you want it."

"Thanks, Ma."

"If I only knew Micky's address, I just know he'd help. He's out of prison but where he's living is anyone's guess."

"Prison, Ma?

"Second home, love," muttered Elsie. "I think I've visited most jails around here. But after I married your Dad, even when I got pregnant with Robert, I still used to visit Mick. I'd take a few provisions, keep his spirits up, you know. Then you were born and it got a bit difficult. Your Father was never happy, he didn't want to be tarred with the same brush."

"Was it to do with fighting," asked the youth, "Uncle Buff being locked up?"

"When he was younger he had a wicked temper. Always in bother that way. Wasn't that good as a fighter, you understand, John, just wouldn't give in. Used to wear down the opposition." Elsie chuckled at the memories. "Up and down like a puppet until the others were weary of hitting him."

"What changed, Ma?"

"Women, pet," sighed Elsie Briggs. "Always to do with women, the last one especially."

"Explain, Ma?"

"I'm sure she was a townie. Her name was Janet or Gemma … whatever," said Elsie, sighing. "But she was hooked on drugs. Took Mick on the same route."

"He an addict, Ma?"

"Addict?" muttered Elsie wistfully. "Who can say with Micky? He burned the candle at both ends. Lived life to the full, wanted to try everything to excess. Addicted to life, wine, woman and song, and things like that aren't free, John. Need money, big money."

107

"Was he a gangster?"

"He wasn't that clever. Worked for gangsters. Brave as a lion was Micky, and people used him."

"He a nice man, Ma?"

"Lovely! Heart so big..." her voice trembled and trailed off as she thought of her wayward brother.

"And he's rich?"

"Not as such, John," said the woman. She fumbled for a handkerchief and wiped her eyes. "He'd do a bit of naughty work, usually for others, and make a bundle. Catch him at the right time and he'd lend you."

"You know his telephone number, Ma? Maybe I can cadge some cash."

Elsie Briggs stared ahead, full of sadness for her brother, her weak lovely brother. "Probably doesn't own a telephone, love."

CHAPTER TWELVE

John left his mother's home and walked to the wagon parked in the back-street. In the distance a lorry screamed its presence as it tore along the narrow lane, music belching so loud the birds took flight. The approaching motor was bulging with assorted scrap - cookers, two washing-machines, a fridge minus a door - plus miscellaneous pieces of decrepit furniture. At the last moment the driver saw the outstretched arm of John Briggs who smiled and waved at the driver. Brakes squealed, the cargo howled and moved, and the vehicle screeched to a halt next to the youth.

"Johnny!" shouted Delbert Hancock. "How you doing?" Glanced at the stationery truck and read the logo, "Shouldn't ask, you must be in the money now that old Dean has kicked the bucket?"

"That'll be the day!" said John. Shrugging his shoulders he spent minutes telling Delbert Hancock the tale. "Six months work down the spout!" he concluded.

From the last house in Moore Terrace a tall thin youth appeared and sauntered along his garden-path. When he saw the two men talking he became impatient and hollered at the top of his voice. Timmy Turten, friend and partner of Delbert Hancock, knew they had to get to Wingate scrap-yard before six-o-clock. They were trading the scrap, plus a little cash, for a small quantity of drugs which the pair would sell and quadruple their money.

Delbert smiled, stuck two fingers in the direction of his frenzied pal, then turned and faced John Briggs. "Timmy won't mind if a tell you," he said. "There's a job on tonight … you want in?"

It took a moment for John to respond. He jumped in with both feet.

At ten-o-clock that evening the trio met at The Palms, near Station Road in Shotton. An hour and three pints later they walked the short distance to the recreation-ground and climbed into the old Cortina. It took the inept group ten minutes to reach Seaside Lane in Easington Colliery and park the car. They were a stone's throw from the intended target. As they left the vehicle the older youths informed John that the car-keys, purely as a precaution, were always hidden behind the back wheel. With a curt nod at the newcomer, Delbert and Timothy sauntered unfazed towards the deserted premises, the pair boasting and bragging about the fortune waiting for them. John Briggs followed quietly. He was worried, the reality was hitting home.

"They're definitely on holiday?" inquired John.

"The Newman's are always on holiday," shouted an emphatic Delbert. "They're absolutely loaded."

"He's right, Johnny," said Timmy. "I went to school with their daughter, Barbara, before they moved to Easington. Called a few times, kept in touch,"

"Definitely touched Barbara!" laughed Delbert.

"That's how I know about the *Chubb.*

"Chubb?" asked John Briggs.

"The *Chubb* safe," uttered Timmy, "in the dining-room, under the stairs."

"Heavy as hell," offered Delbert.

"How will we move it then?" asked John.

"I nicked a steel trolley from Horns Garden Centre last night," grunted Timmy proudly. "You know the kind; it has a long handle, two wheels and a steel lip for carrying paving-stones and the like."

"All we have to do," mouthed Del, "is push the safe backwards so that the front ends lifts an inch or so, shove in the lip of the trolley and ease it down like a pallet. It'll be a doddle."

"Where's the trolley?" asked John.

"Opposite. Dropped it off hours ago," said Timmy. He gestured towards the rows of terraced houses. "Mate works at the colliery. He does me favours, I do him favours."

Timmy Turten hurried to the other side of the road, reached the second house and disappeared into the back-yard. Moments later he returned carrying the trolley.

"But the neighbours!" asked John Briggs. "Won't they hear us?"

"Look for yourself," said Delbert, nodding at the deserted building.

John turned and stared. The targeted building was huge and comprised of three commercial properties. The shop was at one gable-end, hairdressers next to it, and the last building was shuttered and empty. Above Newman's shop and the hairdressers was the huge flat.

"That's where they live," said Timmy, "when they're at home."

"There's no sweat," muttered Delbert. "Next along the street is a butcher's shop and a grocery. Both lock-ups, both empty." He gestured at the flattened acreage beyond the shops, "Nothing but grass after that."

The trio walked to the rear of the building, past the locked back-gate that led into the rear yard and the flat and stood silently in the darkened back-lane. Before them was a small perimeter-wall that gradually rose to the first of the roofs. They stood and gawked as if unsure of their next action.

"You got keys?" whispered John Briggs hopefully.

"Don't need keys," said Timmy. "Only this." He held up a carpet-knife.

John shook his head in disbelief.

"Tim will climb on to the wall," whispered Delbert, "then on to the roof. He'll pull a few tiles off."

"With a knife?" asked the novice.

"Naw, stupid," said Del. "The tiles are rarely nailed down, maybe one in twelve, just a matter of easing enough of them off so that we can get inside. The knife is for the plastic sheet underneath, cut the sheet and we're inside. Tim has a torch so that we can find the hatch-cover. Lift the hatch and we're on the landing."

"What about the alarm?"

"Broken for years," said Timmy. He added dryly, "Old man Newman won't spend a penny on security."

"How do you know?"

"Trust me."

Timmy Turten propped the steel-trolley against the wall and while Delbert held it firm Timmy hoisted his thin frame on to the handle of the contraption, gripped at the brickwork and eased on to the uneven wall. Like an amateur tightrope-walker the youth inched his way towards the first roof, clambered on to the tiles and began easing and twisting at the surface. Ten minutes later he had pulled enough tiles free to allow access; the knife was stabbed and pulled across the thick drapes of plastic. After a few minutes of silent work Timmy wriggled his way through the gap in the roof and disappeared inside the attic. His inept efforts, however, dislodged the pile of loose tiles that were propped like a stack of untidy plates and with a deafening crash the slates crashed noisily on the inside yard of the premises.

John Briggs gasped aguishly, "Maybe we should go?"

Timmy's head appeared through the make-shift hole in the roof. He sprayed a torch-beam at his cringing companions and then probed the immediate area. "What do you think," he said in hushed tones, "stay or go?"

"I think it's okay," whispered Delbert. "Can't see anyone."

"It's alright for you!" gasped Timmy, his voice quavering for the first time. "I'm stuck up here!"

"I'll check!" shouted Del.

Delbert Hancock hurried to the front of the shop, scouted the near vicinity then returned. He nodded at John then beckoned his friend to continue. Timmy Turton eased out of sight.

Using the torch to guide him across the attic, Timmy found the hatch-cover and removed it. Dropping noiselessly to the landing, he ran down the stairs and pulled the set of keys from the wall-hook next to the back door. The door was opened and he reconnoitered the yard. He pointed the torch along the perimeter wall towards the secured solid-wood exit-door. Took moments for Timmy to prise open the bolts and open the door. He called to his comrades then crept back into the home and returned the bunch of keys to their rightful place.

Delbert maneuvered the trolley across the yard and into the entrance to the flat, John Briggs followed nervously behind.

"We'll take a room each," commanded Timmy. "Close all the blinds and curtains upstairs then come back here. We'll take the safe first then if it's still quiet we'll come back and look for jewellery and stuff."

"Where are we taking the safe?" asked John.

"Back to my mate's house across the road," said Tim. "They have an outside toilet. It'll stay there until tomorrow."

"Tomorrow!" replied an incredulous John Briggs.

"Tomorrow night," corrected Delbert.

Tim said, "We'll bring our truck, it's too heavy for a car."

John moaned under his breath. The pains in his stomach were growing.

Minutes later the trio was at ground-level staring open-mouthed at the *Chubb* safe. It filled most of the inner floor of the closet, allowing only one individual at a time to gain access into the confined space.

"No problem," said Timmy, chief thief and brains behind the operation. Placing the trolley inside the closet next to the base of the safe, he wedged his feet either side of the doorway, leaned into the small room until his upper body was parallel to the top of the safe and gripped the safe. He heaved with all of his strength and the front end of the *Chubb* lifted fractionally. Timmy eased it back to the linoleum floor.

"Next time I lift it, Del," said Timmy, "ease between my legs and shove the lip of the trolley into the space underneath the safe."

"How the hell can that be possible?"

"Get on your bloody belly!" snarled Tim. "You'll have to crawl between my legs. I can keep the safe up for a few minutes. Push the trolley between the gap, understand?"

Delbert glanced at John and gestured at the door at the rear of the large room. "Next to the door, you'll see a set of keys on a hook. Take the keys, take a hike over the back-yard, down a set of steps and open the shop. Okay?"

"Right, Del," said the youth. He added lamely, "What do you want me to do when I'm in the shop?"

"The cash-drawer!" snapped Delbert. "It's under the counter, opposite where the customers are served. See if they've left the cash-float."

"On the way," said John Briggs. He left the room.

114

Timmy Turton, legs wide apart, grappled with the floor-safe. His prostrate partner snaked forward and pushed at the steel trolley.

John gingerly shuffled across the darkened yard, inched his way down a small flight of stone steps and unlocked the rear door of the shop. Closing the door behind him he shuffled blindly through the kitchen and reached the main shop. The pungent aroma of stale cooking-fat was everywhere. After a few anguished moments John became acclimatized to the murky interior, saw the frying-range and the counter and slipped towards the cash-drawer. He carefully opened the till and felt for the money. Delbert was right; the float was in the plastic pockets of the drawer. In seconds John had transferred the money to his jacket pockets. He was about to return to the flat when he saw the police-car silently pass the window. Stunned rigid, he could only watch as two uniformed officers stepped out of the vehicle and walked towards the rear of the house. His breath bubbled in his chest and he stood transfixed as the nightmare hit him. Minutes past. There were no sounds of movement. John began to calm, took a solitary step away from the counter and heard the back-gate scraping open. He froze.

Unknown to the thieves, neighbours had telephoned the police when the roof-tiles were displaced.

Delbert and Timothy must have heard movement because they abandoned the safe, stormed up the stairs into the massive flat and searched frantically for an escape route. Pandemonium broke out as the two bungling burglars scattered through the property followed by the agitated and extremely vocal officers. The racket echoing from the rooms upstairs knocked John Briggs into action. He stumbled to the front of the shop and saw the key in the lock of the door. A deft twist, a push, and the youth stepped to freedom. He stood quaking outside the premises. Tried to close the door behind him but his trembling hands made it impossible. John hurried away and didn't look back until he crossed the main road. Moments later a second patrol-car, blue lights flashing, roared past him and headed for the premises.

John slowed and watched the drama unfold. He saw policemen hurrying through the open door of the shop. Suddenly an upstairs window exploded and a murky figure tried to scramble from the upstairs flat but was dragged back into the property. Protestations and blaspheming erupted from the premises as another window-pane cracked and a second figure tried to escape. He too was unsuccessful.

Despite a valiant and courageous attempt at escape Delbert Hancock and Timothy Turton were arrested.

John stumbled towards the car. His eyes filled with tears, his stomach burned with an aching dread. Reached the Cortina, found the keys and drove away.

John Briggs was never caught. Never questioned. He made the princely sum of £23.50 from the botched robbery.

**

CHAPTER THIRTEEN

Days after the botched robbery John knocked on the door of the council house. Avril Jennings, Delbert Hancock's girl-friend answered. Avril, tall, blonde and voluptuous, was dressed provocatively in skimpy shorts and tee-shirt. She stuck her head into view and grinned at the diminutive youth.

Like Jerry Hall standing next to little Mick.

John asked solemnly, "Any news, Avril?"

"Good and bad," she said smiling. "The good news is that Del and Tim are being charged with breaking and entering, assaulting police officers and being in possession of *Class A* drugs."

"And the bad?"

"I'll get no money from Delbert!" Avril shrugged her slim shoulders and moaned, "Chances are I'll have to baby-sit his kid for a year until he gets out of jail!"

"Did you manage to have a talk with him?"

"Don't worry, Johnny," she said, "they'll not mention your name."

He tried again, "Did you talk about the other thing?"

"The wagon?" Avril she scratched at her enormous breasts and began the rehearsed speech. "He wants £500 and no offers. Said he couldn't take less even for you. His mother has the log-book in her name. If you're still keen she'll get your details and post it to Swansea."

John Briggs almost swooned with pleasure, intoxicated at the thought of acquiring the bargain-basement wagon for virtually peanuts. He feigned astonishment, conniving and clever enough to know that Avril Jennings was desperate for cash.

"That's a lot of money for a beat-up wagon!"

Avril grinned impishly. Married to someone as sharp as Delbert Hancock meant she was street-wise and witty. Quick as a flash she retorted, "Short *and* deaf, Johnny, what a combination!"

"£500!" he answered. Shook his head resignedly. He could hardly contain his emotions, "Surely he'll take less?"

"No way!" insisted the young girl. "Del said he wouldn't haggle. That's the rock-bottom price." A big grin covered her face. Avril Jennings teased, "He said the money is mine, said if I could get more for the lorry then I should."

John grimaced.

"£500," she said, teasing. "Plus half an hour with you … now!" Her grin was infectious, "I can sell the wagon for a lot more money and you know it!"

"Avril, if Delbert finds out and I'm as good as dead!"

"He's in Northallerton lock-up. He'll never find out from me."

"There'll be hell to pay, Avril!"

"He never found out about us the first time, did he?"

"Never be as lucky again!" said John. "Your brother Jake almost ruined it for me!"

"He was trying to get into Iris's good books."

"Knickers more like!"

"Iris didn't believe him."

"She bent my ear," John replied. He took a deep breath and added, "No, Iris never knew for sure."

Avril smiled whimsically as she remembered the brief fling. The temptress pushed, "Well, what about my offer then?"

John wanted the wagon so much, knew if he owned his own motor he could stay in business. He was sorely tempted.

"Make up your mind, Johnny!"

"Where's the kid?"

"Delbert junior is at his Mother's house. It's Friday night. There's no way I'm staying in for a year playing merry widows, I'm only eighteen!" Avril folded her arms across her chest, taunting him. "Well?"

John glanced round the immediate area. Apart from two toddlers playing on bikes, the street was deserted. His mind was made up; he had to have the wagon no matter the cost. Without the vehicle he was staring at the dole-queue, state hand-outs and grief from Iris. He would not tell a soul and he knew Avril could not confide in anyone, not with a partner as volatile as Delbert Hancock. John took a deep breath, stepped over the threshold and eased past the lanky female.

"You don't look very happy," quizzed the siren. "Having second thoughts?"

"If Delbert starts sniffing I'll have to buy a passport!"

"Del finds out," said Avril, frowning, "You'll have to buy two, one for you and one for me." She started chortling.

"Don't say that, even in fun, he's one crazy person!"

"Big enough to eat you!" mocked Avril.

"You're right there, Del's some size!"

"Not where it matters," teased the vixen. "He was so disappointing, especially after you!"

"Christ, Avril, you haven't said anything?"

"Not to Delbert," said the girl. She closed the door, "That kind of gossip is strictly taboo." She laughed, "No. I compared notes with Thelma Cruddace!"

John Briggs stayed an hour at the house. It took a further hour before he finally reached home. Iris was waiting, spoiling for a fight. The youth, however, was prepared for any possible spats. After leaving Avril Jennings he had driven to his mother's home and borrowed £600, money enough to cover the purchase of the wagon, car tax and insurance. Then

119

he had called on Delbert's mother, handed over the money, helped her complete the log-book transfer and posted the document. He had only to arrange insurance for the wagon and then talk to Les Green who owned *Tyne-Tees Signs,* about covering Del's old wagon with a new logo. The time away from Avril had allowed his conscience to dissipate. He was composed when he finally reached home, unruffled as he explained where he had been and what he had achieved.

The initial suspicion diluted the more Iris listened to his excuses. Minutes in the conversation the female changed her stance. The warring tones dissolved and the frowns turned to smiles when John told her of the acquisition. Iris was jubilant with her young husband. He was changing so much, taking charge, making decisions, jumping into the unknown. She was seeing another, more mature side of John. Made her love him even more. Iris apologized and pecked him on the lips. She had never been so happy.

John pushed aside the brief dalliance with Avril Jennings. Dug a deep hole and buried his conscience. Convinced himself it had been a one off, a necessary arrangement for him. He had the wagon and the means to a secure future. The temporary agreement, however, was not to Avril's liking. She wanted more of the same, even tried to set up times and dates for future meetings. John stuck to his guns, knowing it was too dangerous to continue the liaison. The village was too small, it was the kind of place where everyone knew everyone's business. Gossipmongers could be found on every street-corner. John Briggs politely declined the offer much to the annoyance of Avril. He had enjoyed the sex but for the first time in his life he had experienced the pang of guilt. He felt close again to Iris. Loved her and prayed she would never find out about his indiscretion.

Morals of a tom-cat, only he didn't know it.

Michael Buff Motson didn't care that he was on his own. Sometimes it was better when there was no one taking the water, when you needed to stay in bed, when your head was aching from too much partying. He didn't need the belly-ache from a woman that spent her day glued in front of the television, whose idea of cooking a meal was to open two microwave-meals bought from the supermarket. Eileen McCufferty had walked out again. Big deal, did he care a damn about her? *Parasites*, he thought, *every last one.*

Micky didn't need a woman telling you how to live your life, demanding you find a job, wash and change everyday. It was non-stop nagging, nothing more. And where was the logic? Point one; there was no possibility of employment for an old lag with a prison tag bright on his shoulder. Point two; what was wrong in trying to get a few days *worth* out of your clothes? Changing clothes every day leads to a mountain of washing which inevitable means using the washing-machine. Not only could he not drive the damn thing but he didn't have the oil to feed it. It was logical therefore to try and get a few extra days wear out of them.

Missed Eileen for some things. Naturally.

He didn't have time to fret however, he had other things to do. Top of the agenda was a visit to an old acquaintance; it was pay-back time for Michael Motson. He would call on Ray Robinson, wanted to see the look of surprise when he knocked at the man's door. Robinson, hypothetically speaking, would shit bricks at the sight of his nemesis, providing he recognised the face. There had been a lot of water under the bridge since the bad old days. Age lines had cut furrows every which way, the hair was thin on top - hence the pony-tail - and the groove that cut across his forehead was still an eye-opener. Sugar Ray would remember the scar. After all, he caused it.

It was time to put the record straight.

Some hours later, in a large estate in one of the seedier parts of Middlesbrough, Raymond Robinson was on the phone. He looked at his wrist-watch and sighed. He'd been talking to his wife, Diane for too long and he was growing impatient. It showed. His tone lacked warmth and caring. He was after all a busy man and, unlike his spendaholic spouse, did not have time to have one holiday never mind the four she'd enjoyed over the past months. Unable to hold his annoyance any longer, Raymond interrupted the woman with a flurry of excuses, bade a gruff farewell and put down the phone. He took a deep breath and tried to settle his nerves. It was a losing battle. He swallowed a mouthful of whiskey and then cursed his wife to the heavens. It was his fault of course for spoiling his family rotten. He took another sip before flopping on to the sofa. Raymond Robinson shook his head despondently and pictured Diane and the two brats spending like there was no tomorrow. Where was it this time, Disneyland? She could have chosen a dozen better, cheaper, locations but no, it had to be Cuckoo-land in Florida. He could say goodbye to five grand, plus change. Another drink was poured.

The attaché case was open on the table. He looked at the piles of cash in the sleek case and sighed jadedly. Closing the briefcase he checked his watch again. Sonny Chin would be calling within the hour to pick up the money for William Garcia. Raymond sat in the big arm-chair and sipped at the drink, his fourth that night. He stared into the big coal-fire, mesmerized by the dancing flames and thought about the girl again. There was something special about Dottie Baxter. He had loved and lost her. He sighed and gulped at the drink. *What the hell went wrong, Ray,* he mused. *Took her away from the hovel in Durham, away from the mad parents, the crazy brother. Bought her everything she wanted; clothes, jewellery, even set her up in that nice flat in Redcar. Paid cash for a damn car and what does she do ... runs off with Hong Kong Phooey! A slit-eyed southerner for Christ Sake! Then she dumps him a couple of months later and grabs Garcia himself! One born every minute, Raymond. One born ... and you're the biggest!*

He pictured his boss, William Garcia. The drug-baron from Leeds was a millionaire many times over. *Should have snitched on him when I was caught,* he mused. *That was a perfect opportunity to send him away forever and take over the business.* He shook his head; it had been another damn mistake. Closed his eyes and thought again of the time ....

Five years ago Sugar-Ray was caught moving a car-load of drugs across town. He was so unlucky that day. Driving along the A66, the main arterial road through Middlesbrough, Robinson broke down and a passing police-cruiser stopped to give assistance and immediately recognized the driver. Second nature for the boys-in-blue to search the vehicle. They hit the jackpot when they opened the car-boot. Could not believe their good fortune, it was Manna falling from Heaven. When Robinson was threatened with a hefty prison stretch he quickly co-operated. He sang like a bird, but not the tune the authorities wanted. Acted the Dodo when they pushed for Garcia's involvement. *'William Garcia,'* he said, smart as a carrot, *'never heard of the man. Hey, if you say the man has a drug empire then I gotta believe you. From Yorkshire to the North-East you say? Tell me what to write and I'll do it ... only it ain't true. I've never heard of Garcia. You want, I'll give you a list of people like me, business-folk, who buy and sell for a living, only you have to look after me, you get my drift, officer. If I squeal on so many my life is worth jack-shit, you know? You scratch my back, officer and I'll scratch yours?* Gave the police a list of small fry who fetched and carried, sacrificed the minions and saved Garcia's precious hide when he acted the part of loyal servant to the Yorkshire drug baron and was dutifully rewarded.

Seven men and one female were arrested and served long jail sentences. Michael Motson was one of the unlucky punters. Named as a major player in the distribution of white powder, his terraced home was raided in the middle of the night by an army of armed officers. (Robinson had gone overboard with his fantasy about Motson) *'Buff Motson has cocaine enough to feed Stockton and Darlington for a month, and he has a sawn-off next to his bed!'* Truth was a mile out. The luckless Buff was a mule, a runner for Garcia's Lieutenant and his house was one of the main storage places for Ray Robinson. Always cool in a crisis, drugged, drunk or sober, Motson clambered into the attic and slipped noiselessly through a roof-window and began to worm his way out of danger. The weather, however, and not the constabulary, beat him. The slate rooftops were glazed with ice and snow and poor Micky Motson lost his balance, back-flipped and smashed through an ancient conservatory. He landed on his head and ended up with more scars and weals than Henry Cooper. The police found a barrow-load of cocaine plus Ray Robinson's shotgun. After three operations and a lengthy stay in hospital Motson was finally hauled in front of the courts. He acted the oaf and refused to name names. Received a ten-year sentence. He served half.

Like Robinson, Motson never betrayed his boss. William Garcia never forgot the kindness of Sugar Ray. Buff never forgot the treachery of Ray Robinson ………….

Micky Motson drove slowly along the main road. It was early still but the roads were almost deserted. He meandered past the flats, turned left at the small shopping arcade and started looking for the club. A big self-satisfied grin covered his pale features when he saw the Grangetown United Club. He continued on his way, recalled the streets had some link with the Lake District. Tried to recall the street names when the road sign, 'Rydal', appeared. He was euphoric. A wave of panic enveloped the man as he fought to remember the link. It was something to do with food. Then he saw the indicator for 'Buttermere,' and he knew he was near. It was the last house before the cul-de-sac, and looked so different when he motored past with Eileen McCufferty. Drove a little way past and parked. He started walking towards the council house, adjusting the woollen hat so that it rested low on his brow and hid most of his head. He pulled on the gloves and sucked in the night air. A cool blustery breeze swilled litter and muck about the darkened street. The moon played hide and seek with the bubbles of grey froth that splattered the skies. The heavenly orb was still hiding when Motson knocked at the door. The weapon, a hammer, was gripped tightly in his hand and was ready to use. He heard the noise of numerous locks being released and took a deep breath. It was pay-back time.

Raymond Robinson wrenched open the front-door and peered into the gloom looking for Sonny Chin. When he saw the hooded figure lunging towards him he instinctively tried to close the door. The ball-hammer missed its target and smacked into the side of the door. The hardwood frame cracked ominously as Robinson flung himself to one side. It was too late to stop the storming, shrieking stranger from entering the house. Motson was hell-bent on retribution and in a desperate act flung the weapon at the retreating victim. Robinson ran along the wide corridor trying to put distance between himself and the attacker. As he stumbled into the living-room he glanced back. It proved fatal. Ray Robinson lost his footing and careered head-first into the marble fire-place. The sound of Robinson's skull hitting the stone was chilling. There was a horrendous *crack* and an almost inaudible gasp from the drug-dealer before he collapsed.

Motson was on him in an instant. One hand grabbed at his tie and hoisted him bodily from the floor, his other raised ready to strike. All of a sudden Motson froze. He knew instinctively that there was something seriously wrong with Ray Robinson. The victim's pate seemed concave, as if his brain had imploded and sucked the skull into a hollow. Blood dripped like a tap from the side of his head. Buff Motson sensed a deep feeling of foreboding. He lowered the unconscious man gently to the floor and began inspecting the unconscious man. Blood was running freely from Robinson's ear.

Motson began to tremble. His chest palpitated like a jack-hammer. Dropping to his knees, with his lips almost touching the silent figure, he whispered, "Ray!" He caressed the waxen flesh, and nudged his old boss, "Wake up, man! Come on, Ray, I was gonna break your legs, nothing more! It wasn't supposed to end this way! I'm sorry man!"

Robinson couldn't answer. His brain was pulp.

Motson stood. He scratched at his stubbled chin and tried to remain calm. He felt nauseous with remorse, closed his eyes and tried to find solutions. Knew that his past record would go against him, knew beyond a shadow of doubt that he would not be believed. Micky shivered involuntary as he surveyed the bloodied body.

At that very moment a car squeaked to a halt outside of the house. Motson moved to the drapes and peered into the street. The motor looked like a *Volvo* with its box-shape and headlights. The engine spluttered to a halt and a mountain of a man struggled free of the cab. The door was elbowed shut and the giant ambled towards the front-door. Micky Motson had seconds to plan his escape. As the front door was pushed open the rear door was closed silently.

"Raymond," called Sonny Chin. One paw pushed ajar the unlocked door, the other inspected the damage. He listened for moments and then whispered, "Ray, everything okay, man?"

Chin pulled out a massive spanner from an inside pocket and stepped into the home. The goliath eased the door shut. He knew something was wrong. Entry into Robinson's home was always slow and irritating, bolts and locks and safety-chains were the usual order of the day. There was too much at stake to allow ease of entry.

The enforcer saw the crumpled body on the living-room floor and approached cautiously, the heavy weapon raised in readiness. He kicked at the lifeless torso, his beady eyes darting from the prone figure to the kitchen-door then back. Easing his huge body on to the carpet Chin placed the palm of his hand against the limp neck of Raymond Robinson. There was a faint pulse. Chin stood, teeth clamping on his lips and weighed up the options. A family dispute perhaps? He shook his head slowly. Diane Robinson was spending Ray's riches somewhere abroad. Instinctively he knew a burglary had gone wrong. He honed in on the attaché case that lay on one side of the fancy table, a spasm hit him and he momentarily lost breath. Sonny Chin focused on the briefcase and his greedy brain festered. Robinson was forgotten as he hurried to the prize. A deft flick opened the case revealing bundles of money. His mind swam with pleasure as he toyed and caressed the cash.

A car back-fired and brought him to his senses. Hurrying to the door he glanced out into the street and saw an old jalopy chugging its way from the lane. A plumage of smoke belched from the wreck as it slowly rounded a corner and disappeared. Sonny Chin shrugged his shoulders and returned to the room. He never gave the motor a second thought as he began systematically checking the house for unwanted visitors.

All the rooms were thoroughly searched. Once Chin was certain that he was alone he started again. The stash downstairs was his to keep, the opportunity too good to ignore. He would somehow convince Garcia that the drug-money had been stolen by the same thief who had tried to snuff the life out of Robinson. Chin systematically examined every nook and cranny and found more treasures. There was £12500 in cash stashed behind the television cabinet. A Tupperware-box filled with a mix of tablets in all sizes and colours was discovered inside a shoe-box. And the Crown Jewels themselves, a half a kilo of pure heroin, was secreted inside an empty sanitary-towel box next to the lavatory basin. As plain as day, the *Tampax* carton had been strategically placed on top of toilet-rolls for all to see. It was a ploy to fool everyone. It took Chin minutes to carry the booty to his car and hide it in the boot.

He phoned William Garcia and told him about the attempted robbery and the missing money. Garcia ordered Chin to search the house for Robinson's business books. Last thing he wanted was the authorities finding enough evidence to sink his empire. Sonny Chin had no need to double-check, the house was clean. He phoned for an ambulance, and completely forgot the police. When they eventually arrived Chin blamed shock for affecting his judgment.

Raymond Robinson never recovered. He was in a coma for eight days. His loyal wife was by his side when he died. Diane held on to the failing body for hours, her lips pressed close as she whispered and wailed. Hospital staff, on permanent watch, praised the grieving woman. They never suspected the real reason behind Diane Robinson's grief. Had the medics eavesdropped on the one-sided conversation between the inconsolable spouse and her gravely-injured husband, they would have revised their initial impressions of the so-called anguished wife.

"Ray," she hissed, "where's the money? Wake up, Raymond, Jesus Christ; I need that cash before the police strip-search the place! Open your bloody eyes!" The woman was demented, "You no-good piece of shit!" She looked round the ward in case of preying eyes. There was no one about. She grabbed at his damp forelocks, "If you've spent it on another whore I'll choke the life out of you! Hear me, Raymond? I .. want .. that .. money! Can you hear me?" Diane lost it totally and in a frenzied, uncontrollable moment of panic, ripped the breathing-tube out of Raymond Robinson's wheezing mouth, "Last chance! If you don't answer I'll tell Sonny Chin how much you've stolen from Garcia over the years! I mean it, Ray."

A nerve-tingling alarm echoed from the apparatus next to the patient's bedside. Diane shuddered and gasped with shock as ward-doors crashed open and doctors and nurses rushed towards the dying Raymond Robinson.

CHAPTER FOURTEEN

On Saturday afternoon Maxi Stubbs left the Safeway Supermarket checkout for his lunch-break. He stood near to the rear-entrance eating the stolen confectionery and drank from the small bottle of limeade. Maxi had no conscience about stealing from his employers; he was on basic wage, a pittance in his opinion, so he stole when and wherever possible.

The youth had recently left his mother's home in Shotton and returned to the town. He liked Peterlee, had spent most of his life there. His old school and his friends were based in the town and he was pleased to get away from the colliery. He hated the pit village but understood why his mother wanted to put distance between herself and Joshua, her no-account husband.

Maxi's Father, Joshua Stubbs, was a vicious bully and had little time for his wife or son. Joshua's parents had left Jamaica in the late fifties and had settled in Forest Gate, London. Joshua ran with the wrong crowd and was always in trouble with the law. When he was old enough Joshua jumped a train and hitched a free ride to Durham, ended up in Peterlee where he wooed and married Winifred Slack. Joshua preferred to party rather than earn an honest crust but had no qualms about his wife working. Winifred soon sickened of the one-sided relationship but every time she tried to leave Joshua threatened her with violence. When her son was fourteen years old the woman packed her bags and moved two miles west to Shotton. Safe and secure, Winifred would not budge from her new home much to the annoyance of Maxi.

Maxi Stubbs lived in a flat in Oakerside Drive, a ten minute walk from Peterlee town-centre. The tenement was neither clean nor quiet but at least it wasn't Shotton Colliery. He'd lived in the Corporation flat for over a year and never once been bothered by his father. His mother should have taken his advice and stayed in the town of 25,000 people, it was big enough to hide from anyone.

Maxi had detested living in the pit village, pleased to leave the place, exhausted by the constant trouble his colour caused, weary of disagreements with local youths. Only person he missed was Iris Briggs. The girl was truly beautiful and the only person he had ever loved. He was sure her second and youngest child was his son, the timing was perfect and the boy's subtle colouring was proof enough for Maxi. He asked Iris to leave her husband, the opportunity was perfect - John Briggs was behind bars for molesting a thirteen-year old - but Iris refused and after a short time stopped seeing him. *'I love Johnny,'* said a determined Iris, *'honest I do.'* Maxi thought her conscience bothered her, and torn between two, she chose the safest option. *'He'll be out in a year, Maxi,'* she said. *'If Johnny behaves himself he might even be free before then. I'm married, got two kids and Johnny thinks he's their father. You and me, Maxi, it can't work. Where would be live ... how could I face people?'* He still saw Iris when she occasionally shopped in the store but almost always she was accompanied by her mother. She still smiled and gave him the look but that was all she gave. There were no liaisons and no intimacy. The good old days were past and gone.

Maxi finished his drink and threw the empty bottle into the bottle-bank, took out the cigarettes and checked his watch. He had plenty of time. He hated Saturdays because the supermarket was so busy; he had to work twice as hard but didn't get twice the pay.

Inside the store, the Brookes family were shopping, Maurice, subdued, subservient, pushed the large shopping-

131

trolley, wishing he were home, praying the expedition wouldn't be too long as he did not want to miss the football. He kept his head down, smiled wearily, regularly checked his wrist-watch and agreed with everything his wife, Josephine, said. Their only daughter, Julie, guided the push-chair single-handed, ignored the wailing infant and tried to concentrate on the problem-page of the magazine. The family stopped next to the toiletries and mother and daughter started discussing the merits of the latest own-brand shampoo. Maurice Brookes lowered his head with embarrassment, forgot he had marooned the laden trolley mid-way in the aisle, and rested forlornly on the contraption. A mother and daughter whizzed into view and collided with Maurice's skewed trolley, knocking the man sideways and lifting him out of his stupor.

Iris Briggs glowered at Julie Brooks. She hated the girl who had seduced her husband and then had him locked up for a year. Detested the whole family, especially the snobbish bitch of a mother.

"Excuse me!" demanded an agitated Iris and she gently but firmly prodded at the man's trolley. The noise of the impact was alarming. "Can you not keep to one side of the aisle?" she growled, all the while her eyes roasted on the teenage witch.

Maurice, in a pickle of embarrassment, pulled and pushed the lop-side trolley to one side.

Iris's Mother, Nancy Evans, an old neighbour of Josephine Brooks, tried to disarm the situation. She smiled and acknowledged the woman, "Josephine, how are you?" she asked.

"As well as can be expected, Nancy," whined the woman. She glanced at Maurice who was again checking his watch, 'No use moaning, no one listens."

Nancy, always the peace-maker and negotiator, closed on the push-chair and fondled the whimpering child. "So this is Sheila?" She turned and smiled warmly at her pouting daughter, "Come and have a look, Iris, she's the double of John."

Iris stood as if shackled to her trolley, her features set in stone.

"The bairn still hasn't seen her father?" said a smirking Josephine. She glanced at her daughter, "He hasn't called has he, Julie?"

Julie, knowing Iris's reputation, shook her head nervously then looked at the floor.

"Young lady," said an incensed Josephine, "I'm talking to you."

"John called!" interrupted Iris. She glared at Josephine Brooks, "He called at Grange Terrace … you'd moved! He asked the neighbour but she didn't know your new address."

"Of course, love," said a sarcastic Josephine. Turning to her husband she barked, "Let them past Maurice."

Josephine Brooks turned away and began studying the merchandise. The conversation was over. Iris and her mother stole a knowing glance at one another before trundling along the isle.

Out of earshot, Josephine Brooks jibed, "Called to see his own daughter! Do you believe that?"

"Mother!" said Julie. "Best to bite your tongue when Iris is about."

"I'm not frightened of that young floozy!" She looked at her husband. "I'll not be intimidated by anyone, will I, Maurice?"

"No, love," soothed the hen-pecked husband. He looked at his wrist-watch knowing if they didn't hurry and finish the shopping he'd miss the results.

"Look at that watch again, Maurice," threatened Josephine, "and I'll personally smash it!"

*

"You can't simply walk off the job, said a seething Beatrice Crumplin. "You and Kenny have to give notice. What about your entitlements?"

"Entitlements," asked John Briggs, dwarfed next to Kenny Wilkinson. He was still counting his wages. Worked five and a half days and received a paltry £100. It made him even more determined. "And what would they be, Missus?" he asked.

"Holidays… and things," stumbled Beatrice, annoyed that the young upstart had the audacity to ruin her plans. "You'll both lose your holiday pay."

"You can stick your holidays!" said a resolute John Briggs.

"How dare you talk to me like that!" she whined.

John turned to leave the kitchen, Kenny pirouetted like a ballet-dancer wearing pit-boots, the linoleum squeaking loudly as he tapped after his companion.

"Kenneth!" said a desperate Beatrice. She physically grabbed at his jacket, "You don't have to go … I'll make you manager."

"Get off me!" barked the beanpole

"But you haven't got a job!" said an incensed Beatrice. "Are you bloody mad?"

"Don't like you, Missus," grunted the youth, "and I won't work for you!"

"Go!" shrieked Beatrice. "The pair of you can join the dole queue!" The frustrated female followed them into the back-yard, shouting and goading the youths. "Mark my words you two, you'll never get another job in Shotton!"

"Go play with yourself!" retorted Kenny Wilkinson.

"Leave it," said John Briggs and he grabbed his friend in an effort to subdue him.

"I'm seeing George Jones this very day!" shouted Beatrice Crumplin venomously. "I'll personally see to it that he does not employ you two! You're finished in the coal business!"

John smiled smugly. He walked away and Kenny followed.

The pair trooped around the corner into the maze of council houses and slowed at the top of the cul-de-sac. Hopper Terrace was Kenny's home.

"Back to normal, Monday, then?" asked the taller youth.

"Yes. I'm collecting Delbert's lorry in an hour. The printer is putting the logo on now."

"Right then," said the taller youth, "nothing changes?"

"There's one change, Kenny," said Johnny Briggs determinedly. "You've got a raise and a weekly bonus!"

*

Elsie Briggs had made tea for herself. She carried the laden tray to the living-room, determined to spend a pleasant hour snacking, watching the television and reading the paper. It was Saturday afternoon and she had a routine. Frank had been gone a few hours and he would not return before tea-time. She had cleaned, in a fashion, and was now going to savour the remainder of the afternoon. The banging at the door alarmed Elsie; no one bothered knocking at her home, she had an open-door policy, '*Come in, you're not a stranger*,' she would always say to any callers. The old

135

woman muttered oaths under her breath as she heaved her bulk from the sofa and waddled towards the rear door.

"Dorothy!" uttered a surprised Elsie Briggs. Her daughter-in-law was an infrequent visitor, never before calling on her own. She peered over the woman's shoulders, "Robert not with you?"

"He's at the colliery," said Dorothy. She heaved her bulky frame into the small kitchen, "Practically lives there!"

"Working on a Saturday?"

"Four hours at double time, Elsie! Well worth it," she answered with a smile. Dorothy was twenty-five years old and already on the fast lane to middle-age. Took a deep breath and continued, "Robert told me about young John's dilemma?"

"Dilemma, pet, how so?" answered a bemused Elsie Briggs.

"Trying to start his own business?"

"Poor Mr. Crumplin dropping dead like that," mused the older woman. "Did you know our John gave him the kiss-of-life?"

Dorothy nodded. She had heard the tale from half of the village and every time something more was added to the heroic tale. Rummaging through her hand-bag, she pulled out a cheque and handed it to Elsie.

"Here we are," said Dorothy proudly. "We thought it best to give young John a helping hand. I called at Victoria Street but there's no one in, so if you could give…."

John Briggs burst through the door and almost collided with Dorothy. His eyes were wide with surprise.

"The man himself, eh?" smiled the younger woman.

"Hello, Dorothy," said the suspicious youth.

"Dorothy called to see you," intervened Elsie. "She's got a lovely surprise for you."

The trio was still talking ten minutes later. Dorothy was truly amazed at the fortitude of the youngster. She listened intently as John regurgitated his trials and tribulations. Told her about his unsuccessful negotiations with Dean Crumplin's wife, then making appointments with the major banks and failing miserably. He then concluded the tale by mentioning the quirk of fate that allowed him to acquire a wagon but didn't elaborate on the failed exploits of Delbert Hancock and Timmy Turton that gave him access to the vehicle. He took Dorothy to the living-room, stood by the big window and pointed to his new acquisition. The coal wagon was smothered in the new logo. He was as proud as a peacock.

John was still grinning when Dorothy grabbed and cuddled him, almost squeezing his breath from him.

"Robert will be so proud of you, John! I'm so proud of you!" She pulled away, embarrassed at the show of emotion, her voice still pitched. "I hope everything works out for you."

"Thanks, Dorothy, and thanks for offering the cheque."

"If you change your mind, call in and see us. The money is there for you, okay?"

Dorothy Briggs tousled his thinning locks, turned and headed out of the room. She opened the door, turned, smiled at the boy and then she was gone.

Elsie said, "Can't believe what I've just witnessed! Dorothy offering money. It has to be a first!"

"She said the cheque is there if I want it, Ma!"

"You know what," said Elsie, "I think she means it."

"You don't think our Robert was the instigator? It's a lot of money to be lending?"

Elsie smiled, eased past her son and switched on the television. "There's only one boss in that marriage," she said, "and it's not Robert."

"I thought she never liked me."

"Maybe she's turned over a new leaf?"

He nodded then moved to the door, "Better go, Mother, I'm collecting the kids."

"Will you be calling tomorrow?"

"Maybe Monday, Mother. I'll tell you how my first day has gone."

"Okay, love," said Elsie, flopping into the arm-chair and staring at the television.

The local news channel was repeating news about the Middlesbrough murder. Mother and son were suddenly glued to the screen.

Elsie said, 'It's awful, and on our doorstep!"

"The man who was killed was a drug-dealer."

Every time drugs and crime were mentioned in the region, Elsie always said a silent prayer for her beloved brother.

John sniggered. "Good riddance!" he said.

Elsie blanched and prodded a finger at her youngest, "Stop it, John!" She filled her chest, "It could be Micky!"

"Uncle Buff," retorted the lad, "I thought you didn't know where he lived, Ma?" Shook his head, "He still into drugs?"

"I don't know," groaned Elsie Briggs, awash with emotion. "I don't know anything!" She sighed loudly, "I worry, John, I always worry about Micky!"

The woman turned and stared at the small screen, mesmerized. John took his leave, promising to return Monday.

The back-door banged leaving Elsie alone with her thoughts. She stared at the television, at the street scene, and observed the tiers of yellow tape and the many police vehicles. A reporter appeared on the small screen. She was young and attractive. She spoke in hurried tones about the bungled robbery. The journalist was joined by a dour, cadaverous detective. The officer dwarfed the waif-life

138

reporter, *'Drug-related,'* he grunted sardonically. His waxen features told it all. *'When the next-of-kin are informed I'll be able to give more details of the deceased man'.* There was a brief nod from the gaunt officer before he ambled away.

Elsie's face furrowed with stress lines. Her wayward brother resided somewhere in the Teesside area and didn't work nine till five. Micky Motson mixed with the wrong crowd in a big way. Her hands subconsciously covered her gaping mouth as she fretted and worried for her brother.

"Say a bloody name, you fool!" groaned Elsie Briggs. "Say a name!"

**

CHAPTER FIFTEEN

"Pal, you wanna wrap or what?" asked the shaven-headed neighbour.

Maxi Stubbs smiled as he swapped money for drugs. The slim muscular youth intrigued him. He was polite and spotlessly clean. Maxi had actually been in the upstairs flat several times buying dope and was amazed how meticulous he was. Couldn't understand, however, the lad's insistence on calling himself *Sandy* and not Simon Baxter because he certainly wasn't fair-haired. Despite having his head shaved the hue of crimson still smudged his skull. The close-cropped head also showed white jagged scars criss-crossing his pate like some grotesque spider's web. His lower jaw was misshapen and gave him a menacing appearance. When Maxi eventually inquired about the injuries, Sandy Baxter boasted that it took six baton-welding warders to subdue him when he was resident at Medomsley Young Offender's Institution.

"Is that where you belong, Sandy," asked Maxi, "west of Durham?"

Maxi Stubbs was trying to be sociable, thinking his neighbour might fancy a few pints at the Hearts of Oak pub only minutes away. It was Saturday night and Maxi was bored and a little lonely for company. Any company. He still felt an outsider because of his colour; count on one hand the number of coloured kids residing in the town. Maxi couldn't quite work out the stranger. The way he looked you up and down was off-putting. Wanted to ask Sandy Baxter if he were a homosexual because his neighbour never talked about girls or boasted how much of a stud he was which was unusual for one so young. Too frightened to ask about his neighbour's sexuality, Maxi kept his thoughts to himself.

"In that area," answered Baxter. "Wolsingham. You heard of it?"

Maxi shook his head. He'd never travelled beyond Durham. Knew Sunderland and Newcastle were north. South was Hartlepool and Middlesbrough. But west of Durham was unknown territory.

"You an import, pal?" asked the drug-dealer.

"Why you say that, Sandy?"

"Dumb question. You're not a true-blue Aryan are you?"

Maxi Stubbs knew his deficiencies in the physical game. He had tried hard but had never won a fight in his life. Knew enough to hold his tongue.

"Born in Peterlee, Sandy," answered Maxi. "Cumbrian Way, about a minute's walk from your old bail-hostel in Eden Hill."

"Right."

Maxi said, "I'm as English as Randolph Turpin!"

"Who the hell is he?"

"He was a boxer. A champion boxer."

"I'm not into boxing, pal," smirked Sandy.

"Kenny Lynch! Charlie Williams!"

"I remember the singer?" He scratched his skull, "Charlie who?"

"You fancy a pint, Sandy," asked Maxi, trying desperately to deflect the snide remarks.

"Why not," said the smaller lad. He turned as if to leave then asked flippantly, "You read, man?"

"Now and again," replied Maxi Stubbs. "I've nicked the odd book from the library."

"I'll lend you some, eh?"

"Thanks Sandy," said an exuberant Maxi, "appreciate that."

"You ever read Alex Haley?"

The taller youth shook his head, "No," he replied, "never heard of that one."

"Have a squint," said Baxter, leering. "Might open your mind, might even persuade you to check your roots!"

"You're a pal, Sandy," replied the naïve Maxi Stubbs.

*

The vehicle crawled along Belvedere Gardens, a two street enclave of private homes situated at the northern end of Shotton.

"When we reach the house," ordered Beatrice Crumplin, "stay in the car!"

Sammy Bruce sat poker-faced in the passenger-seat. He asked carefully, "Will you be long, Beatrice?"

"Long as it takes!"

Beatrice saw the house-number and ordered Sammy to stop. She climbed out of the driver's seat, glowered at her companion before slamming the door and proceeding along the path towards the semi-detached house.

Sammy Bruce crunched his face with suppressed anger. There were times when he detested Beatrice, when he hated her to distraction. He'd left her twice in ten years. Second time he hadn't even packed a bag. Told his mother the relationship was too much like hard work, that there had been too many rows and disagreements to make the liaison work. His mother knew the truth, '*Where did you get those bruises, Samuel,*' she had asked one time. '*Beatrice hit you again, son?*' His mother was the only one who knew about Beatrice's temper tantrums. A few days would pass and Beatrice would phone his mother and inquire after him, then she'd call around and see him, and always full of remorse, crying and humble with him. Trouble was, Sammy loved

142

Beatrice, the only girl he'd courted properly. There'd been others but that was school-days and didn't count. Beatrice was his first full-blown affair. He always felt guilty about their relationship. Dean Crumplin had been his friend, the pair work-mates at Horden Colliery years ago. The three of them would often go out drinking together. Sammy had no idea that Beatrice had held a torch for him until one night when the inevitable happened. They had returned to the house in Shotton, Dean out for the count again, drunk as a skunk, and Beatrice had that funny look in her eyes.......

Sammy checked his watch. It was 6.30pm. He was meeting his pals at the Workingman's Club in an hour and Beatrice knew about the snooker match. Trouble was Beatrice's love of money. She was mad for the stuff. Wasn't content at cleaning out Dean's house even though they'd found the mother lode. Sammy Bruce had never seen as much cash in his life. His old pal had been a right skin-flint, a modern-day Scrooge. £23,235 had been discovered in Dean's hiding-places. Beatrice knew them all: behind the sink, under the floor-boards where the television stood, and in the loft. Sammy had been given the task of crawling on his belly to the furthest corner in the loft, covered from head to foot in yellow insulation fibres. He had successfully retrieved the biggest haul, and coughed muck for days afterwards.

Despite the windfall Beatrice wasn't happy, wanting every last penny she could get. Sammy would have asked for a nominal sum to off-load the coal-business. Wanted to give it to the young lad but Beatrice wouldn't contemplate such foolishness. She wrongly imagined the youngster would have found some funds to buy the business. Fell flat on her face and she wasn't happy, spitting blood and bile, even threatened to slap Sammy if he mentioned again selling Dean's business for a give-away price.

Sammy Bruce flushed with embarrassment as he watched Beatrice knocking seven bells out of the door. When the burly figure of coalman George Jones eased into view he slumped deeper into the seat and shook his head despairingly at the desperate antics of his partner.

Beatrice Crumplin said, "Hello George."

"Beatrice," said George Jones, a little awkward at seeing his late-rival's estranged wife.

"I couldn't come inside for a moment, George?" asked Beatrice, stepping into the landing of the home. "I have a business proposition that might interest you."

She'll never change, thought George Jones.

"What a lovely home you have George," said Beatrice. Took it on herself to saunter through the big house meticulously inspecting and assimilating, only stopping when she had reached the living-room. Easing on to the giant settee, she inquired, "Susan not at home, George?"

"Shopping, Beatrice," answered the stocky coalman. "She'll not be long."

"You'll have heard about Dean?"

"I'm sorry, Beatrice, he was a decent man. Hell of a worker."

"Dean in a nutshell," said Beatrice. "Worked himself into an early grave. Lived for work ... you know he sometimes worked a fifteen hour shift."

"He liked to make money, Beatrice," said the coal merchant sympathetically. "Don't we all?"

"There's work, George," said the woman, "and there's obsession. In the end he only thought of how much money he was making and not about the people who cared for him. You'll know I left him?"

"That was a shame Beatrice; he thought the world of you."

The woman signalled the end of the niceties by coughing and shaking her head. "The reason I called, George," said Beatrice, fixating on the standing figure, "Dean's business is going for sale and I wondered if you'd like to purchase it? Lock, stock and barrel, I'd like £5000, and that would include the wagon."

"No thanks, Beatrice," said the man. "Got enough on my plate."

George Jones had heard all the gossip. He did not like the woman's attitude nor her ruthlessness. George was an acquaintance of Frank Briggs and knew all of what had occurred between Frank's youngest son and Beatrice. That very day he had driven through the village and seen the youngster's valiant effort at sprucing-up an old wagon. Truth be told, George Jones admired the youngster, thought him a better man than his layabout father.

"Pardon me?"

"I'm a one-man business, Beatrice," explained George quietly. "I have an established round. No way as big as Dean's but it gives me a comfortable living."

"Do you know how much Dean was making, George?" said the woman. "Do you know how many customers he has?"

"I work alone, Beatrice," said the merchant. "It suits me."

"But the money, George?" Her tone echoed disbelief, "It's for nothing!"

"And end up in the graveyard next to Dean?"

"£3000 and that's my final offer."

"Beatrice, love," insisted the coalman. "I'm really not interested."

"You're a fool, George Jones!" barked the woman.

145

Beatrice Crumplin stood, brushed herself down and hurried from the room. George followed her to the door.

"I'm sorry, Beatrice," he said and watched the woman wrench open the front door.

"You will be!"

George Jones grimaced and held his tongue. Last thing he wanted was a full-blown argument with Beatrice.

"You'll find a buyer, Beatrice," he said carefully. "I'm sure someone will buy the business …"

George Jones wasn't allowed to finish the sentence.

"I used to tell Dean you'd never amount to anything!" barked Beatrice, interrupting the man. "I was right! I don't know why I bothered!"

The woman stormed away, her features flushed with anger.

"Goodbye, Beatrice," said George. He closed the door, thankful that his visitor had not overstayed her welcome.

*

The Hearts of Oak tavern was a man's pub, an old-fashioned drinking- den and the regulars enjoyed the warmth and genuine cheer of the place as well as the strong ale that was served. The interior of the bar area was ancient; the leather bench skirting two sides of the room was threadbare and patched in places. Near to the door was the regulation billiard table. About the place was a hotchpotch of stools, chairs and arm-chairs apparently arranged with no sense of order or grouping. The locals however, knew the pecking-order, understood that certain seats were branded with invisible name-tags and belonged to regular customers, and woe betide any stranger who stepped out of line and ignored tradition.

By 9.30pm Sandy Baxter had ruffled a few feathers. Intentionally.

Billy Warren, thirty-plus, was top-dog and ruled the pub with an iron fist. Tall, lean and heavily tattooed, Bill could out-drink and out-fight all-comers. Sixteen pints a session was a regular occurrence for the imposing figure, and he could still find his way home. Warren didn't suffer fools gladly. He was neither a bully nor a braggart but push him too far and sparks would fly. It was mid-evening when the brawler sauntered towards the lavatories. Passing the two young lads playing snooker, Warren nodded at the strangers before he disappeared into the lavatory.

"Sick of this," muttered Sandy. He threw the cue noisily across the billiard-table and smiled at the sea of faces turning his way. He strode away, pint in hand before flopping on to the battered arm-chair.

Maxi Stubbs, who had visited the pub several times in the past and understood instinctively the ethos of the place, made a bee-line towards the seated figure and begged him to find another seat.

"On your bike, Maxi," replied the stubborn Simon Baxter. He smiled coldly as the big fellow strode towards him. Raising his glass, he said mockingly, "Cheers, fella."

The entire room went a deathly silence. There was not a sound as everyone in the bar watched and waited.

"Move, lad!" grunted Billy Warren. He shook Baxter's chair. Gesturing at his beer and cigarettes that stood centre-stage on the small table next to Baxter, he continued, "That's my pint, lad, and you're in my seat!"

Sandy Baxter smiled as sweetly as a choir-boy, "Join me, friend," and nodded at an adjoining chair. "Take a pew."

"Move, punk," grunted the taller figure, "or there'll be trouble!"

"Come on, Sandy," begged Maxi Stubbs, "there's other seats."

"I like this chair, man!" The youth smiled cockily at Warren.

"Won't tell you again," muttered the older man. He was fuming.

"Won't tell me what, pal?" goaded the youth.

"I'm not your pal!"

"Go and play dominoes, old man!"

Warrren swung an almighty punch at the seated figure. There was no prior warning. The noise as knuckle hit bone and gristle was sickening. The onlookers rose as one and watched the spectacle; it had been a while since Wild Billy lost his temper.

*

An hour after the pub brawl, two females headed towards the public-house in the nearby town-centre. It was 10.00 and Thelma Cruddace was in a foul mood and about to throw in the towel. The evening, in her opinion, had been a write-off. The pair had tried most of the pubs in the place and were desperate for a little action. It was Saturday night, supposedly the best night of the week. Persuaded by Tammy to forgo the delights of Sunderland in favour of a cheaper evening closer to home Thelma had encountered only morons and skip-rats. She'd spend a small fortune and not once been offered a drink from the cheap-skates they'd encountered. The night had been an unmitigated disaster.

"The Gamecock is always full, Thelma," said Tammy hopefully. "Guaranteed!"

"Pigs fly, Tam," muttered the despondent female, annoyed that she'd worn her most expensive *Anne Summers* underwear, more annoyed she couldn't flaunt it to some gorgeous hunk. She relented, "One more try," she whined, "and then I'm off home!"

Their luck was in; they hit the jackpot at the very last venue. The place was packed and the atmosphere excellent. The juke-box played so loud it smothered the crowd close to the bar. At the opposite end of the room gyrating bodies bounced and shook to the beat. The females watched as a couple left their seats and headed for the door.

"Grab those chairs, Thelma!" shouted Tammy and she waded expertly towards the bar-counter.

There were four stools strategically placed around the table, the two opposite were occupied by a coloured youth and his battered friend. Thelma Cruddace focused on the shaven-headed lad, saw the bruised, swollen eyes and smelled trouble. Told herself that she would move as soon as Tammy returned with the drinks. She didn't notice the attention she was getting from the other youth.

"Thelma?" asked the black lad and smiled like a prospector who'd found gold. "Thelma Cruddace, isn't it?"

The female glanced at the youth, sneering at the audacity of the stranger and then the stupor of the alcohol lifted enough for her to realise he had called her by her name. She looked again and it suddenly dawned on her; the colour, the mischievous smile. "Maxi Stubbs," she laughed, "it's been a year!"

Tammy Bryce tottered to the table. She recognized Maxi immediately, still fancied him and grinned excitedly. The gloom of the night lifting as quickly as a whore's skirts. Tammy knew where she was spending the night. Introductions were made and the gossip started in earnest, apart from the rather sullen skin-head called Sandy Baxter.

149

Maxi Stubbs started to regurgitate the evening's entertainment but was interrupted by the female.

"The Hearts of Oak is a dive, Max," whined Tammy.

"It's a man's pub," he replied. "Darts, dominoes and pool, the only thing missing is women."

"That's not a bad thing," mouthed his companion. He glared at the two girls.

Tammy, tall and beautiful and full of a youthful arrogance was not in awe of the stranger, she retaliated, "Win, lose or draw?" and gestured at his damaged features.

"What do you think, sweetie?" said Baxter, seething.

"Judging by your face," answered the female, "I'd definitely say you came out second-best."

Simon Baxter glowered. Glancing at his companion, he spat, "Tell him Maxi!"

"Sandy was caught with a sucker punch," said the coloured youth. "Knocked him off the chair," Maxi was in full flow, loud and buoyant, the evening suddenly illuminated with the thought of proper company. "All hell broke loose! Sandy started fighting back and the whole pub seemed to join in! I separated the pair of them but then we were thrown out!"

"I'll be back tomorrow," vowed Baxter. "Face to face, see what he can do."

Tammy had little interest in the obnoxious little man with the obvious chip on his shoulder. She turned and raised her glass to his companion, "Hope I'm not wasting my time, Max?"

"How so, Tammy?"

"Tell me that you've lost interest in that little madam."

"Which little girl would that be," said Maxi Stubbs, suddenly realizing that the girl was interested in him and not his companion. "Jog my memory, Tammy."

"Iris Briggs."

Sandy Baxter was only half listening, glancing around the crowds of folk, looking for some real company, male company.

"Iris, eh?"

"Rumour is, Max," laughed Thelma, joining in with the banter, "her youngest boy is not kosher?" The female winked at her friend, "Little Frank?"

Tammy smiled wantonly. "Frank … Farouk," she answered. "Whatever. He's definitely not pukka."

"You don't say?" replied Maxi brusquely. Took a deep breath and fired a broadside, "Tittle-tattle, nothing more. It might be the same folk linking you and Johnny!"

"If John ever finds out," interrupted Thelma, ignoring the jibe at her friend, "I reckon he'll kill you!"

"I'm not frightened of Johnny Briggs," answered the lad, feigning bravery. Chest out, chin jutting, he spat, "Anyway, he's chased and caught most of the skirts in the place!" He stared too long at the tallest girl, asked, "Isn't that a fact, Tammy?" It was his turn to twist the knife.

It was becoming awkward for Tammy Bryce. Colliery gossip had so far eluded the girl's earlier dalliance with the diminutive lothario. Wanting to keep it that way she changed the record slightly, "Johnny Briggs gets out of Medomsley," she said, chortling, "and you leave Shotton. Coincidence, Maxi?"

"Medomsley," intervened Simon Baxter. He leaned across the table like a human pit bull, eyes wide with interest as the fog of alcohol lifted. "Run that past me again, girl. Who did you say left the lock-up?"

Maxi Stubbs replied, "No one you'll know, Sandy. He's a local boy."

"Name?" grunted the pugnacious Baxter.

Tammy Bryce interrupted, "Johnny Briggs," she said.

151

Baxter's body spasmed and he almost dropped his drink. "The would-be footballer?" he barked.

Tammy nodded, uncomfortable now, "You know him?"

"Best friend," said the brawler, regaining his composure. "Lost touch though!"

Thelma Cruddace smiled, "Everyone knows Johnny Briggs.

Tammy seized the opportunity to silence gossip-monger Max. She nudged the stranger, "Between you and me, Rocky, there's a bit of history between Maxi and John Briggs!"

Baxter grinned manically, "I'm all ears!" he said.

**

CHAPTER SIXTEEN

If he had not walked the short distance to the newsagent shop that morning Michael Motson would have been pulled for questioning. It was Sunday morning, the two-minute constitutional to the shop for papers and fags was completed and Micky was returning home. He turned a corner and saw the jumble of police-cars parked outside his house either side of his clapped-out *Hillman Imp.* Cool as a cucumber, Micky casually crossed the back street; his head stuck in the newspaper and strolled out of sight. He stopped at the bus-stand, the last in a long line of passengers, and smiled thankfully when the double-decker pulled up. *'Where to?'* asked the coloured driver with the Birmingham accent. The bedraggled passenger handed over coins: *'As far as this will take me, friend.'* Micky found a seat, put his head between his hands and prayed.

A short while later Micky Motson was standing at Hartlepool's main bus terminal. His thoughts were in freefall, bordering on paranoia. He was only a few miles north of Raymond Robinson's home! Then his luck changed, a single-decked bus roared into view and Buff watched as the driver altered the designation plates from Hartlepool to Sunderland and then listed various drop-zones. The town of Peterlee stood out like a beacon. The place was a mile east of Shotton, and his sister, Elsie lived in Shotton. He thought that if the police were going to look for him they would check his old haunts in Wingate. He decided to visit Elsie knowing she would always help him. His sister wasn't short of a bob or two, she would lend him money, enough to get him away from the North-East.

"How much to Peterlee?" he asked.

153

Michael watched as the driver inspected him, visibly wincing at his appearance as he quoted the fare. It was too much for the ex-con.

"You got a problem?" he grunted, and gave the man a dark look.

The tubby bus-driver suddenly realised the gravity of the situation. Not about to step into the minefield he nervously asked for the fare. The money was thrown down and the ticket snatched from quivering fingers before the passenger found a seat.

The episode made Micky conscious about his personal hygiene. Thought perhaps Eileen McCufferty was right, maybe he had let things slide. He shrugged his shoulders, thought it was time to get his act together. Elsie would sort it out. He'd have a bath and spruce himself up, might even borrow a few of Frank's clothes. They'd be the wrong size and shape but at least he would be clean.

An hour later Michael Motson was speed-walking from Peterlee town centre towards Shotton. The town was a busy place. Two minutes into his journey and he had counted three police-cars and a cruiser. He felt sick to his bones, regretting his earlier, impulsive action. Knew he should have waited a little longer before visiting Robinson, waited and planned and thought more about the implications of his recklessness. Not that it would not have altered anything. The end result would have been the same; Robinson would have suffered for betraying him. Broken bones, disfigurement and humiliation was the order of the day. He sighed loudly; a little planning might have changed the outcome. Didn't want to kill Sugar Ray, wanted to hurt him. It was never his intention to put his former boss in a coffin. That was the trouble with a long prison sentence; the festering got inside your head and made you a little crazy.

He pushed aside negative thoughts and tried to be positive. What was done was done. Giving Sugar the kiss of life forever and a day would not bring him back. Robinson was stone dead. Micky nodded stoically, he thought the turncoat deserved to die. The same man had destroyed umpteen lives. He pictured Justin West, the late partner of Robinson. Thanks to Sugar Ray's testimonial, West had been given fourteen years behind bars. The ex-accountant had not survived two years. Unable to adapt to prison life Justin West had hung himself. Lisa Coxon, Robinson's secretary and occasional lover, had suffered the same fate as Motson. Found in possession of Class A drugs she was locked up for eight years. She left a young family on the outside. The list of casualties was endless. Motson grimaced; he had nailed the grass, not only for his sake, but for all the others. He thought about Robinson's boss, the gangster, William Garcia from Leeds, and wondered about possible repercussions.

An ice-cream van pulled up alongside the striding figure. A switch was activated by the driver and manic tune suddenly engulfed the immediate vicinity. Michael Motson quaked with shock and his legs buckled. He turned and glowered at the vehicle.

"Buff!" shouted Anthony Dixon, the owner of *Antonio's Ice Cream*. Born and bred in Wingate, he'd owned the van long enough to earn the name Antonio. When he served kiddies he played with the accent, and fooled no one but himself. An Italian Geordie, *'I Antonio, what's tha ganna have, like?'*

"Tony," gasped Motson, "you scared the hell out of me!"

"Been years, Buff, where you been hiding?"

"A lift, Tony," asked the pedestrian, already opening the side-door. "Need a lift to Shotton, man."

155

"No problem," said the driver, "I'm on the way to Wingate. Shotton main street okay?

Minutes later Anthony Dixon dropped his old friend in *Potto Street,* close to the Post Office. He drove the van out of sight then stopped in a side street. He opened all the windows allowing fresh air into the putrid cab. *Never again*, thought Antonio, *stinks worse than a tramp.* He remembered how the man used to be; fiery-tempered, brash, ignorant but always spotlessly clean. *Buff's wearing a pony-tail,* mused Anthony, *and he's got no hair!*

Michael Motson knocked on the door then waltzed into the terraced house like he owned it. "Elsie, love," he called, "you about?"

"Mick!" gasped the incredulous woman. She hurried to his side, grasped and held him to her ample chest, "Micky, where've you been all this time?"

"Things went a bit pear-shaped, Elsie."

"Jesus, Mick," said Elsie, frowning at the stench of unwashed clothes. "When was the last time you washed?"

"Few days," he answered brightly. "You know how it is, Elsie?"

"Get upstairs," she ordered, "the bath is in the same place!" She pushed her brother towards the stairs. "Go, and leave all your clothes on the landing. Soak yourself, okay?"

"Where's Frank?" asked the man. "Won't he mind?"

"Bugger Frank, you're my brother. Now go!"

Elsie waited a prudent five minutes before following him up the stairs. Saw the pile of festering clothes, wrapped in the old jacket, and the decrepit brogues perched on top of the pile. The woman bit her lips in an effort to stop the tears. Her brother appeared exhausted, dirty and gaunt; his thinning locks tied in a silly plait made him look foolish. Elsie coughed and wiped the tears on to her sleeve.

"Mick," she said loudly, unable to hide the quiver in her voice, "you in the bath yet?"

"Having a soak, Elsie."

"Still a size 7 shoes, Mick?"

"Yeah."

"Inside leg still 27?"

"Stopped growing when I was fourteen, Elsie," he chuckled. "Still hoping for a miracle."

"I'll put the kettle on, love," she said. "You'll be hungry?"

"Eat a horse." *Saddle, reins, bridle*, he thought. *Anything!*

Elsie shuffled to her bedroom, pulled and plucked and found enough to clothe her brother. Frank's cast-offs from a decade ago when he was a smaller and slimmer version of himself. The shoes were a size too big but two pairs of socks would cure that hiccup. The trousers were six inches too long; twenty minutes with the needle and thread would rectify the fault. She hurried to the kitchen, turned on the cooker, filled the big frying-pan and switched on the kettle. The woman climbed the stairs again, listened outside the bathroom and heard the activity.

Elsie nodded with approval. "Mick," she said, "underwear and socks are outside of the door. Put on Frank's dressing-gown until I alter some trousers, okay?"

"Thanks, Elsie. Appreciated, love."

"Food will be ready in a few minutes." She remembered. "Mick," put on both sets of socks, Frank is a size 8, okay?"

"Okay."

"Mick?" Elsie had to ask.

"Elsie?"

157

"You heard about that trouble in Middlesbrough?"

There was silence for a few moments as he tried to think of a plausible answer.

"Mick?" she called.

A decade ago Mick had driven a top-of-the range *Mercedes* around Shotton before parking outside his sister's house in *Moore Terrace.* His antics had the whole street talking. She still recalled the man being chauffeured by her brother, remembered his silly name, Sugar Ray, the same name that *Look North* broadcast hours ago, the drug baron, Raymond Robinson, from Middlesbrough.

"Mick!"

"Hear you Elsie," answered Micky, "loud and clear."

"We have to talk, Mick."

Elsie Briggs sighed and left the landing. It was cards on the table time.

As Elsie cooked her brother's breakfast a young man approached one of the houses in nearby Victoria Terrace. He carried duct-tape and rope. Smiling and whistling merrily, Simon Baxter could have easily passed as a workman if it had been a workday and his face wasn't swollen and bruised from the mayhem of the previous evening. It was early morning, Sunday, few people were about and Baxter was on a mission. Fortune had played into his hands the previous evening. The chance meeting with the girls in the pub was a Godsend; he had gleaned so much information from the females and the coloured youth. He'd enjoyed his time with Maxi Stubbs until an unfortunate altercation in the toilets ruined the evening. Stubbs, filled with alcohol and false courage, had foolishly stood his ground when the name-calling became too much for him. Maxi retaliated and threw a punch at the shaven-headed psychopath and suffered the consequences.

158

"Morning, love," said the stranger as the young mother opened the door. "John told me to call."

Iris Briggs said, "He didn't tell me." Couldn't help but stare at the injuries to the man's face. "John's at the recreation-ground with the boys. They're watching the football. Can I help?"

"He'll be watching, not playing," said the skinhead brusquely. "I guess that would be my fault ... I was the one who smashed his knees!"

Baxter darted forward, struck the woman's face with a knuckled fist and knocked her into the kitchen. Iris was unconscious before she hit the floor.

When she regained consciousness, Iris was tied securely to a kitchen-chair, propped in the centre of the sitting-room. Rope was wrapped around her arms and feet and sticky-tape covered her mouth. She was in her underclothes, her dress was draped over an arm-chair, the television had been switched on and the stranger was sprawled across the sofa, apple in one hand and a large knife in the other. He appeared to be engrossed with the programme.

Iris wept uncontrollably.

Forty-five minutes later John Briggs and his two sons burst through the door. They were laughing and joking; exhausted, happy, and very hungry.

"Ma," shouted a mischievous Eddie, "Dad says if the dinner isn't ready he's gonna eat Frank ...." He froze and clamped his hands over his mouth at the horrific scene that greeted him.

Close behind, his face obscured as his youngest squirmed in his gasp, John Briggs stumbled into his first-born. He started to complain and then stopped, immobilized at the macabre sight before him. Saw Iris stripped and bound, and

159

next to her, the leering face of Simon Baxter. The intruder had one hand gripping her hair and the other held a knife.

"Shut the door!" hissed the intruder.

The door was closed. The young father stood dumbfounded and silent with his arms around his boys.

"Johnny No Luck!" said Baxter. "Remember me?"

John tried to speak but his mouth was as dry as tinder. His whole body trembled. Stood helpless as his boys wrapped their arms around him. Eddie clung to his legs, his eyes closed, calling for his Mother. Frank, still gripping his Dad's throat, stared wide-eyed at the grotesque image before him.

"Sit down!" demanded Sandy Baxter. He pulled the knife gently across Iris's neck. A faint red weal appeared as the girl convulsed and fought to escape her binds but the intruder stared at the youth as if the woman did not exist, "Won't ask again."

John Briggs shuffled towards the sofa as the children clung to him for dear life. Both boys started crying.

"What do you want, Sandy," John asked said. The strain was telling. He was so frightened his voice raised an octave, "I've done nothing."

Sandy Baxter released his grip on Iris and her head flopped forward. A deft pull and the adhesive masking-tape was ripped free of her mouth. The girl gulped open-mouthed like a dying fish. The maniac leaned close to her waxen face until he was almost touching her cracked lips. Grinning wolfishly, he asked, "Better for you?"

Iris focused on John and her sons. "Don't cry, boys," she gasped unconvincingly. "Everything will be okay." Big tears rolled down her face.

"Didn't your husband tell you about Sandy Baxter?" asked the demented intruder. A surreal glow emanated from his glazed eyes.

Moments passed and the only sounds in the room were the soft unremitting sobs and sniffles from the children.

"Let them go, Sandy," pleaded John. "It's me you want."

The stupor lifted. The deranged youth focused again on the woman. "Look, girl," whined Baxter. He flicked his tongue against his top dentures, manipulating them until they loosened and rested on his lips in a monstrous smile, "False teeth!" A long pause before he added, "Your husband knocked them out." His eyes rolled momentarily as the images washed over him; "I was a long time in hospital... a long time."

"Please let them go," begged John Briggs.

Sandy Baxter straightened and stretched to his full height, scratched the long blade over his scalp and said, "The scars," he tapped the knife noisily against his shaven skull, "always itch."

"Let her go, Sandy."

"You think so much about her, Johnny?"

The young father grimaced and waited.

"You don't *love* her, do you?" said the knife-man. His languid tones echoed derision.

John Briggs caressed his sons. He stared intently at this captor, unable to speak.

"Mr. Briggs," said Baxter, mocking. He smoothed Iris's hair with the flat side of the blade, "She's not worth the trouble. Want to know why?" He paused, grinned insanely, leaned close to Iris and whispered the name of Maxi Stubbs. So close their lips almost touched, "You like black, don't you, girl," he continued, "isn't black your favourite colour?"

"Let her alone," begged John. "Let her be!"

"Maxi Stubbs, Iris," chuckled Sandy. He licked her nose, "You'll remember him?"

161

The girl's eyes widened with revulsion, speechless as she squirmed open-mouthed at the smell and touch of the tormentor's tongue on her face.

"Dad," stammered Eddie, his whole body shaking with fear, "stop him!"

"Please, Sandy," begged John, "let Iris go."

The intruder ignored the pleading, enjoying the persecution and the distress. He smiled wildly at all present, enveloped in the sensuous, heavenly cloak of mania.

Baxter kissed her ear wantonly. He whispered, "Maxi Stubbs is my neighbour. He told me so much." Stood erect, turned and stared intently at his victims huddled on the sofa. "Men … such braggarts, aren't they, Johnny?" he said icily.

John Briggs paled. His breath laboured as his mind festered.

Baxter continued bating, "You'll think Maxi has been boasting, believe it's hot air from the nigger?"

"Maxi Stubbs is a liar!" gasped Iris and she twisted her frantic face towards her husband. "It's not true, John! Whatever he tells you it's not true!"

Baxter said, "Want to know what your wife was doing when you were stuck in Medomsley?" He was ecstatic, enjoying the cruel game, "The import from the Indies told me all about his play for your girl, Johnny. Don't it turn your stomach, man, your little wife being chased by a half-caste?"

"Maxi Stubbs is a liar," moaned the demented girl.

"Chase me, Uncle Remus," mimicked Baxter, his tone pitched high. "If I run slow enough you'll catch me!" His body began twitching with sordid pleasure, "Maxi Stubbs has some mouth."

"I want my mom!" sobbed Frank and he hid his terrified head in his father's chest.

"You want more," asked Baxter, eyes rolling with delight, "because those coloured have a way with our women don't you know?"

Simon Baxter's body began to twitch, then as if a switch in his brain had suddenly fused, the spasms stopped. He stared blankly at his captives and saw the disbelief registering. It brought a smile to his evil face. He moved the knife until it was touching Iris's nostril and watched her flinch with fear. Made him grin with pleasure.

"You think I'm a liar?" Baxter grunted as he came out of the stupor. His eyes feasted on John Briggs, "Maxi wasn't the only one who was loose with his tongue. I talked to some of your friends. Two girls who know you well."

Iris closed her eyes. John stared at his tormentor.

Baxter focused on Iris. "Open your eyes, girl," he said, slapping the blade against her head. "You gotta hear this!"

John struggled from the sofa but stopped when Baxter shook his head wilfully and pointed the knife at Iris's bulging eyes. He returned to the seat.

"I'm sorry!" whined Iris, gaping frantically at her husband,

"Thelma," said the psychopath, "I'm sure her name was Thelma. And Tammy ... Tammy Bryce. He paused while the words registered. Added contemptuously, "Both girls had so much to say don't you know!"

John Briggs groaned, his features crunched with apprehension. Iris screamed hysterically and fought against the bonds. The two small boys wept uncontrollably.

Made Baxter chortle.

**

163

CHAPTER SEVENTEEN

"Elsie," said Michael Motson, "Ray Robinson was the lowest of the low. He was a snitch. Grassed on a load of people, some of them close friends. He didn't care who he hurt as long as it saved his own skin!"

"But Mick, if you'd called the police and explained...."

"Listen, sis," interrupted the man. "Eight decent people were locked up because of Robinson; one of them was a woman with a young family. They were locked up for a total of 96 years!"

"Each?" asked an incredulous Elsie. The eldest of the Motson girls was not the brightest of stars in the sky, "Mary Mother of God!"

"No, in total! I got ten years! Lisa Coxon got eight years. She left three kids to be shuffled around foster-homes!"

"You could have explained it was all a terrible accident, Mick."

"And they would have listened?"

"Sure they would have!"

"I put a hammer through his front-door. I chased him, Elsie! Christ, if I'd caught him I would have put him in traction!"

"End of the day you didn't kill him! It was a terrible mistake!"

"Elsie, I can't put it right, I can't put back the clock!"

Elsie grimaced and nodded sympathetically.

"Robinson cost me five years," Michael Motson pointed at his forehead, "He gave me more scars than Frankenstein! You know I've got a permanent headache through him?"

Elsie said patiently, "What will you do?"

"I need to disappear."

"They'll think you're guilty …"

He interrupted, "I left the claw-hammer …finger-prints!"

Elsie Briggs reached for her purse. A wad of money was handed over. "Sorry there's not more."

"The £120 will get me to London. Lenny Jobson got out of clink a few months before me. Lives in Hayes, near Heathrow, said I could look him up any time."

Elsie said, "The rest of my money went to John for his coal-wagon. You know that, Mick, don't you?"

"I'm happy, Elsie."

"Right then," she said. "You'll be off to Durham Station?" She left the sofa, cuddled and kissed her brother. "Keep in touch."

Micky squeezed her tight, "I'll write," he said.

"Let me phone John's house," said Elsie. "It'll save you walking to Victoria Street. He'll not mind picking you up."

"It'll take all of three minutes, sis," he said. "I need the exercise."

"I'll phone him, eh, just in case they're out?"

"Leave it, Elsie," he said, chortling. "I want to see the look on his face when he sees his mad uncle."

"I'm so proud of him, Mick. He seems to be getting his life back."

"Maybe I'll do the same, Elsie," he answered half-heartedly. "Once I get to London."

Minutes later Michael Motson had reached his nephew's home. He tapped and opened the door. Laughing softly, he mimicked his sister, '*Come in,*' he shouted, '*you're not a stranger.*' Dressed like some reject from Carnaby Street, he stepped in to the small living-room and froze. The smile turned to a grimace as he witnessed the nightmare.

"Well, well," smirked the knife-wielding youth, "Rip Van Winkle in the flesh or is it Beau Brummell. Come in and close the door."

Micky assessed the situation in moments, his mind cold and calculating as he plotted and planned. Raising his arms high in the air he feigned surrender. "I want no trouble, lad, I'm not a fighter!" he stammered. He acted like a frightened clown when he wailed pathetically, "Bad with my nerves," he wailed. "I'm bad with my nerves!"

"Uncle Buff?" said John Briggs, gaping at the comical figure that dithered and whimpered before the captor. He barely recognized the balding hippie. His uncle looked small and frail, and so different from his memories.

Sandy Baxter glanced at the seated youth who clung to his two sons. He chuckled and said, "Uncle Buff … kind of name is that?"

A moment's distraction was all it took for Michael Motson to dive headlong at the intruder. Fists flew as the two adversaries struggled for control. Iris, strapped to the chair centre-stage, was knocked to the floor, the television cracked noisily against the wall. It was bedlam. The Wingate brawler was ferocious as he attacked; the speed and doggedness of the shrieking Motson unnerved his younger opponent. It took moments of intense hand-to-hand fighting before Baxter was driven back, both men still battling as they toppled headlong into the fireplace. Motson, sensing victory, grabbed the steel poker and hit Simon Baxter across the head. The blow knocked Baxter senseless. The fight was over. Micky Motson struggled to his feet.

Little Eddie screamed with delight. His baby brother covered his face with a pillow and cried for his mother. John Briggs came out of the stupor, jumped off the couch and kicked at the unconscious figure. Satisfied, he fell to his knees, untied the bonds that held the wailing Iris and hoisted her gently to her feet. Only then did he see the knife wedged in the side of his uncle's waist. Michael Motson's midriff was soaked with blood.

The older man said reassuringly, "It's nothing we can't fix." He glanced at the flustered, weeping female, "Iris, find a dressing!"

Iris bolted up the stairs. The two boys ran after their mother.

Micky stripped off the ruined shirt, lay on the settee and stuffed the garment into a ball and placed it close to the wound. Smiled at his nephew through gritted teeth and slowly pulled the blade free. He then pushed the bloodied cloth into the seeping wound.

Iris hurried down the staircase, the boys in fast pursuit. In one hand was the box of sanitary towels, in the other she held several thick pads.

"I've only got these," said the female. "For emergencies."

"Perfect," said the injured man. He instructed her to fill a dish with warm water and salt. "I want you to clean it first. It's a flesh wound, only went in an inch before it came out the side." Then he instructed his nephew to shackle the unconscious figure, "Don't want the cracker to get free. Tie it good and tight."

"Shall I call the police?" John asked.

"Not yet." He saw the puzzled look and explained, "It's not the first time I've cracked someone's head on a fire-side. Long story John, I'll tell you sometime."

Sandy Baxter started groaning. John grabbed at the coil of rope and moved to the prostrate figure.

Twenty minutes later the jobs were done. The moaning figure of Baxter was trussed up, and Michael Motson's wound was staunched and bound. The injured man, oblivious to the pain, asked his startled nephew to take him to Durham Railway Station.

"You want to go to the station," said the youth, trying to dissuade the injured man, "not the hospital?"

Motson smiled genuinely, "Son, if the cut was bad, I'd be the first to see a doctor, okay?"

Iris inspected the dressing. Four sanitary-towels were secured with copious amounts of yellow masking-tape strapped round his waist.

Iris said, "Like a bumble-bee, but at least it's stopped the blood."

The man fastened the shirt, a gift from the youth. It was a tight-fit but much more fashionable than the discarded, garment. He shook hands with the two boys, kissed the girl and shuffled from the house.

"How long do I wait?" asked Iris and gestured at the bound figure stuck safely in one corner of the room.

Baxter's arms were tied behind his back, rope coiled about his lower legs, and sticky-tape jammed across his mouth. The psychopath was going nowhere.

"Half an hour, said John. "Tell the police what happened, say I've gone to the hospital … Don't mention Buff."

John Briggs drove through the streets of the colliery, reached the Fleming Hotel junction and slowed as a nearing vehicle indicated then changed its mind. John hesitated before inching forward. When his injured uncle lifted a cautionary arm he braked the wagon for the second time and waited. The hesitancy proved calamitous; a driver behind the wagon lost concentration and slid into the rear of the lorry. The noise of the shunt was horrendous. John winced, Michael Motson cursed, and the female driver of the dented Mercedes screamed in anger.

The damage was minimal but the woman was livid. She stumbled from the car, inspected the damage, then ran to the passenger-door of the lorry and started remonstrating. Josephine Brooks ranted and raved, pulled open the door and continued with the verbal assault.

"Look what you've done!" she screamed. "Are you drunk …."

"Josephine," interrupted a perspiring Micky Motson. His head swam with discomfort, "Is that you?"

The woman spluttered into a dazed, surreal silence as she suddenly recognised the voice from the past. She stared with utter disbelief at the ruined looks of the older figure, incredulous with shock.

"Michael?" she said, gaping at the older man.

"Hello, Josephine." Micky Motson cradled the wound and tried to smile. "It's been a while."

"Michael," stammered the bewildered woman, "is that you?"

He tried again, "It's really me." The words were soft like treacle.

"I couldn't find you, Michael," said the woman, the road accident forgotten as her emotions started on a roller-coaster ride. Still in turmoil after years of frustration she stammered, "You almost destroyed me …"

Michael interrupted, "I'm on the way to hospital, love." He opened his jacket and pointed a shaking hand at the bloody shirt. A scoundrel to the end, he whispered, "I'll call you."

"Michael!" Stared at the man she had loved, who had hurt her so much. "I was pregnant! I was fifteen and pregnant! You left me!"

"I didn't know!" pleaded the man straight-faced. He had forgotten about the baby.

"How could you?"

169

"I had no option, Josephine," he answered. Tried to act normal despite the terrible pain in his side, "I was in Deerbolt."

The woman frowned, confused.

He told her about the Young Offender's Institution near Barnard Castle in West Durham.

John reluctantly climbed out of the truck. Julie Brooks's mother was the last person he wanted to see. He walked to the rear of the truck and inspected the damage. The coal-wagon was unmarked. The Mercedes fender was bent. The damage was minor. Taking a deep breath to steady his nerves he approached the woman. The sight of the youth jolted Josephine Brooks back to the present.

"You!" she bellowed. "Of all the people!"

Michael Motson intervened, "My nephew, Josephine."

"Nephew," gasped an incredulous Josephine Brooks, "I don't understand?"

"John is my nephew."

Dumbstruck, Josephine Brooks looked at the boy and then at the man. Her jaw dropped. The groan spilling from her lips was almost inaudible.

Michael Motson repeated the news, "He's my sister Elsie's son."

Josephine came out of the trance, her fuddled brain slowly assimilating the information. The pair had the same blue eyes, receding fair hair, identical stature. She felt faint. It was all too much. She tried to move away. Pushing aside the youth she stumbled to her car. Tears fell like rain.

Michael Motson told his nephew to get back in the cab. He had a train to catch. He had to escape. Nothing else mattered.

The wagon disappeared in a cloud of smoke leaving the woman broken and weeping. Spread-eagled over the bonnet of the motor, she wailed to the heavens.

"God help me," she sobbed, "this is not happening to me!"

All of a sudden the realization hit her as her thoughts spiralled out of control. Michael Motson had been her lover. He was her daughter's father. Julie's father was Michael Motson and he was related to the horrid John Briggs! The men were blood related! Her eyes closed as she tried to assimilate the awful truth. John Briggs had got her daughter pregnant, and her daughter Julie shared the same blood line as the animal that had impregnated her! Her grandchild's father was.......

"No!" she called to the skies. "No! Dear God please don't let this be true!"

**

(

CHAPTER EIGHTEEN

They stood together on the lonely platform at Durham Railway Station, waited twenty tortuous minutes with no conversation and the nephew was concerned.

John Briggs said, "I'm sorry about bringing up the past."

Micky Motson exhaled noisily, the irritation evident, "Old news, okay?"

The youth regretted his inquisitiveness. It had been obvious that his queries about Julie Brooks's mother had annoyed his uncle. The brief journey to Durham had been awkward, marred by his casual, innocent probing. Reached the outskirts of the city and was told in no uncertain terms to change the record. The older man did not want to talk about his past.

John, trying to make amends, changed tact, "Buff," he said quietly, observing the waxen features, "you don't look well."

Michael Motson smiled. He now regretted his earlier outburst. His nephew had not meant to embarrass him, the boy was naturally curious.

"Johnny," replied the injured man, "I'm fine. Need a dose of medicine and plenty of sleep. Don't worry yourself, I've been in tougher scrapes."

The noise of the approaching coaches echoed around the place, the squeal and rumble enveloped the station as the train slowed and then stopped. There was a final caress before the two men parted company. The walk to the nearest carriage was slow and painful for the older man. Michael Motson moaned softly as he struggled on board. The door closed and the older man disappeared inside.

The train chugged away. John waited until the last of the carriages disappeared from sight. He stood a while, looking at nothing, dazed and stiff from the events of the day. His mind began to crowd with awful images. Torturous pictures filled his thoughts: Simon Baxter was taunting, Josephine Brooks was bawling; saw Maxi Stubbs with Iris, his Uncle Micky arguing with Josephine Brooks. The collage was bizarre, the facts, real and imagined, were all too weird to absorb.

John thought about Sandy Baxter, imagined the bedlam that would arise when the police began their interrogation. He turned and walked slowly towards the wagon, his thoughts jumping through hoops. Remembered the confrontation with Mrs. Brooks, Julie's mother. He tried to imagine Josephine Brooks with Michael Motson. The pair had been an item once, intimate once. In love! Mrs. Brooks became pregnant and the father was his Uncle. *How could that be*, he thought, *there was only one daughter and that was Julie?* Did Josephine Brooks have an abortion or was Julie Brooks the daughter of Buff Motson? *'Jesus,'* he gasped, *'we could be related!'* The youth climbed into the cab and grimaced at the ludicrous thoughts bombarding his head. Shook his head with disbelief, *'It could be true,'* he said out loud. *'Maybe that's why Buff lost his temper with me?'*

The motor spluttered into life and John slowly manoeuvered the wagon down the steep decline from the train-station, engaged the brakes and waited at the junction. He thought of Michael Motson. His mother had been so honest about the man; he had a heart of gold and would help anyone. The older man had been fearless, so brave against Simon Baxter. He'd laughed at Iris when she called him a hero, wouldn't talk about his heroic, unselfish act. Iris was right; Buff Motson had saved their lives. Without a second thought he had risked his life against a much stronger and

173

younger opponent. John shuddered. Had his uncle had not
arrived at that very moment Sandy Baxter might have killed
them all.

John was unable to move away from the junction, his
head spinning with an aching and troubled heart. He saw the
leering face of Baxter goading him about Iris. He winced at
the images of Iris with Maxi Stubbs. Made his head throb
with the uncertainty, knowing his wife could never admit to
any wrongdoing. His mind filled with putrid thoughts. All too
real. He switched on the radio and pressed frantically through
the channels until he found music. The volume was cranked
high. He wanted any noise, any sound to blank his head. The
pictures, however, would not leave. Saw Baxter and heard his
accusations about his youngest son. John groaned out loud,
his heart heavy with grief.

Michael Motson eased gratefully into the first available
seat and watched as the city was left behind and the green
fields blossomed into view. Perspiration ran down his burning
torso and his head swam in a comforting haze. He gently
touched the mound of bandages. The wound was still dry. He
sighed with relief. Despite the discomfort Michael began to
plan for his future. He would phone Lenny Jobson as soon as
the train reached King's Cross. Lenny's missus had been a
community nurse who got caught with her hands in the
pharmaceutical till. She would tend his wound. He smiled, felt
as if providence was on his side. After all, he had money in
his pocket, and after a few hours on the train, a nurse and bed
and board … maybe even a job would be waiting for him. It
could easily have gone belly-up. He was one lucky man.

He thought of Josephine Brooks. After a lifetime apart
he'd seen her again. He shook his head as the memories
returned. When Josephine got pregnant he disappeared. He

followed his nature and ran from responsibility. He had always wondered what she had done, whether or not she had seen the pregnancy through and had the child. The thought made him smile. Michael Motson a father, it would have been a first. He'd had his share of pretty girls but never had a kid. Thought about the infant and wondered whether it was a boy or a girl and struggled to work out its age.

Michael began reminiscing. He grimaced. He was an absent parent, a scoundrel. The poor mite was better without him. He thought of Josephine. She was still a picture, the kind of woman who always made the effort and kept up appearances. The rosy image lasted moments before reality scrapped sense into his jumbled brain. The female had always been a handful. Despite her young years, she knew what she wanted and usually got it. Micky shook his head knowing the relationship would never have survived his gallivanting ways, not that he would have ever married her, even when she had reached the legal age. Consummating a union with such legal niceties was never an option he had ever contemplated. Truth be told he was a rogue and would never change.

He thought again of the ex-con. Lenny Jobson knew people who knew people. It wouldn't be too long before he had a car licence, National Insurance Card, references … the whole caboodle. It was good to have friends like Jobson.

He closed his eyes as tiredness cloaked him, his thoughts jumbled and senseless. Saw images of Josephine and the child, the baby older now, perhaps young John's age. He wondered if the pair knew each other … stranger things had happened. His mind wafted and waned. Ray Robinson appeared. Sugar Ray scared rigid at his doorstep, Ray bolting like a rabbit chased by hounds. Micky groaned as the nightmare raked his conscience. He was in a mess, never known a hole so deep, and it was all his own doing. He wondered about possible repercussions. Wasn't too concerned about the law. The worst that could happen was a long drawn-out trial with some snotty-nosed barrister half-heartedly pleading for leniency followed by an inevitable prison sentence. He could plead insanity; blame his upbringing, use any excuse to wangle leniency. The only certainty was the outcome of the trial. He would be locked up. It was only the length of the sentence that was debatable. No, the law did not frighten him. It was people like William Garcia, and more especially the muscle they employed to settle scores, who made him jittery.

Michael fell into a deep, uncomfortable sleep.

**

CHAPTER NINETEEN

John was worried, the reality of leaving Simon Baxter in the same house as his family was hitting home. He parked the wagon close to his house and saw a fidgeting Iris waiting at the open door. She was crimson-faced and stammering explanations about the escape of the psychopath. Shock enveloped John Briggs, shock and a gut feeling that something was amiss.

The news was incredible. Make-believe, according to John Briggs who barged past his wife and entered the living-room. Baxter was gone; the place was empty. John rounded on his wife demanding explanations because she had that look again, the same remorseful look she had when he confronted her months ago about her supposed philandering. Iris's blustering, over-the-top excuses did nothing to allay John's fears. With bloodied, bandaged arms wrapped around her chest, Iris looked decidedly uncomfortable.

"The plaster around his mouth was loose," she said. Stood high on the gallows, noose around her neck, spittle covering her dithering lips about to take the plunge. "I tried to cover his mouth, tried to shut him up!" She stopped abruptly, the glowering looks from her husband unnerving her. "What … what's the matter?"

He looked around the room. The place was in chaos. An over-turned chair and miscellaneous cushions littered the floor, the television leaned perilously against the far wall and the fireplace was strewn with abandoned duct-tape, brushes and the solitary poker.

"The police are on the way, John!" said an emotional Iris.

He slumped on the sofa, his eyes focussed on the wall-clock. He had been gone almost two hours and the police were finally on their way. It did not make sense.

He said, "You want to tell me what really happened, Iris?"

"He was shouting! The boys were scared! I sent them to your mother's house as soon as you left …"

He interrupted, "Where's Ma … where are the kids, Iris?"

"Your mother phoned, I told her to look after Eddie and Frank because the police were coming,"

Iris starting pacing the room, her steps manic as she circled in ever-decreasing circles.

"But you hadn't phoned the police!"

"I was going to phone but Baxter was shouting louder and louder. I thought I'd push the tape over his mouth." Iris stopped suddenly, her voice dipped as she confronted her very own Doubting Thomas. "When I got close he lunged at me like a dog! Bit me! Wouldn't let go of my wrist …said he'd bite through an artery if I didn't release him!" Her hands went to her quivering mouth, the soiled bandage hung loose from left wrist. "He wouldn't release me, John. I had to untie the rope one-handed."

"He left the house?" His tone was sceptical, "He left you?"

"He heard your mother on the phone! Perhaps he thought she would call!" she said. "Probably thought you'd be back any second! He untied his legs and ran out the door!"

The noise of screaming brakes and doors slamming stopped all conversation. The police had finally arrived. The lies stopped. Iris was taken to hospital.

By midnight the battle lines had been mapped and drawn. The marital wall had been unconsciously built dividing the

178

double bed equally. Each lay stiff and fretting either side of the boundary. It was the man who finally succumbed to sleep, the stress and weariness of the day's events was too much for John. His breathing changed from fitful and erratic into something more rhythmic and shallow, his body slowly relaxed as he drifted into slumber.

Iris could not sleep, her conscience nagging her. Regret was paramount in her thoughts knowing she had blundered. It had been an act of madness, she could see now but fear and desperation made her act the way she did. Iris had to find out how much Sandy Baxter knew about her affair with Maxi Stubbs. Baxter had been safely secured so Iris imagined it would have been easy to discover the truth, knew that in order to fight her corner she had to be ready with answers. Iris was not about to give up John Briggs without a fight. Every scrap of information discovered would be used by her to keep her marriage intact. Maxi Stubbs was in the past and she was determined to keep him there, at any cost.

She had paced the floor for an age, watched and followed by her frightened boys. Iris agonising at the earlier conversation between the intruder and her husband, trying to recall, verbatim, what had been said or inferred. Baxter had goaded them with his poison, '*Maxi was making a play for her, Johnny. He was always chasing her.*' Almost, but not quite a damming confession, '*What do you think she was doing when you were locked up, Johnny Briggs.* The inference that Thelma Cruddace knew about her dalliance with Maxi Stubbs was worrying. Iris had to find out things.

She had been gentle but firm with her children. Reassured them, told the boys their father and the police were on their way. Iris ordered her sons to Grandmother Briggs' house. She didn't have to tell them twice. They obeyed her without fuss or fight. When Iris opened the back-door the pair careered through the streets leaving her alone with Simon Baxter.

'I'm going to pull back the plaster, you hear?' Iris said to Baxter. She held the steel poker in her hand, ready to strike if he tried to escape. *'I want to know what Maxi Stubbs has told you. If you move I'll hit you!'* He had nodded in sullen agreement, trussed and tied safely, his fighting spirit seemingly spent. The last thing Iris expected was an attack. The speed and frenzy of the strike scuttled her plans, the pain of the bite had been excruciating; the weapon abandoned as she fought to free her arm. It was too late, she had gambled and lost. *'Untie me or I'll bite off your hand!'* he had screamed, his words almost incomprehensible as he clung to her flesh. Iris understood, her mind registered every distorted syllable as he repeated his threat. Meant it too because he gnawed at her flesh and didn't stop until the bonds were loosened. Then Baxter surprised her. She waited with eyes tightly closed for her world to end and heard the door slam. The maniac had gone. Iris grabbed the phone, sucked in air to steady her shattered nerves, *'Hello, police, could you please come to 100, Victoria Street, Shotton. Break-in... yes, but more than that. Assault, yes, but more than that. The man was called Simon Baxter. He tried to kill us!'*

The worst part for Iris was waiting for John's return. Her conscience plagued her knowing how he might react. She was right to worry. The verbal torture started immediately and continued throughout the following day. John was unpleasant, malicious and distant. The situation deteriorated when the police returned the next day. The officers were overtly cynical; they could find neither rhyme nor reason in the young couple's version of the *alleged* assault. Neighbours were interviewed, photographs of Simon Baxter were shown but nothing had been heard or seen. The police were at a loss.

John Briggs was in a dark world all of his own making. The barracking from the officers did not affect him; the chiding went over his head. He cared less when the police rebuked him for leaving his wife alone with the criminal. His thoughts were elsewhere, his mind filled with uncertainty about his wife. Her explanations didn't make sense, her words didn't gel. He knew Iris enough to know something was wrong, married to her long enough to believe she was hiding something. His wife was covered in bruising and had a badly cut wrist yet neither the wounds nor the discomfort appeared to bother Iris. She showed discomfort when his questions became personal, only then did she visibly squirm.

The officers plied him with innuendo. "You couldn't wait until we arrived, Mr. Briggs? You left your wife alone with someone as deranged as Baxter? Odd, to say the least!"

"He was securely tied!" John replied. He gingerly caressed his stomach. "He'd kicked and punched me. I felt ill."

The constable's smirk was buttered with liberal layers of disbelief. He tried to embarrass John when he asked to see the bruising. Didn't expect the rebuke.

"Part-time doctor are you?" said the youth.

It went downhill when one of the local constables recalled John Briggs' tainted history. The conversation steered away from the so-so assault on the husband to the battered and obviously bloodied wife.

"No hanky-panky, son?" queried the middle-aged policeman. Shrugged his shoulders, showing he was a man of the world and knew all about domestic discord. 'Shoe on the other foot, Briggs, your missus was playing away and you caught them at it? Spit it out, laddie, Baxter is your wife's boyfriend, isn't he?'

John protested vehemently but his protestations fell on deaf ears. .

"One thing puzzles me, son," said the barrel-shaped constable, "Baxter was out for revenge and yet it was your wife who was assaulted. Odd, don't you think?"

His cadaverous companion, sporting an over-sized helmet that covered most of his forehead, joined the argument. "There was a massive argument that spilled into a brawl," he said, smiling. "You beat Baxter, tied him hand and foot … and then drove all the way to Durham Hospital!"

The roly-poly officer interrupted. "Fought with a so-called lunatic and yet there's not a bruise on your pretty face?"

His companion said sardonically, "Maybe your wife should have had priority, sir?" He looked at Iris's swollen features and gestured at her neat bandaged arm. He glared at John, "It doesn't add up!"

Iris intervened. She snapped, "Last night everyone was sympathetic."

The thick-set policeman retorted quickly, "We've found Baxter's address in Peterlee but he's missing. Talked to most of the residents living in the flats and no one seems to have a bad word for Simon Baxter. They said he was very quiet, a model neighbour."

The beanpole constable focussed on the woman. "Little Johnny hasn't been up to his old tricks again? Few years ago his hand was forever on his trouser-zip, Mrs. Briggs. We don't want to be opening a can of worms because of some incensed husband."

Iris interjected angrily, "You don't believe us?"

John brought the tumultuous meeting to an abrupt end. He stormed to the door informing the constables he was going to make a formal complaint. He disappeared.

An hour later a relieved and buoyant Iris joined her husband at the police-station. Despite the sutures, bandages and the aches and pains the girl had used her time well. Alone for the first time that day she used all of her guile and cunning to cover past transgressions. It had not taken long to plot and plan and make the necessary phone-calls and now she had the strength to continue with the cover-up. Told John about Maxi Stubbs's dogged persistence in trying to woo her. Brash too, informing him about John's so-called friends who knocked on her door late at night, who telephoned or caught her on the street, and all offering comfort and companionship to the lone woman. Iris was confident the camouflage would work, especially if Maxi Stubbs remained quiet and Baxter escaped the police net. She needed time on her side; time for memories to fade and the rift to heal.

The chirpy couple, arm-in-arm, waltzed away from the police-station. Iris was filled with buoyant optimism and about to play her trump card.

She said, "Simon Baxter told you straight, John. Sure Maxi Stubbs made a play for me, in front of my mother when we shopped! We'll go there now, John. I'll wait outside while you confront her. I've got nothing to hide. And while you're checking I want you to call on Thelma Cruddace and Tammy Bryce, you hear. You ask them anything you want. I haven't seen the girls for months. Cards on the table, John, I've got nothing to hide.'

"It's okay, Iris," he replied. John was exhausted, "I didn't mean to act so stupid."

They walked into the police car-park and headed for the coal-wagon. A police cruiser eased from the main road and parked close to the strolling couple. Another minute and the couple would have missed the vehicle and avoided the passenger. The fickle hand of fate, however, intervened. Two officers stepped out of car and beckoned at the rear passenger. Maxi Stubbs struggled out of the car and into the path of Iris and John Briggs.

A few moments was all it took to change lives forever.

Maxi Stubbs had been dragged from his tenement and driven to the police-station. Maxi's fault. He was the worst for wear. It wasn't only the alcohol the previous night that made him sullen and irritable, it was the thrashing by Baxter that left him wallowing in self-pity. The police visit the following morning was the final straw. An ill-tempered Maxi refused to answer any questions so the police had little option but to escort him to the station. When he climbed out of the police-car and saw the battered features of Iris Briggs, Maxi Stubbs felt utter despair. He gawked at her and then at the stone-faced John Briggs. Bewildered, ignorant and very frightened he panicked. Imagining that Iris's husband had been told the truth by Sandy Baxter Maxi lost his nerve.

"Johnny," he pleaded, "Baxter made me tell him! I'm sorry!" His eyes rolled with fear. He had been attacked by the madman the night before and it now appeared John Briggs was after his blood. "I won't fight you, man! Iris and me…it's been over for years, honest to God!" Maxi Stubbs stared at the girl, "Tell him, Iris, tell him there's nothing to worry about! I don't want any more trouble!"

The policemen grabbed the jabbering prisoner and frog-marched him towards the main building. John and Iris stood and gaped as Maxi was dragged through the double doors of the police station.

Iris could not speak. Her head was tortured, she felt nauseous and weak. She heard the wagon-door open and close, listened to the roar as the engine was gunned. Iris started to cry.

John was grief-stricken. Emotions bounced and jarred in every direction. He was confused and hurt and needed to be alone. He tore out of the car-park like a madman, his mind racked with a terrible foreboding. Selfish and secretive about his own inadequacies John drove away knowing he had to put distance between himself and Iris.

One thing he knew. Their marriage was over.

**

CHAPTER TWENTY

After the break-up, John went cap in hand to his parent's home. He needed temporary lodgings and although his mother understood his plight his father did not. The truce lasted two weeks before Frank Briggs showed his true colours. John had hinted he would stay a week or two but never thought his dad was counting the days. He gave half his wages to his parents hoping it would sweeten the pill at having his youngest staying with them. He was wrong. Strolled down the path after an early finish and heard his parents arguing loud enough for the street to hear. The vitriol from his father's mouth made him stop in his tracks.

"I'm not having it, woman!" said Frank Briggs. "It's been two weeks, almost three! Once they've flown the nest, you don't expect them to come back. It's all wrong, Elsie, only you're so bloody close to him you can't see it. You're making it too easy for him, he'll never want to go back to Iris!'

John had not told them why he had left. He thought they might have guessed; imagined the entire colliery knew his business. He still couldn't quite grasp the fact that Iris had betrayed him or the way lies and deceit rolled off her tongue as if it were second nature. He'd not had a decent night's sleep since he'd packed his bags and walked the short distance to Moore Terrace. He looked the same, tried to act the same but inside he boiled with insatiable, horrid images. Every second of every hour the torture was regurgitated. He continued working and acting as if nothing troubled him but an incessant bombardment of misery rocked him. He was exhausted but unable to rest.

Heard his dad's deep tones, "He's got to go, Elsie!"

John returned to the wagon, unable to face his father. He drove away in shock, only returning when he knew his mother was alone. He gave her the news; he would pack his bags and be gone within days.

Elsie Briggs, peacemaker, tried to mend bridges.

"Why not see Iris?" said the woman. "Chances are you'll be able to talk now that tempers have eased." Elsie touched her son's arm lovingly. "It's not only Iris, John. You've got two lovely boys, you can't abandon them."

Her words cut him. John dropped his head as the tears suddenly flowed. He moved to his mother's side and held her tight, a child again, his desperate cries gouged from a broken heart.

Elsie Briggs wept with her son. Minutes passed and still they embraced. Heartbroken, he opened his soul to her. Slowly the tears subsided into sniffles and coughs and still the pair clung to one another.

Elsie gently eased her son from her bosom. It was time to face demons. She found the handkerchief and wiped away the tears.

"I'm all mixed up, Ma," said a distraught John.

Elsie nodded sympathetically, "I know, son."

His words were whispered, heartfelt, "I don't trust Iris."

The woman sighed and held his hands.

He took a deep breath, "Frank is not my son," John groaned.

"You don't know that to be true, son!"

"It's true, Mother, Maxi Stubbs said as much!"

"Honey, I know one thing for sure, men always exaggerate," answered Elsie. She took a deep breath, "Anyway, it was years ago, and she was so young."

"Ma!"

"Don't expect sympathy, son," said Elsie. She smiled as she offered the gentle rebuke, "Iris had your baby and as soon as she was sixteen she walked down the aisle!"

"Her mother wasn't keen to sign the marriage certificate!"

"Stop it, John! It was your fault! What you did with the baby-sitter was awful! Julie Brooks was thirteen when you made her pregnant!"

"I went to prison!"

"Poor Iris got some flack because of you!"

"She wasn't loyal, Ma!" he said venomously.

"Iris told me all the gossip," offered Elsie. She was desperate to alter his stubborn attitude and perhaps persuade him to return to his marital home. "There were queues of people telling her all about you. She knows more than you think!"

"Tell me?"

"Tammy Bryce for one!"

"Right!" He grimaced at the news. Knew Tammy was a blabbermouth but didn't realise how far the gossip had spread.

"Thelma Cruddance was another!"

"Iris knew about Thelma?"

"Sure." Elsie chortled, "Iris called her Olive Oyl."

John grimaced and waited for more.

"And when you worked at Suncrest Fire Surrounds…."

"She knows about Alice Drinkwater?"

"Yes," said Elsie. She was calm and non-judgemental. John's answer was to retaliate the only way he could.

"Iris went with Maxi Stubbs!"

"You're very like your Uncle Mick," she said matter of fact. "There's a law for you and a different law for everyone else!"

"Maxi Stubbs is black!" hissed John Briggs, acting like a paid-up member of the Ku Klux Klan.

"Been different had he been white, eh?" Elsie chuckled, "Sidney Poitier asked me for a date I'd have to give him the okay. Johnny Mathis sing me a song and I'd definitely have to think about it!"

"Stop it, Mother!"

"You stop it, son!" Elsie was resolute, "What's good for the goose!"

"What about Frank?"

"Your son, what about him?"

"He's coloured. Ma!" moaned the youth. "He can't be mine!"

"Don't talk so stupid!" she chided. "He has a healthy complexion."

"He's not my son!"

"You can't wait two years and then make a decision like that!"

"I've always had my doubts about Frank."

"He's your double, you idiot!"

"Mother!"

"Shut up and face your responsibilities! We all make mistakes in life! Make mistakes until the day we die and that's a fact! Truth is, Eddie and Frank are your kids and it's a bit late in the day to start disowning one of them. You want an excuse to leave Iris, pull something else out of the hat because I won't ever agree with you on that. I'll tell you something for free. There's a lot worse than Iris. Look what she's been through these past weeks."

"That's something else! Baxter escaping! I never believed Iris. He was tied hand and foot; it would have been impossible to get free!"

"He grabbed Iris, forced her to untie him! Hell, John, she had to go to hospital. There were bloody teeth marks on her arm! You'd think she'd been savaged by a dog!"

189

"Ma, he was tied and gagged when we left! Remember, Baxter was the one who spilt the beans on Iris. I'll tell you what I think happened …"

Elsie had heard enough. She stood and moved to the kitchen, "You're too like Micky Motson," she snapped, "and that's a fact!"

John lowered his head, knew he was wasting his time trying to convince his mother.

Elsie glanced at her son. Realised she had said enough. "I'll make tea, okay?" she said softly.

John nodded glumly. He asked half-heartedly about his uncle

"Mick will phone when he's ready." Elsie said. "I expect he's hospitalised."

"I thought it wasn't serious."

"That's Micky. Thinks he's Dr. Kildare." Elsie suddenly weakened, wanted to unburden her worries about her delinquent brother. Looked at her son and knew it wasn't the right time.

Elsie said, "See Iris, eh. Do it for me, son."

John shook his head.

"We'll talk later," she replied and busied herself at the sink.

Days later John Briggs had made up his mind. He was abandoning Durham and his family, and moving out of the area. He sat in his coal-wagon with co-worker Kenny Wilkinson and gave him the news. It was Saturday afternoon, their final shift was at an end and the pair squatted in the motor close to Hopper Terrace, Kenny's home. The younger lad seemed reluctant to leave the wagon even though the talking was over. Kenny's mood had fluctuated from depression to euphoric then back again. John offered the business for peanuts he had initially baulked at the prospects of self-employment and then, with a little persuasion from his young boss, had hesitantly agreed. Still he sat, pensive and apprehensive, unable to accept the inevitable, and once again tried to dissuade John Briggs.

"Fair enough, John, you're leaving Iris, but that doesn't mean the business has to be over?"

"It's not over, Kenny," Grit and determination came from the young entrepreneur. "I've told you, it's yours."

"Not fair," muttered a distressed Kenny. "I gave up a job to work for you."

"You'll still have a job. In fact you'll have your own business."

"I'm not eighteen!"

"You've got a driving licence, and that's all that matters."

"I'll need help!"

"Hire someone, it's easy enough."

Kenny threw in the towel, "When will you leave?" he asked.

"Tomorrow."

"Definite?"

John ignored the question, "I want £500 for the wagon. The coal-round is yours. It's for nothing Kenny."

The young driver gunned the engine and gave his worker the goodbye look. Kenny shrugged his shoulders, climbed out of the cab and walked away from the motor.

When John reached his parent's home his mother was busy on the phone. He mimed, '*Bath, okay,*' part-stripped and hurried up the stairs. He soaked for half an hour, shaved, dressed and hurried downstairs, ravenous for food, and found his mother still with the telephone jammed against her face.

"Any chance of food, Ma?" he asked.

"It's Micky," said Elsie, clamping her hand over the mouth-piece. "Give me a minute, love."

"Uncle Buff," said John, "is he's okay?"

Elsie nodded then continued with the telephone conversation. "Right, I'll give you a call! Give me the number and the name of the street.' Elsie wrote furiously then hung up.

Mother and son ate together. Elsie talked non-stop about her wayward brother.

"He's staying near London," she said. "Been poorly for a few days but he's okay now. Living in Southall." She glanced at the hand-written note, "Greenford Avenue, that's the address. Micky's okay, apart from being broke. Oh, almost forget, he's calling himself Milson, Michael Milson." Elsie Briggs saw the shock register on her son's face and knew it was time to explain a few home-truths about her criminal brother.

John listened agog, a surreal smile on his angelic face. He suddenly knew where his destiny lay.

Impulsive and reckless, said his mother when John told her. She tried but failed to dissuade her youngest son. Despite tantrums, arguments and tears Elsie could not change his mind. Even her directness could not alter his impetuous plans. Told John he was running away from his obligations, wanted him to bide his time and allow old wounds to mend but his mind was made up. The humiliation and pain of the broken marriage was the driving-force behind his decision. Few people knew of his plans: family members, his parents naturally, and his brother, Robert. On the day of his departure, Kenny's Wilkinson's father, a coal-hewer at Horden Colliery, had called at the Moore Terrace address with a bundle of cash for John's wagon. The lanky miner handed over the money, shook hands on the deal and left.

The worst part was the journey to the train station. John's father chauffeured him to Durham with hardly any conversation. Frank Briggs was an embarrassed mute until they reached their destination. There was a brief handshake and a hesitant, half-hearted blessing from the parent and then he was gone. John waited almost an hour for the train. When it arrived he hurried into the first carriage, slumped into the empty seat and promptly fell asleep.

Fortune smiled on John Briggs. Had the youth decided on the fourth carriage and not the first, he would have met his arch-rival, Simon Baxter. The fellow had been in hiding for weeks before making good his escape. He had boarded the train ten minutes earlier in Chester-le Street having arranged to meet his sister, Dottie, at York where he would be chauffeured to nearby Leeds. Dottie Baxter, ex-lover of bouncer, Alex Heslop and hard-man, Sonny Chin, was now living with one of the North's biggest criminals, William Garcia. She had come a long way since leaving her hovel of a home in West Durham. Never forgot her roots and never gave up on her baby brother.

Four carriages separated Baxter and Briggs. John would never be as lucky again.

**

CHAPTER TWENTY ONE

"Let's forget the uncle, eh," said the man. "Call me Buff."

John placed the suitcase on the single bed in the cramped downstairs room of the terraced house. He gazed around and counted; there were six beds in total.

"Hey, Johnny," said the older man, chortling. "Do I smell regret?" He folded his arms around his chest, his smile wide and infectious.

"I never expected…." Couldn't finish the sentence, he'd imagined they would have some privacy.

"The real world, kiddio," said Michael Motson. He flopped on to the nearest bed and ordered his nephew to follow suit. "Listen up, son; this is what you have to do …"

Motson was a wily old dog. Knew he was a wanted man and didn't want any harm falling on himself, his friends or his relations. He began to go through the ground rules for survival.

"First of all, kid, you don't know me, and you've never met my friend Lenny. Okay? Personal trouble made you leave Durham and seek your fortune elsewhere. Trial and error led you to the lodging house. As luck would have it there are two vacant beds - one upstairs and one downstairs - so when I answer the door to you you'll think it's Christmas. It's like finding gold dust getting bed and board around here. You get the drift? I'll introduce you to the landlady. Slip her a month's money in advance and you're in. When you drop your suitcase on the bed we start talking. You're looking for work … my firm needs a jobbing labourer / fork-lift driver. Bingo, your luck is in!"

Michael Motson led the youngster back to the front door, "Stay there, I'll find Norah." He disappeared leaving an anxious John Briggs, suitcase by his side, standing at the doorstep.

Norah Flannigan was the owner of the property. The woman suffered the same genetic blight as Phil Lynott; she was black and Irish but without a hope of auditioning for Thin Lizzie. The cross-eyes were icing on the devil's plate because the disfigurement gave the stout, middle-aged woman a fiendish appearance. John handed over a wad of cash and tried valiantly to focus on the landlady's one good eye. It was unnerving. The landlady, oblivious to the scrutiny, counted the cash as expertly as a bank-teller, the moon-faced proprietor unperturbed, her eyes darting from one lodger to the other, tallying and talking.

"You're charmed, son, it's rare we have vacancies. The rules … No eating or drinking in the rooms and definitely no women, okay?"

The landlady nodded curtly, turned and tramped up the stairs, her enormous rump moving from side to side as if manipulated by some mystical, mechanical ram.

"The door is locked at midnight!" she called out. "Wake me up once and you'll be on the pavement before you can break wind!"

John wandered into the side room and placed the suitcase on the allotted bed. Micky Motson stood, pulled on his jacket and informed his nephew they were visiting the local pub and meeting room-mate, Lenny Jobson. As they headed for the rendezvous Micky told him the gossip.

"When Lenny was released he found his missus shacked up with some shark. His old haunt in Hayes was out of bounds so he found lodgings in Southall."

"Where does Lenny stay?"

"Next bed to you," answered the man. "By the way, don't mention Lenny's missus, it's a bit of a sore point."

"Six of us in one room, Buff," he queried. "That's a lot of bodies!"

"Hey, you've hit the jackpot. This is London. Finding a decent kip is not easy!" He nudged John, "Don't fret about Norah, her bark is worse than her bite. As long as we behave we have a free hand. If you catch some nookie, sneak it in and keep it quiet. Norah turns a blind eye."

"Those eyes!"

"Don't forget the arse!" laughed Michael Motson.

The corner pub was minutes away. It was packed, and there wasn't a white face in sight. Michael Motson pushed his way to the crowded bar, ordered three pints and gazed around the room looking for his pal.

John said, "Everyone's coloured!"

"Southall, Johnny … A Caribbean curry with the odd white bean thrown in for taste. It's a melting-pot. You'll get used to it. Peel away the top layer and you'll find real people underneath."

Lenny Jobson materialised. He was average height, bald, gaunt-looking and without an ounce of fat. He gestured and shuffled towards them. Introductions were made as they found seats.

"So you're Buff's relation," said the man. His birthplace was indeterminate because of the lilting tones, his eyes a piercing blue that sparkled with fun, "You as daft as?"

John lifted his beer. "I thought I was," he said, "until Ma told me all about her mad brother."

"Hey, steady on." laughed Michael Motson, "or I might just send you back!" He quizzed his nephew, "What exactly did Elsie say about me?"

"Nothing much," said John. "Does Middlesbrough ring a bell?"

Micky Motson blanched and almost choked on his drink, "Elsie told you?"

"Told you what?" interjected Lenny. He looked at John, "He's a bit of a rascal. Come on tell me."

Micky chortled, said, "Another time, Lenny, eh?"

The trio talked for an hour and then left the pub. They wandered aimlessly along the main street of Southall. The older men talked and, for the most part, the youth listened and tried to assimilate his new surroundings. They passed a huge cinema whose billboards and hoarding advertised films in a foreign language; sauntered past a butcher's shop whose fluorescent panelling above the place was in some unknown dialect. Everywhere John looked appeared foreign; bus-drivers wearing turbans, taxi-drivers likewise. It was an eerie introduction to the streets of West London.

Lenny mentioned work in a factory in Hayes. The prison after-care service had worked with the Social Services and helped secure employment at a firm called Firestone Tyres.

"It's called Metro-Store," said an exuberant Lenny. "It's a subsidiary of Firestone. You'll like it, John." He saw the look of surprise register on the lad's face. "Buff didn't tell you? Still, it only happened today. Thought he might have told you at the train station. It's on a trading estate, few miles away in Hayes, next to the Airport. Decent money and all the overtime you want. Buff's been there a week, gets his National insurance Card and P45 in a few days … even got himself a new name! It cost me a packet but I owe your uncle."

Micky Motson grunted, "Hey, the Indian doctor fixed my cut for free and you said you'd pay for it!"

Lenny Jobson smiled wickedly, "Only because you offered to fix his little problem," he said.

Both men exchanged knowing glances.

"Tell me?" said John. He glanced at both men who seemed content to shrug shoulders in shared understanding. "What did you do for the Indian Doctor?"

"I had a quiet word with a troublesome patient," said Micky.

The men turned off the Uxbridge Road and trundled along on one of the many side streets, "Greenford Avenue, John," reminded his uncle. "This is our new address. Don't want you getting lost and Elsie getting on my case, okay?"

Some time later, John had washed and changed and sat relaxing on his designated bed. Lenny was on one side, his uncle on the other.

John said, "There's only one bath and there's no shower, there's six beds downstairs and the same number upstairs. How do we manage?"

Lenny answered stoically, "When in India, do as the natives do."

"Have a bath once a week," said Micky Motson. "Friday night is best, that way you're clean for the weekend."

"Wash-basin, Monday to Friday," offered Lenny. "Same with your clothes. Work all week and change at the weekend. The laundries charge a fortune. Once a week, John, bath and change, okay?"

Lenny Jobson saw the look of despair on the kid's face. "Hey," he said kindly, "you want a few tablets to help you sleep?"

**

CHAPTER TWENTY TWO

Harold Steinbeck, General Manager of Metro-Store, had the look of a meatier version of Eric Morecambe. The appearance of the comedian but nothing else. Steinbeck was a hardnosed, conniving businessman. He sat relaxed in the small office situated in the top storey of the huge warehouse. Minus coat and with shirt-sleeves at half-mast Harold Steinbeck smiled approvingly at the young, nervous stranger. The interview had lasted minutes.

"Mr. Briggs," he said politely, "it's been a pleasure." Easing forward he pressed a buzzer, "The manager, Mr. Pickett, will show you around the building. Your friend, Mr. Jobson, informs me that you've had experience driving fork-lift trucks, so most of your working-day will be based in and around the yard-area. The work is basic. Articulated lorries will be arriving throughout the day and your task will be to off-load the pallets of tyres and place them on the raised landing next to the two lifts. Labourers will then take the tyres in the elevators for storage on the top two floors of the building."

John asked, "Are all the other floors stacked with tyres?"

"No, Mr. Briggs. We are a tenant and rent the top floors only. The warehouse, together with the building at the entrance to the yard, is owned by the music conglomerate, E.M.I. The present set-up is essentially temporary and when we have secured more suitable premises we will be moving."

There was a timid knock at the office door and the work-manager entered the room. Harold Steinbeck acknowledged the man with the slightest of head movement. "Mr. Pickett," he said, "I'll leave Mr. Briggs in your capable hands." He smiled at the youth and said dismissively, "If you would like to follow the manager."

Oliver Pickett was below-average height, overweight, olive-tanned and with a permanent shine of perspiration over his jowely, anxious face. The under-manager speed-walked through the enormous warehouse with the young trainee trying to match his stride. As Pickett walked he washed his hands with invisible soap. He was in his fifties with thinning jet-black hair plastered over his pate. In a constant state of panic and flux he garbled and gesticulated at the long aisles of stacked pallets filled with innumerable tyres of all girths and sizes. John glanced, nodded and tried to assimilate the jumble of information. There was so much to remember and so many types and sizes of tyres. Some were so large a child could easily stand inside and stretch to their full height and still not touch the opposite rim. The young man from Durham was impressed.

They reached one of the empty elevators and the manager hurried inside. He pressed a dial and the pair were whisked to ground-level. Oliver Picket continued with his staccato explanations and the youth continued to nod appreciatively, only fearful that the fretful manager might ask him to verify or regurgitate his newly-acquired wisdom. Luck was on the youngster's side as he was neither asked nor given any chance to pontificate on his new role. The lift-door clanked to a halt then rattled noisily as it was opened. The older man gestured at the trainee who stepped out of the lift and on to a concrete ramp that looked down on to a large yard.

In the distance, two coloured workers, dressed in regulation blue overalls, stood next to the smaller figure of Michael Motson. The trio were lounging against a bright yellow fork-lift, talking and laughing with the driver, Lenny Jobson.

"You are acquainted with the folk-lift trucks, son?" asked the under-manager.

The youth nodded nervously, hoping he would not have to give a trial demonstration of his driving ability.

"Yes, Mr. Pickett," he answered hoarsely. "I drove them when I was employed at the colliery." He hurried down the concrete ramp putting distance between himself and the boss and joined the crew of Metro-Store.

The elevator-door closed noisily. Oliver Pickett disappeared and John sighed with relief.

Unknown to the managers, John, together with Micky and Lenny, had been at the firm since seven-o-clock that morning. As no one clocked-in until eight, Lenny had one hour to instruct the youngster in the basics of fork-lift driving. The brief introduction proved illuminating for the pair. It had been a stressful hour of training for both Lenny and his apprentice.

Michael Motson introduced the two strangers. The tallest, meanest looking of the pair, wearing a bright red and yellow woollen beret, skin like black pearl with patchy wiry face-fuzz, was Griffith Edwards, a thirty year old Jamaican who hesitantly shook the youth's hand.

"Okay, man," muttered Edwards. His tone was awkward. "Folks call me Griff."

His companion, Freddie Lakunda, spoke. "Me is from Jamaica too," he chortled. "Don't mind Griff, he don't smile till long after breakfast!" Short and slim with a permanent smile on his round young face Freddie shook the youth's hand like a hand-pump.

Lenny slapped a playful arm on John's shoulder, "Come on kid," he said earnestly. "Get on board and let's see how much you've remembered." He lifted his frame from the fork-lift seat and clung perilously to the steel safety-canopy with

201

one hand, gesturing to a nearby articulated wagon, "Slow drive over there, we'll unload those pallets."

"See you in a bit," laughed Micky Motson, nodding at the pair. "We've got some business with one of the drivers."

The trio, led by the balding pony-tailed self-appointed leader, hurried towards the ramp and the elevator.

Lenny saw the look of bewilderment on the lad's face, "A little scam, Johnny," he explained. "Pocket-money for the workers."

"Pocket-money?"

Lenny explained, "The floor below Steinbeck's office is full of the commercial stuff … car tyres to be precise. Griff and Freddie and Lamont King…"

The youth interrupted, "Lamont King?"

"Lamont runs the show. He's late today. Caught a dose of the pox off a working-girl." He laughed, adding, "She'll not be working for a long time, not after the slapping he gave her. Lamont has been here for years, should be in charge but they're racist bastards round here, son. Every time a supervisor leaves Lamont applies for the job and every time he's overruled. Last month, old Jamie Carruthers croaked on the job. Lamont had a strong word with Oliver Picket, the under-manager. Waste of time, Steinbeck says piss and Oliver wets his pants. They hired a bloody Scotsman, Frazier Tubbs! Frazier! Now what kind of name is that? Anyway, the Jock is useless … worse than useless. After that, Lamont decided to get even and started selling tyres for cash." Lenny shrugged his shoulders. "Life's a bitch, Johnny."

A tall, thick-set man of mixed race turned a distant corner of the complex. Head down, body swinging to some invisible beat, the fellow approached the pair.

"That him, Lenny?"

"Uglier than Leon Spinks, reckon?" chortled Lenny Jobson. Leaning forward he turned off the ignition. "Yeah, that's Lamont."

"Looks evil, Lenny."

"He is that," answered his companion. "Not many would cross Lamont?"

"Uncle Buff?"

A quizzical smile from Lenny Jobson, "Lamont's Division two material, but Micky Motson, sorry, Milson, he's Division One!"

"Buff looks so quiet," said John Briggs, "and he's small."

"All in the mind, son. Buff doesn't know when he's licked."

The stranger slowed next to them and growled a greeting at Lenny.

"What?" protested Lenny Jobson, big smile on his face.

"Bloody lies you tell, man!" spat the Jamaican. "Shove a wire down me dick! Man, ain't slept a wink all night thinkin' 'bout that wire!"

"What, no plunger down the old spout?"

Lamont King pulled out a small bottle of tablets. "Pills, man! Dose of penicillin is all me got to worry 'bout!"

"Progress, Lamont," said Lenny. "Honest, last time I paid a visit I was opened up with a wire down Mr. Dinkle. I screamed so much they had to gag me, swear to God!"

"When was that, man, or is you playin' tricks agin?"

"Fifteen years ago, Lamont. Merchant Navy, Hong Kong. God she was worth the pain." Lenny Jobson turned to the lad, "Trouble with those Chinese whores John, all their pussies are horizontal!"

Lamont grunted and moved off, "Better clock me in. See ya!"

203

The steel lift-doors opened noisily. Micky, Griffith and Freddie simultaneously stuck their heads into view. Not a word was spoken as the thieves quickly reconnoitred the yard area. Satisfied, they started pushing tyres, three and four at a time, on to the raised walkway, down the ramp and towards a nearby articulated truck. Lamont suddenly pirouetted and hurried to the stationary wagon, jumped into the empty trailer and began accepting the stolen tyres like some circus juggler. Minutes later the stolen property was covered with tarpaulin.

"Another ten," shouted Freddie, "quick as you like!"

The three men hurried to the elevator for their second sortie. The driver of the truck sauntered into view, munching on a steaming hot pie. Lamont King left the truck and strolled towards newcomer. The driver paused, wiped his mouth, then stuck his hand in his coat-pockets and pulled out a bundle of cash which was handed to Lamont. The money was counted then pocketed. The ringleader walked towards the empty lift.

Lamont King glanced at Lenny. "See you in a while, man," he said. "We split it fair.' He stepped into the elevator and was gone.

"Right, lad," said Lenny, resorting to his role as training instructor. Switching on the fork-lift truck, he said, "Let's see you slowly drive to the wagon, hoist the spades slowly and remove that full pallet, okay?"

John smiled, crunched the gears loudly, and hiccupped the truck towards the wagon. His head buzzed with excitement. He had been employed only a few hours and already had met the co-workers, learned to drive a truck, and had been involved with skulduggery and theft. It was his first taste of life in the big city. The previous night he'd tossed and turned thinking about Iris and the boys but today his thoughts were elsewhere. Preoccupied with his job, new faces, and the

204

shenanigans at Metro-Store, all thoughts of his family were temporarily shelved.

**

CHAPTER TWENTY THREE

Leeds town-centre was choc-a-bloc with people meandering through the busy streets. Couples, old and young, some linking arms, others holding hands, enjoyed the buzz and excitement of the city. The sun burned from a brilliant blue sky and a gentle warm breeze filtered through the streets and walkways. Too hot to venture inside the near-empty shops, it was a time to passively sit and take refreshment and view the delights of the cosmopolitan town.

At one end of the main shopping area, three people sat around the inadequate table next to the cafe, sandwiches in their hands, their refreshments filling the miniature table-top as the constant queue of folk wandered aimlessly by. The youth sat between the older pair, satisfied he had said enough and now listened to his eldest sister, Dorothy Baxter, discussing his case with Sonny Chin. Sonny was enormous in every sense: massive torso, thighs so thick they stretched his trousers to bursting, head big and fat with crease-marks caressing his brow making a frown a permanent fixture on his face. Thick locks ran like tributaries down past his wide shoulders, his hair was as black as pitch and liberally oiled. Seated, he spilled either side of his flimsy chair which shuddered as if waiting to collapse under his weight; when he stood, his six feet four frame put the fear of God in most people. Chin was employed by the biggest racketeer in Leeds, William Garcia.

Dottie said, "Bill Garcia wants it done, Simon."

Dottie Baxter was a tall, smouldering beauty whose dark locks spilled over delicate shoulders. Her piercing blue eyes had a magical quality; her skin was porcelain perfect and her voluptuous figure was guaranteed to turn heads. The woman had an aura of bewitching sensuality about her. Still under thirty, Dorothy Baxter had destroyed countless marriages when bedazzled suitors abandoned their wives in the vain hope of snaring the ultimate prize. Years earlier, working in the night-clubs in Middlesbrough, she had started a torrid affair with Ray Robinson, one of Garcia's lieutenants. The affair wasn't permanent, but lasted long enough to move her from a rented council semi to a small apartment overlooking Redcar's golden sands. For the occasional favour Dottie had her rent paid and was given an allowance. That was how she met Sonny Chin. Moving a consignment of drugs from Middlesbrough to Leeds, she was escorted by the huge Oriental and an immediate bonding took place and Dottie and Chin became lovers. When she eventually met the crime-lord himself, Dottie unceremoniously ditched Sonny Chin and moved into one of Garcia's plush apartments. Dottie became Garcia's plaything, did occasional errands for the criminal and even slept with the odd customer when Garcia asked.

Dorothy Baxter had dragged herself from life's sink and made good. Knew what she wanted, knew what she had to do to achieve her goal. One day soon she would marry William Garcia.

Weeks earlier pandemonium had erupted in the back streets of Middlesbrough when Ray Robinson lost his life. Rumours abounded that some rival team was trying to take over the Boro operations but were soon discounted when Garcia called in favours from crooked policemen. It wasn't the demise of Robinson that incensed the Leeds gangster nor the money that had been stolen, it was the information that the police discovered at Robinson's house. Ledgers and files were found in the loft and all of William Garcia's influence and bribes counted for nothing as addresses were raided and men arrested. Business was badly disrupted. The only good thing that came to light was the name of the hot-head who had killed Sugar-Ray. Garcia was livid when he discovered that the lunatic had once worked indirectly for him. Michael Motson was his name.

There was a huge reward for the head of Buff Motson.

Sonny Chin nodded solemnly and said in an effeminate, high-pitched voice, "I'll see Mr. Garcia, ask how he's going to use you." He glanced at the battered, swollen features of Simon Baxter, observed the shaven skull displaying the weals of scar tissue, saw the wide vacant eyes burrowing into him and could sense trouble. He asked, "You got a problem, kid?"

With a gun to his head, Simon Baxter could not change his manic nature no matter the size or the look of the adversary.

"Hey, fella," Baxter retorted with savage gusto, "I haven't a problem and I'm not your kid so stop the tough-guy routine, okay?"

Sonny Chin felt a tremble in his chest as he struggled to hold his temper. His squat face took on a crimson hue as rage welled inside his head. Placing the snack on the table he looked venomously at the female.

"That's the only chance he gets, Dottie," he growled, "and that's because he's your brother!"

"Don't talk to her," growled Sandy Baxter, jutting out a jaundiced jaw, "talk to me!"

Dorothy Baxter defused the situation. With an ominous grunt she slapped a bejewelled hand across her brother's bristled head and watched him flinch with the discomfort.

"Another wisecrack and you're on the next train back," snapped Dottie. "Do you understand?"

"He was staring at me, Dorothy!"

The female fumed. "Last chance!" she snapped, "I want an apology!"

The youth grimaced. He wavered for a brief moment before backing down. The North-East was the last place he wanted posting.

Dottie continued, "If you have to take smarties, wait till bed time, Simon. They're starting to fry your brain!"

Sonny Chin said to Baxter, "Mr. Garcia is anxious to find Motson. If he gives the nod, you'll have to show me where he lives!"

"Hey man, that's risky, y'know," muttered Simon Baxter. He added lamely, "All I know is the address of his relations!"

Chin said brusquely, "You can stay in the car and point your finger. I'll do the rest."

"There's more than a few people after my blood!".

"Simon," she said softly, "Mr. Garcia asks you to jump through a hoop you jump. You don't ever refuse!"

The youth became agitated and began to scratch at his scalp.

"Simon!" shouted the woman. "Don't do that!"

*

Iris Briggs knocked on the door in Moore Terrace, stepped inside and saw Elsie standing next to the sink. The two boys ran past their mother and flung themselves around the stout figure of their favourite grandma. Eddie and Frank pulled at her skirts and begged for loose-change, ice-cream, sweets … anything. The bulging purse was found, coins handed over and the pair vanished like a whirlwind to the nearest shop. Iris sat at the kitchen-table like she did most days, anxious for any crumbs of gossip about John. Her face was still swollen from the assault, her wrist was still bandaged but she didn't seem to care. All Iris talked about was her

209

missing husband. Days ago, when Elsie told her about her son's journey to London Iris had been heartbroken.

"Any news, Elsie?" asked the girl.

The older woman made tea and joined the girl at the table. "He phoned last night, love," said Elsie. "He's working with our Micky in a warehouse near Heathrow. Don't think he's too happy with the arrangement. Apparently there's half a dozen men in every room in the lodging-house … and one toilet and one bath! The owner charges £100 a week, and there's not a bite to eat!"

"Do you think he's having second thoughts, Elsie." Iris bit her lip in anticipation, "Think he might come home?"

"He's so stubborn, love. Typical man. There's one rule for them and one for us!" She paused and found the cigarettes and lighter and sucked in a lungful of smoke. "It's a pride thing, Iris. I tried to tell John, probably told him too much. Told him you knew about his little flings." The woman smoked for seconds, contemplating. "Might have stayed a while longer but his Dad wasn't happy with him here." Elsie shook her head morosely. "His own bloody son!"

"Did he ask about me?" Iris said a silent prayer. Never realised the pain of losing could hurt her so much. "Tell me, Elsie!"

"Asked if you were okay," she replied. "Even asked about the boys." She looked at the girl and saw the shock registering.

"He asked about Eddie and Frank?" Iris could scarcely believe it. "John asked about Frank, honest Elsie? Don't lie to me, please!"

"Asked if Eddie was still kicking the football, asked if Frank's asthma was any better." Elsie sighed. "Men, neither rhyme nor reason to them!"

Iris could not stop the tears. She dropped her head and began to weep.

The older woman's eyes filled. She wiped away the wetness, "Married for years, pet," she said, "and I never once cried like you." She sucked long and deep on the cigarette before continuing. "Frank was always selfish. Push come to shove, he's not like his son. John's been a rascal but there's no one quite like him. Heart of gold he has and I know he loves you Iris. It's just different for some men."

Iris began to shake. With her head downcast and eyes blinded by the flood of tears, she began to wail softly.

"John will come back, love," sympathised Elsie. "He's paranoid at the moment, thinks everyone in the place is talking about him."

"Don't know what to do!" cried Iris. "Can't live without him, Elsie, I really can't!"

*

Metro-Store used a small back room on the top floor as a make-shift canteen. The place consisted of a few tables and chairs, a smattering of cups and plates and a *Baby-Belling* cooker stuck on a bench next to the lavatory. There were no real cooking facilities so Old Jim, an arthritic consumptive, was employed as the tea-boy for the staff. Orders were taken early and the old man shuffled out of the huge site, trundled along the road, past workshops and smaller factories and stood in the queue at the take-away van. Jim Vasey, a taller version of old Steptoe, with the same permanent whiskered scowl, made the journey twice every day; first for the ten-o-clock break and then for the lunch-break. The choice on the menu was limited to miscellaneous burgers, pies and hot-dogs. Few of the permanent staff used Jim for the purchase of food, mainly because of the pensioner's continuous, phlegmatic cough. '*I'll pay for pies,*' said Lamont to an attentive John Briggs. '*But man, gimme salt and sauce not spittle, it ain't no delicacy!*' Jim's others tasks consisted of throwing Domestos around the toilet-bowl whenever the inclination took him, and occasionally brushing the accumulated garbage out of the canteen.

John liked the old man. In between the retching and coughing he took the youth aside and told him the gossip about the place. '*Steinbeck used to be a big man at Firestone some years ago, John, but he was doctoring the books and flogging the odd consignment. Didn't catch him with his hands in the till, but almost. Him and Oliver Pickett like two peas in a pod. They were demoted and moved here, the pair of them, both serving out their time until retirement. Steinbeck is a cool character, shifted the blame to some of the night-shift. Management had no alternative but to sack half a dozen decent men.*' Jim Vasey told John about the new works-manager, the Scotsman, Frazier Tubbs. '*He's a boss's man, son, up their arses as far as he can go! Don't trust him or confide in him. And the Caribbean Crew, they're all thieves and vagabonds, especially Reggie Lamont. He's out of his head on smack most days, doped up like Bob Marley. Had my way, I'd ship 'em all back!*'

John was out of favour with his uncle because he wouldn't take a penny from the sale of the stolen tyres. '*You don't have to take it as such, Johnny,*' said Michael Motson. '*Accept it and hand it over to Lenny and me.*' John 's honesty suited Lamont, he didn't want the youth involved because the split was becoming too wide and the profits were diminishing. He laughed at the white boys, '*Kid got principles, man. Be a betta world wi more like he. Chances are he'll sleep comfortable in his bed nights not takin' booty.*'

Frazier Tubbs appeared in the afternoon of the second day. His wife worked as a district nurse and couldn't take time off work. Frazier could and did, and with three young daughters he had persuaded Steinbeck to grant him the occasional leave of absence. He didn't look the stereotype Scotsman with his thick mane of luxuriant hair, ear-rings and medallions and casual style of dress. He was small and petite and Hackney born and bred, unlike his Paisley-reared parents. The greeting was casual and cautious.

"No one told me," he said when Lenny introduced the newcomer to the foreman. He glanced uncomfortably in the direction of Motson who struggled to push an enormous tyre up the steep concrete ramp towards the waiting escalator. "Same with that bloke! People are being hired and fired without consulting me!"

Lenny Jobson smiled icily, "Take it easy Frazier! Meet John Briggs, our new fork-lift operative."

The pretend Scots was livid, "I should have been at the interviews, it's all-day wrong!"

Michael Motson shouted over, "Hey, Hamish, stop the foolish talk! How can you be at the interview when you're never at work!"

"That's enough from you, Milson," said the diminutive ganger, his voice edgy with anxiety. He'd heard enough about the bully-boy to hold on to his emotions. Turning away from the agitator he asked John, "You can drive competently?"

"Frazier," interrupted Lenny Jobson, "the lad is better than me for God's sake!"

Tubbs relented. He had little alternative. Closing on the newcomer he hissed ominously, "Suppose we can try you on one week's probation, see if you're any good!" He shook his head and said, "Got my eye on you, Laddie!"

213

"Come again," growled Michael Motson, suddenly next to the Scot, his features twisted with anger. "You tartan pixie," he grunted and pulled the charge-hand close to him. "Just because he's a bairn don't ever think you can throw your weight around! Hear me, Hamish?"

"My name is Frazier!" spluttered the man. "Please let go of me!"

The second elevator banged its presence. Motson released his grip on Tubbs as three bodies spilled on to the ramp.

Hurrying from the melee, Frazier Tubbs barked commands at the Jamaicans, "Get back inside, there's work to be done on the third floor! You!" he bawled at Freddie Lakunda who drove the internal fork-lift truck. "There's a whole pallet of radials smashed in aisle ten!"

Freddie Lakunda creased his features in feigned hurt as he glanced at Tubbs, "You know 'bout smashed pallet, boss?"

"It's my job to know everything!" bawled the naive foreman. "Now let's get it tidied before Steinbeck makes his rounds!"

The lift-doors closed on the feuding workers.

A worried Lenny called top Lamont King, "Tubbs has seen the pallet already. What if he checks the day's invoices?"

King appeared unconcerned, "There's no problem. Overturned pallet don't mean jack-shit. Can't tell there be missin' stock. Hell, those tyres coulda been sold months ago. Fool Freddie could have caught the aisle with his dodgem-truck. Quit with the worryin' man, leads to ulcers."

"He's got a point, Len," said Micky Motson. "Leave well alone, eh?"

A relieved Lenny Jobson turned to the silent, observant youth, "John," he said, a hint of a smile creased his gaunt features, "the boys are havin' a party tonight, you want in?"

"Boys?"

214

"Boys from the beautiful Caribbean," said an enthusiastic Micky Motson. "Lamont always puts on a good spread, food, drink … chill!"

Lenny smiled wickedly, "You ever tasted black, Johnny?" He guffawed, "It's the best taste in the world."

"Don't follow, Lenny?" said the youth.

"Women!" said the man, chortling. "What else?"

John's mood suddenly plummeted. He imagined Iris with Maxi Stubbs. Mixed-raced Maxi! Bile racked his brain as he heard Lenny's words. *Black is best, best taste in the world!* Wondered if that had been the attraction for his wife.

"You okay, John," asked his uncle. "If Frazier Tubbs has upset you I'll sort it?"

"No," he said, "nothing's wrong."

"So what's the plan, kid," asked Micky Motson. "Fancy a night out?"

"I'll think about it."

John did not go to the celebrations. He chose instead to wander the streets of the neighbourhood. By eight-o-clock, exhausted, he made his way back to the lodging-house. The sortie had filled him with a glum realisation that his mother had been correct about his impulsive behaviour. He had abandoned family, work and friends and now he was regretting it. The more he wandered the more depressed he became. He had foolishly imagined that the streets of London would be paved with gold, that it was a vibrant, vivacious place, filled with thrills, spills and good cheer, where everything was possible, a place where he could start afresh and make a new life for himself. The naive teenager was beginning to see the reality, the rawness of bed-sit land, the scramble for employment and long hours simply to survive. Loneliness enveloped him; the feeling of isolation was tangible. He felt isolated and adrift in a strange place and without a real friend in the world.

A little after eight he weakened and phoned Iris. He couldn't stop himself. All he wanted was to hear her familiar voice again. Missed Iris so much it hurt. Stubborn to the end, filled with foolish pride, the youth made blurted out excuses when she spoke.

"Iris?"

"John," gushed Iris, almost fainting with gratitude, "you've phoned!"

"Iris!" said the lad, over-the-top with feigned exasperation. "What are you doing at Ma's house?" He held his breath, prayed that the ploy worked and that Iris would talk to him.

"You've phoned home!" said an excitable Iris. "Don't hang up, John, the boys want to talk to you! How are you? Are you eating? Your mother said you're sharing your room with a load of men, John, are you still there?"

He drank her voice like nectar. The familiarity, the lilting tones, the knowledge that someone was still interested made him shake with stupefying emotion. Waves of pleasure washed over him and still he fought the impulse to show his true feelings. "Iris, how are you?" he said, struggling to regain control, captivated by the sound of her sweet voice. "Is Ma there?"

Iris was in seventh heaven, thrilled that he'd called, reading him like a book. Never hurt him again, no matter what the outcome. She started sobbing uncontrollably. "Pleased you've called," she sobbed, "even if you wanted your mother." Played to his whims, anything to keep him talking, "Will you talk to the boys, John. They really miss their dad! Please John!"

He stood in the phone-box, his eyes closed as he milked her presence. Couldn't help himself, "How are you, Iris?" he said, tears running down his face, hands clamping over the receiver until he regained control of his spiralling emotions. "Another week and I'll be able to send you some money."

"Don't want money, John, we want you back!" She was begging now, unable to stop, didn't care how she sounded. Wanted her husband back no matter, the humiliation not important. She would have sold her soul to start again. "I'm sorry, John," she sobbed. "Give me another chance, please!" The pain so bad she began to cry like a child. The line went dead and she became hysterical with grief.

The phone-call was cut short because John couldn't control his tears. He didn't want Iris to hear his grief.

Hundreds of miles apart and the pair cried for one another.

**

CHAPTER TWENTY FOUR

The living-room of the palatial mansion on the outskirts of Leeds dripped of class and money. Luxurious carpets, ornate, expensive furnishings; the sweet smell of power and success was everywhere. William Garcia sat quietly, small cigar in one hand, a glass of red wine in the other and watched the youth intently. Opposite, relaxed on the enormous sofa, sat Dottie Baxter and Sonny Chin, the gruesome figure of the oriental filling two-thirds of the seating-space.

Garcia waited and listened patiently to the tale of woe from the youngster, no expression on his sturdy face; he was alert, intuitive, and his feelings were masked. William Garcia had the look of Huntz Hall, of *The Bowery-Boys* fame ... a menacing, intimidating incarnation of the cinema star. He stood a shade under six feet, thick-set, fifty, with thick salt and pepper hair. When Simon Baxter had finished, Garcia studied him. He didn't like what he saw; the blazing eyes, the arrogance, and the suppressed anger that radiated from Dorothy's brother.

Moments past and still the gangster pondered. The silence was frustrating for the boy as he glanced earnestly from the crime-lord to his sister then back again. Baxter grimaced, irritated at being on show. He tried to appear relaxed but his body squirmed and moved against his will. As a last resort, the youth wrapped his arms around his chest and stared at the floor.

"Sonny," said William Garcia, finally breaking the silence, "an orange-juice for the boy."

Sonny Chin moved effortlessly from the settee and slipped from the room. Garcia sipped at his drink, his eyes moved from the fidgeting youth to the female. Couldn't believe they were brother and sister; Dottie was so regal and serene, aloof and yet filled with poise and charm and an inner resolve. The youth was a manic jack-in-the-box, ready to pounce and purge on a whim, a volatile and dangerous young man. Despite initial reservations Garcia decided to employ Baxter once Motson had been found. The organisation always needed cannon-fodder and mules and Dottie could be so persuasive when she set her mind to something.

Sonny entered the room carrying the refreshment which he handed to the boy. Garcia gestured to the sofa and watched as the youth sat next to his sister, an embarrassed grin cracking over his bruised features.

"If I send Sonny to the North-East," said Garcia passively, his gaze on the youth, "you are quite sure the house could be located easily?"

"Yes, Mr. Garcia."

"And Sonny could glean all of the information from those residing there?"

"Positive." answered Sandy Baxter. "The man you want is related, an uncle." His shaven head nodded impatiently, pleased that things were about to happen, retribution now a certainty. *Kill two birds with one stone,* he mused. *Odd-job could deal with Motson and I could have a piece of Johnny Briggs' hide. Perfect, another chance to put things right!*

"Okay," said William Garcia, "might as well get started, Sonny."

"I go now?" queried the giant, rising like a ghost.

"Yes, the boy too." said Garcia. "Take the Peugeot. If there are complications it can be ditched."

"You want Motson brought to you, Mr. Garcia?"

"No, I think I'll let you deal with the problem," said Garcia. He turned to the youth who jumped to his feet in anticipation, "Have you quite finished with your drink,

219

Simon?" and watched as the boy greedily gulped at the remainder of the orange-juice. "Good, good. Now, I'd like you to wait outside for a moment, I need to talk to Sonny."

Dorothy stood and led her brother through the huge conservatory and in to the garden area.

"Play it anyway you want, Sonny," said Garcia. "I don't mind if you use the boy to do the dirty work. Things go pear-shaped then he'll not be missed." He sighed, added, "Questions?"

"Should be safe enough, Mr. Garcia. Time we get there it'll be dark so there's little chance of me being recognised."

William Garcia smiled. "Sonny, night or day, you'll always stand out in a crowd."

Chin smiled. "I'll be thorough if information is withheld," he said coldly. "I'll frighten people enough to guarantee there'll be no witnesses. And I don't have a single conviction. I'm not on any police computer for any kind of crime …"

"Of course, Sonny," answered William Garcia, interrupting. "I will leave it in your capable hands."

*

"I've made up my mind, Elsie," she answered quietly. Her tone was resolute.

Elsie Briggs smiled. She was warming to Iris, admired her gumption, "If you're sure?" she said.

"When John phoned last night I could sense something was wrong."

Elsie recalled the panic in Iris's voice the previous evening. It was ten o'clock at night and Elsie was in dressing-down and curlers quietly clipping at her toe-nails waiting for her drunk of a husband to return home when Iris burst through the door. The young girl was filled with woe about her absentee husband.

"I haven't slept all night, Elsie," said the girl. "Something about his voice seemed uncertain. John sounded upset and then the phone went dead."

"You'll need this," said the older woman, handing over the piece of crumpled paper. "Name and address of his lodging-house. Landlady is called Flannigan, Greenford Avenue, Southall, West London. Think it's near to Heathrow."

"I'll find the airport," said a determined Iris, "then I'll ask directions."

"You're sure about this, Iris?" quizzed the woman. "You thought this through?"

"Nothing to think about!"

"Suppose you travel all that way and John doesn't want to see you? Have you thought about that, all that way for nothing?" She touched the girls arm tenderly, "John is so stubborn. Maybe if you wait awhile he'll come back of his own accord?"

"I can tell, Elsie," said Iris. "He misses me." She looked away, her voice faltering as heartache raked her body, "Longer he's in London the more chance he'll meet up with someone."

"That's a fact," agreed Elsie. "When were you going?"

"Eddie will be out of school soon. I'll pick up Frank from my mother's house … then we'll be off."

"We!" said an incredulous Elsie.

"If I take the boys…" Iris wasn't allowed to finish.

"Not for a moment, girl," interrupted a resolute Elsie Briggs. She shook her head resolutely, "No!"

"I've made my mind up!"

"Not with the boys, Iris," said the mother-in-law. "And certainly not with that car of yours! God, it's held together with rust and glue!"

"John had the Mini serviced a month ago," replied Iris. "It sailed through the M.O.T. first time!"

"Get real, Iris," grunted Elsie sarcastically. "Sailed my arse!"

"I'll show you the certificate if you don't believe me!"

"Girl," said Elsie stoically, "you got brains or sawdust in there," prodding a finger at her skull. "Or do you think John drove all the way to Seaham for the fun of it. There's two good garages in Shotton both offering M.O.T. and my boy drives to Seaham Harbour to have the Test? He's going to leave the car in a strange place because he fancies a stroll along the harbour wall?"

Iris looked crestfallen. "I didn't know the certificate was bent. It drives so well for a twelve year old car. You think it could break down?"

"Take the train, pet," said Elsie, "and bring the boys here tonight."

"Shouldn't you ask John's Dad first? You know what he's like!"

"When it comes to my family, pet," said Elsie Briggs, "Frank hasn't a look-in. Drop the kids off if you decide to go." She paused then added. "Why don't you phone John and tell him?"

"I don't have his number," replied Iris, "He phoned from a call-box."

"So it'll be a surprise?"

"Something like that," said Iris.

"Like David Frost," chortled Elsie. "Hello, good evening and welcome!" She grabbed the girl and cuddled her tight.

The vehicle stopped close to the terraced house. Car lights were extinguished, the engine died and both occupants reconnoitred.

"That's the house, friend," whispered Sandy Baxter, gesturing at the terraced property. "They must go to bed early around here."

"Call me Sonny," growled the enforcer, "or Mr. Chin!"

"Sonny, eh?" said the youth. He found his accomplice annoying, arrogant and condescending. Wanted to say so much but knew better. He held his tongue, there would be other times.

"Sonny will do fine."

"That's not Chinese, so what's with the real name?"

"Mind your business!" grunted the oriental.

Sonny Chin was English. Born in Brighton of mixed parentage, he was named after his worthless father, Stephen Chiningham, a waiter in the Merchant Navy. Stephen senior skipped ship en-route to Canada and never returned to his wife and five year old son.

"Don't be so touchy, man …"

Chin ignored the questioning. Shifting his bulk, he stared at the row of terraced houses. It was a little after ten and most house-lights were either dimmed or extinguished.

Filling his chest, Chin glowered at the youth. "The house is in the dark, the folks must be in bed." he said. "Knock loud enough to wake those inside." He handed Baxter an adjustable spanner, "Use this on them. Don't worry, I'll be behind you!"

"Stay in the car, man." said Baxter. He toyed with the weapon, "One clout with this and they'll be unconscious!"

"Do it!"

"Hey," grunted Simon Baxter, "take it easy!"

Baxter eased out of the Peugeot, pulled a felt cap from his jacket-pocket and donned it. He started walking towards the house then stopped suddenly and returned to the car. Sonny Chin wound down the window.

"What now?"

"Sayonara," whispered Baxter. His body stooped, palms clasped together as if following some kind of ritual, "Goodbye," he whispered, grinning from ear to ear. The youth hurried away.

"Certifiable!" gasped the seated figure.

As Chin wound up the window Simon Baxter was banging at the house door. After some moments a neighbour's head appeared from an upstairs window. The youth was prepared, knew exactly what to say.

"Evening!" shouted Baxter.

"What the hell do you want at this time of night," shouted the woman. "Iris is out!"

"She told me to call!"

"She's nothing but a minx!" The crone started closing the window.

"Any idea where I might find her?" pleaded Baxter. He glanced across the road at his accomplice. Took a deep breath and tried again. "It's important I see her. John Briggs sent me with a message!"

"That little nuisance! He's another one! Up and leaving his kids like that, it was disgraceful!"

"That's why I'm here! I need to see Iris!"

"One second!" she retorted and disappeared inside to ask her husband directions. Knew Elsie Briggs lived in Moore Terrace but didn't know the street number.

Minutes later a buoyant Simon Baxter was striding towards the stationary car. In a world of his own he jabbered nonsense verse, *'Odd-job, I bring you great and bountiful news! Make you rejoice next to the Tree of Wisdom and Knowledge.'* He couldn't stop chortling at the humour.

"What the hell are you whispering?" asked Sonny Chin as the youth climbed into the Peugeot.

"Never said a word!" replied Baxter. He frowned, *I was thinking, not talking, Charlie Chan!* he mused and gestured ahead. "Follow the road to the bend, there's a Nursing-Home on the corner, take a left on Moore Terrace." He grinned wickedly, "Briggs' parents' house is halfway along the street." He was excited, ecstatic at the prospects of the coming trouble. Glancing at his companion he said, "Sonny, what's Japanese for *Hello*?"

Chin groaned, "Why the hell would you want to know?"

Baxter smiled at his grimacing companion, "Got to be authentic, Sonny. I want to sound Japanese."

"You sound like Bobby Thompson!" spat Sonny Chin. Remembered sitting bemused watching videos with Dottie Baxter, the north-east comedian pronunciations beyond Chin's comprehension. "Or like the skinny one from the Likely Lads!"

Simon Baxter was on a high, the rebuke ignored. He pondered for a moment; a wide grin covered his face when he uttered, "You and me could be trainee Triads?"

"Triads?"

Simon started laughing hysterically, "We could be The Seven Samurai … if five were lost!"

A despairing Sonny Chin shook his head.

CHAPTER TWENTY FIVE

A little before ten, Iris finally left Shotton for the long journey to London. She had meant to depart hours earlier but both boys had responded badly to the news of their mother leaving them, albeit for one night. It was Iris's fault, she had told them the stark truth instead of fairy-tales and so bedlam ensured for hours as the children pleaded that they be allowed to accompany their mother. Too late, Iris realised her mistake. Elsie tried to rectify the deteriorating situation by offering carrots and assorted sweeteners. It didn't work. Then Elsie dug more holes by telling little white lies, told the boys that their mother really wanted an evening out with the girls and that the London excursion was a ploy to calm them. The charm offensive was wasted on the children; it was a passport to pandemonium. The turmoil was excuse enough for Frank Briggs to make a hasty retreat from his home and have an early night at the pub. By nine-o-clock Iris was forced to change tactics. She used her womanly guile to quell the discontent. Fed and fussed and feigned defeat and then informed the boys that they would all leave for the Capital the following morning. It took an age to convince Eddie, older and more worldly wise than his younger brother, that she was indeed postponing her journey. She then gave her solemn word that the family would leave for London bright and early. Both boys were exhausted when they finally climbed into the spare bed in their grandmother's home, never questioning the fact that they were not returning to their home in Victoria Street. Well past their bedtimes, the children were fast asleep in minutes leaving Iris to bid a quick, tearful farewell to Elsie Briggs.

"Give him my love, Iris," she sobbed. "Tell him to come home."

"I'll phone you when I reach London."

"Drive carefully," begged the older woman. "There's plenty of Motorway cafés, make sure you have lots of breaks. Driving at night is awful, okay, pet?"

"Promise, Elsie," she answered, kissed her again and left.

She drove along Moore Terrace and almost scrapped into the big *Peugeot* that meandered dangerously along the back-street. The Peugeot's windows were open as driver and passenger tried to read street numbers using a torch. Predator and prey passed one another, so close, so far apart.

"We should have waved down that Mini," said Baxter. "Could have asked directions instead of farting about with a torch!"

"That would be foolish," grunted Sonny Chin. He sprayed the probing beam against a nearby door, "Showing your ugly face to a possible witness is all we need!"

"You look in the mirror lately, pal?"

The car came to a halt in the middle of the street. Sonny Chin started to heave his large frame out of the car, his temper at breaking-point with his manic accomplice. Realising he had overstepped the threshold of endurance, Baxter decided it would be prudent to eat humble-pie.

"A joke, Sonny!" whined the youth. "Nothing meant, I'm sorry!"

Get back in the car, Bluto, he mused. *You slept with my sister! Do I mind, do I say anything?*

Sonny Chin seemed to waver for an eternity. He fumed and fought against his natural instincts, stood half in, half out the car for an age wanting to crush the wind out of the irritating, repulsive specimen. William Garcia's face appeared, telling him, warning him against failure. The assignment had to be completed, there was no question about that and Chin knew well the frightening consequences of displeasing his boss. He closed his eyes, sucked greedily at the night air and climbed back into the car.

"There's the house!" hissed the giant, suppressing his temper. "Get started, I'll follow you. Don't use too much force, we want them to talk."

I look a complete fool, thought Baxter, easing out of the cab. *How can unconscious people have a conversation?*

Sonny repeated the warning, "Did you hear what I said?"

"Okay! Give me a minute!"

Baxter walked quickly along the path to the rear door of the house, a fixed, pained smile across his wild features. The door opened at the first knock. Elsie Briggs was in the kitchen preparing supper for her husband.

"Hello, love," said Elsie, "can I help you?"

Sandy Baxter forgot the script as he stared at the rotund, solid woman whose eyes sparkled like someone he knew from the past. The image of Micky Motson suddenly blossomed inside his head; the silly man with the receding hair, the obnoxious pony-tail... and the beautiful eyes! Mentally alert he matched the pair; the woman had to be the sister of the wild clown who shouted when he fought!

"Buff Motson!" he blurted out accidentally.

Elsie became uneasy, "Are you looking for Micky?"

"Yes, love, Buff sent me to see you…"

Reality hit Elsie Briggs. Realising something was wrong she tried to shut the door. Suddenly a massive shadow shot past a faltering Simon Baxter and smashed into the door. The woman was knocked to the floor. Wood broke into splinters as Sonny Chin stepped into the small kitchen and stood like a giant obelisk glowering at the prostrate, frightened female.

"Lock the door!" he muttered to his diminutive accomplice.

Sandy Baxter pushed the door shut.

"I need the address of Michael Motson," said Sonny Chin calmly.

Elsie Briggs moaned with pain. She imagined the intruders were somehow linked with the Middlesbrough criminal, Raymond Robinson. Knew it was an act of vengeance and that they were after her brother. Elsie shook her head and refused to speak.

Sonny Chin struck with the speed of a rattlesnake. His boot clipped at the stubborn features of the spread-eagled woman knocking her front teeth into bloody splinters. Elsie collapsed in a dead faint. Chin ordered Baxter to search the house for evidence of Motson's whereabouts. The youth disappeared into another room searching for clues. The damaged back-door eased open and a cooling breeze filtered through the rooms. Chin slammed the door shut, grabbed the chair and made a temporary wedge against the splintered door-handle, moved to the sink and filled a cup with cold tap-water and poured it over the unconscious figure.

Elsie struggled to a seated position, her hand inspecting the damage to her mouth, wincing as the images tormented her. She muttered weakly, "I've never seen my brother in years!"

"You've lost your teeth, girl," spat Sonny Chin. He bent his muscled torso close to the ruined face, "Do you want more?"

Chin didn't allow the woman time to answer. An enormous fist smashed the bridge of her nose. The noise of broken cartilage was horrendous. Blood and snot burst over Elsie's startled face as she fell back heavily against the linoleum. She was knocked out cold for the second time in minutes.

The back-door squeaked noisily as Frank Briggs, inebriated and full of good cheer, pushed at the jammed door, dislodging the chair which tumbled to the side of his unconscious wife. Hardly had time to protest before he was grabbed and hoisted bodily into the room. All it took was a mighty slap across the waxen jowls to turn the fellow into a whimpering informer. With feet kicking madly to find the floor Frank begged for mercy. He was slapped again and immediately ceased his pleading. The numbness of the alcohol disappeared and he became a craven coward.

"Michael Motson!" hissed the brute, pulling the hysterical wheezing figure close to his cold leering face until his breath permeated the victim's open mouth.

"Yes!" wailed Frank Briggs. "Just tell me what you want!'

He was lowered to the floor, the grip released and for the first time he saw the crumpled, insentient body of Elsie. His legs buckled and he slumped to the floor. He began to weep uncontrollably.

Sandy Baxter returned. "Nothing at all," he said, gazing at the couple filling floor-space. "There's two brats asleep upstairs. Oh, I forgot, I found this, Sonny." He handed Chin a photograph of Elsie standing with her brother, Michael.

Sonny Chin gasped in astonishment. His dizzy accomplice had mentioned his name and blown his cover! His temper broken, Chin rammed an elbow into the startled face of his partner. The youth collapsed in a heap. He turned his attention to Frank Briggs and ordered him to stand. The cowardly ex-collier struggled to his feet, his face downcast, unable to look at the maniac.

"Michael Motson," grunted Sonny Chin. "I want his address!"

"He doesn't live here, he's moved to London."

"Where in London?"

"I don't know," stammered a frantic Frank Briggs. "My wife has an address."

"You want to live," said Sonny Chin, "you'd better wake her up."

Frank groaned out loud, he knew his wife too well.

The mayhem downstairs began to disturb the children. Young Frank groaned and began to turn and twist as the nightmare shook him. The racket woke Eddie who sat upright, rubbed the sleep from his eyes and began to complain and snipe about his horrible parents. Then the reality hit him for six, he was not at home, he was staying at his Nana's house. Eddie clamped his hands over his mouth to stop himself from crying out. Moments past and still the sounds of argument continued. An inner resolve gave him the strength to steal out of bed and creep to the landing where he stood listening as the noise wafted from the rooms below. Eddie's eyes widened with fear and his mouth opened with shock. There were strangers in the house and they were threatening his grandparents. Inch by inch the terrified boy retreated, reached the bed and slipped under the mound of blankets. He wrapped his arms around his young brother and finally broke down. Eddie Briggs began to call out for his mother.

*

The five hour journey turned into a Herculean struggle between willpower and growing fatigue. Iris lasted hours as the excitement of seeing John spurred her on. Half-way into the expedition she was fighting to stay awake, drifting and

231

coasting between lanes and jarred into consciousness as other drivers blared and honked at her erratic behaviour. An articulated wagon, with fog-horn screaming like a coming blitzkrieg, forced its way past the meandering Mini and jerked Iris awake. The heart-stopping shock of seeing the huge truck careering past proved too much. Iris realised she had to rest. She pulled off the motorway, ate and drank in a futile attempt to revive her flagging body, returned to the deserted car-park and immediately fell into a dead sleep.

Iris awoke in the early hours of the grey cold morning and continued the journey. After umpteen errors and a multitude of willing helpers pointing the way she finally reached her destination at seven-thirty and then sat outside the terraced house for an age trying to find the courage to confront her husband.

A hiccupping line of male traffic left the front door of the house on Greenford Avenue. Some in pairs, gossiping loudly despite the early hour, sometimes a lone individual in work-clothes and battered travelling-bag, meandered forth. Old and young left the semi-detached, the door like some giant magician's top-hat as it regurgitated a seemingly endless troop of workers. Iris counted ten people, all males, which made her thankful for small mercies. There appeared to be little temptation for John at the lodging-house.

The early smog and clinging damp of mist lifted. A searing shard of sunlight suddenly illuminated the drab street and probed the decrepit Mini. Iris struggled from the cab, away from the stultifying glare and stood in front of the property. Taking a long intake of breath, she gingerly approached the door and stood frozen on the front-step trying to pluck up the courage to knock. Suddenly the door opened and a bald, scowling man appeared. In an instant the gruesome grimace was transformed into a beaming smile. The sight of the beautiful girl altered the whole demeanour of the stranger. As Iris spluttered an apology the fellow was jostled from behind and a second figure pushed his way into view.

"Come in, you're not a stranger!" said a chortling Michael Motson. As Iris gawked and struggled with embarrassment, the newcomer shrugged his shoulders, added, 'It's me, Iris!'

It was John's uncle! The encounter proved too emotional for her. Iris stammered a greeting as he eyes filled with tears.

Michael Motson chuckled, eased forward and pecked her on the cheek, "Jesus, girl, how did you find us?" His head clearing from the smog of alcohol, he added quizzically, "There's nothing wrong is there?"

A gentle flush crept over Iris's face. "Wanted to see John," she stuttered, "that's all."

"The bruising has almost gone," said Michael. He stroked a finger across her jaw.

"Makeup can hide anything," she said, chortling.

Lenny Jobson said, "I wish someone would travel hundreds of miles to see me …"

The banter stopped abruptly when the bleary-eyed youth appeared. John Briggs saw the familiar face of Iris standing between the two jabbering men. He gaped with incredulity; she flushed with a heady mix of hope and desperation.

"Cat got your tongue, Johnny?" said a beaming Michael, his rough hands scratching at the boy's tousled locks.

"Come on, Mick," said Lenny Jobson. "Let's leave the kids to talk."

"John," said the uncle, "I'll clock you in at work in case you decide to come in, okay." He nodded at the woman, "Nice to see you, Iris." He turned to the youth and said, "Take her into our room, John. Everybody's gone to work and Norah doesn't get out of bed before ten, okay?"

Lenny was already walking away when he shouted, "Take a day off, Johnny, show your girl the delights of London."

Michael Motson hurried away leaving the youngsters alone on the landing.

"I'll show you where we live, Iris," said John. He took her into the adapted living-room.

When Iris saw the lines of single beds and the single dilapidated wardrobe she gasped in disbelief.

"What's the matter?" he asked, squatting on his unmade mattress.

"It's like the Army," she replied, sitting next to him. "Like a barracks!"

The talk was subdued and hesitant. Both sides reluctant to make the initial sortie into the emotional minefield and then slowly the magnet of unmitigated bliss pushed aside doubts and uncertainties. At first the discussions were shallow and safe, with talk centred on home and children, families and gossip. Then it happened, spontaneous and combustible, as fingers hesitantly touched and probed and bodies groaned with the ache of their separation and loss and two hearts came together. In the stranger's house, in the small and cluttered barrack-room, the couple found each other, discovered again a joyful sensuous reunion. The past, with its murky and clinging mire, was temporarily cast aside, tears and pain shelved as the couple made love. And for a short time nothing else mattered.

It was John's idea to follow Lenny Jobson's advice and spend the day together. It was still early and the street traffic was rising in crescendo as the working-day cranked into action. The young couple left the terraced property intending to drive into the city. Iris was the driver and John the route-planner as they turned into the Uxbridge Road and headed for Ealing, en-route to the city-centre. Minutes into the journey they paused at traffic-lights near Hanwell. The pair were blissfully happy and chattered incessantly as they waited for the lights to change. Anything and everything was on the menu. John asked about his parents, Iris's mother, his coal-business, all drab and mundane stuff yet somehow it felt special and interesting as he soaked up news from home like a bee sucking nectar.

It was Iris who spotted the big car facing them. It was a maroon-coloured Peugeot. The driver was enormous, and foreign, his knotted locks cascaded over stone features. He was staring intently ahead. Next to him, a youth sat upright, his head slightly skewed and resting against the window. He was fast asleep. Simon Baxter, even in slumber, looked unmistakably evil.

"Look!" she gasped, her eyes wide with shock as she gestured to the car facing them. "It's him!"

The lights turned green. The couple stared in disbelief as the Peugeot shot past them heading in the direction of Southall. Only when a multitude of irate motorists began to sound their horns did the battered Mini jerk forward.

"I have to contact Ma!" said John. "She's the only one who knows my address!"

It took a short time to find a phone-box and wasted minutes trying to get in touch with his parents. John was in a quandary.

Iris confirmed his fears, "It's after eight, the boys should be out of bed!" she said.

He dialled again and again and each time was unsuccessful. He closed his eyes, concentrated and tried to recall his parent's neighbour's name.

John suddenly remembered. He tried twice before he was connected and then listened despairingly as Jemima Simpson shouted frantically down the phone-line. Iris saw the signs of

235

panic in his face and prodded him with nervous impatience. She saw tears welling in his face, the open mouth, the occasional nod, the slow descent of the telephone.

"Ma is in hospital, critically injured. Dad's okay ….."

"What about the boys?" interrupted Iris.

"Eddie and Frank are with your mother. Dad's in hospital too, not serious!"

"Oh, God!"

"Eddie heard them. The noise woke him! He ran down stairs and found them!"

Iris wrapped her arms around John and began to cry.

"You'll not believe it," he said. He pushed Iris to arm's length, "Eddie called the police! My little boy called the police and then he went back upstairs and dragged Frank under the bed to hide. They stayed there until the police came. My boy! A hero, Iris! He's the talk of the colliery!"

"What's happening, John?" said Iris. She followed her husband back to the car. "What's going on?"

"Dad told the police that a Chinese man is after Uncle Buff! We'll have to warn him!"

Iris looked at John, her features masked with bewilderment. "Simon Baxter was in the car too," she gasped. "It doesn't make sense!"

**

236

CHAPTER TWENTY SIX

Lamont King was ecstatic, "The deal's done and dusted, man, pure perfect. Motor man callin' here right now." He glanced at his wrist- watch, "We got all the time in the world."

Lenny Jobson intervened, "We got half an hour before the management show their faces!"

"That's the beauty of my wicked organisation skills, man," chortled the exuberant Lamont King. "I done an excellent deal wi' driver. Fella is on the way to Heathrow, goin' directly to Wimpey. He be callin' here first, doin' detour, and will be makin' donation to Lamont's favourite charity! A'm talkin' 'bout £2000 cash!"

Michael Motson gawked at the amount. Lenny Jobson grinned. It was their biggest payday to date.

"Same fella couldn't do deals like me," said Lamont wryly. "Could spout good enough but money-makin' … the dude lacks talent!"

Lenny Jobson was puzzled. "Not quite with you on this one, Lamont?" he said.

"Want me to be the man to explain Lamont's jibe," interjected Freddie Lakunda. "Me thinks the ganja still roosting inside his skull!"

"Tell me while you're at it, Freddie," said Micky Motson.

"Load of tyres is supposed to be dropped off here, put in damn warehouse, signed and invoiced," said Freddie. "Lamont has done the deal with some shrewd operator at the Wimpey site inside Heathrow Airport. When management gets here at nine, invoice will be on office table for filing. Impossible for them to check cos I rearranged pallets last night!"

"Like a game of draughts, man, shufflin' decks!" said Lamont, "When the man wi' kilt has a shuffty he'll be well pleased at the new pallets … only a few will be as empty as a bitch's head!"

"I be puttin' tampered pallets on bottom of pile, man," said an exuberant Freddie. "Even eagle-eye Frazier will never guess!"

"Ain't empty as such," interrupted Lamont, "we just scooped out middle of damn pallets! Outside lookin' in it still looks filled wi' tyres on account of management scrutiny."

Freddie Lakunda glowered at his partner, impatient to continue. "There be tyres on view, no fret," he said. "Pallets look as full as Old Jim's chest on a rainy day. Take top pallets away and see the middle be empty, but there be no worry cos we not be reaching bottom pallets for months. Anyways, I be re-jigging the aisles periodically."

A large articulated truck swung into view and trundled towards them. When it reached the huge concrete quadrangle the vehicle started a three-point turn. Within minutes the driver had turned the juggernaut and was facing the exit route. Lamont was like a hound-dog following scent as he chased after the cab. The exchange took place. Cash was swapped for invoices which were duly signed. Three top copies went into Lamont King's pocket, the fourth copy was retained by the anxious driver. After a brief verbal exchange between the two the truck moved off. The deal was completed in minutes.

The four men moved to the safety of the open elevator and the money was shared equally, Freddie Lakunda holding Griffith's cut until he showed his face.

Lamont grinned like a buffoon, "Like takin' candy from a baby," he said. "Ain't that the truth …"

Suddenly an old car roared into view, rattling gravel and dirt into a cloud and leaving long skid marks across the yard.

The four employees of Metro-Store watched in shared fascination.

"More of your white-trash Lenny," muttered Freddie Lakunda. "Honky always tryin' to impress the babes!"

John Briggs leapt out of one side of the small saloon, Iris out of the other and both ran towards the ramp.

Micky and Lenny exchanged worried looks.

"That boy is in some hurry, man" said Lamont, watching the fracas. "Reckon he runnin' from her or she be chasin' him?"

"Too much testosterone turnin' her pretty little head!" grunted Freddie. His eyes were cold, knew something was amiss. "Girl could be pregnant the way she looks!"

John reached his uncle. He was agitated and breathless. "There's been trouble!" he shouted.

Micky Motson winced. "Tell me, son," he said calmly. "Nice and slow."

"Guess who we saw …" John never finished the sentence.

"Baxter!" bawled Iris, interrupting. "Simon Baxter and a big Chinese man were heading for Southall!"

*

A few miles east of Hayes the big saloon trawled the quiet streets of Southall as the car's occupants reconnoitred. The criminals finally found the road, parked and began the methodical search along the long stretch of terrace. The task was painstakingly slow as each door was approached and inmates questioned. Sonny Chin was in a foul mood, he had never known a job take as long, never driven so far to find his victim; Leeds to Durham, Durham to London, it was becoming a test of endurance and stamina. He thought about the old woman, Motson's sister. Admired her, admired anyone with spunk and grit. He had beaten her until he was tired but the girl wouldn't talk. She was loyal to the end. Even when her bones were cracked she wouldn't divulge a thing. Screamed like a pig in an abattoir but refused to give a scrap of information about her beloved brother. The husband, however, was a whining bag of wind and quickly regurgitated the information. Motson was residing in Greenford Avenue, Southall. Sonny Chin sighed knowing the job would soon be completed.

Glancing across the street Chin observed his shaven-headed crony gesticulating wildly at some perplexed tenant. Sandy Baxter's facial injuries were growing by the week. Chin pondered, Baxter had been very quiet since his beating the previous night. He wondered if he had learned anything since revealing Sonny's identity to the husband. Baxter had regained consciousness in the house and had been dragged into the rear yard and left there to learn the error of his ways. The youth had sat on the cold path staring at the night-sky, head screaming with pain because of the assault, still uncertain as to why he was assaulted. *'Why did you hit me?'* he shrieked. *'What did I do wrong?'* When Sonny whispered his reply, Baxter barked the sarcastic reply, *'You're worried because I mentioned your name? Sonny, the cops' couldn't begin to find enough bodies in the whole county to start an Identity Parade with people who looked like you!'*

Baxter struck gold half-way along the street. He waved the photograph of Motson with his sister inches from an agitated tenant and saw recognition registering. The woman, bleary-eyed from sleep and oozing of sweat and alcohol, fumbled with cigarette and lighter. The female, annoyed at being awoken at such an ungodly hour, nodded impatiently. Finally managing to light the cigarette, Norah Flannigan inhaled deep into her lungs and blew smoke into the stranger's face.

Sonny Chin hurried across the road, head down until he reached the dishevelled, demented-looking landlady.

"Police!" grunted Chin.

Norah Flannigan was not impressed. She folded her arms, glared at the enforcer and said defiantly, "If you're a cop I'm Shirley Bassey!" Took another suck at the cigarette and demanded to see a warrant-card.

Sandy Baxter, smiling icily, flashed a £20 note in her face. "Flying Squad," he said.

Her patience at an end, Norah snarled a reply, "You must think I'm as green as cabbage-looking!"

Baxter toyed with her, "More like black and cross-eyed, Missy!"

Norah Flannigan had carried the affliction all of her life. The disfigurement had made her tough as leather. Used to cry when she was a child, used to run away from the hurtful comments, until the day she faced her tormentors. When she'd finished with them they never called her again. Norah Flannigan was a pugnacious, proud woman who could stand her ground with most. The hurtful comment from the stranger spurred her into action. Her temper broken, Norah launched herself from the doorway, flew past the Oriental and hit the shorter man as hard as she could. Simon Baxter felt the full weight of the blow. Caught off-guard, he stumbled and fell to his knees. Chin's reaction was lightning fast. He grabbed the landlady, hoisted her aloft and bundled her into the house. Baxter struggled from the pavement, wiped his bloodied mouth and sheepishly followed.

Chin subdued Norah with a punch into her stomach. Retching and gasping for air, the woman crumpled on to the floor. Baxter swung a boot at the moaning figure and heard the awful sound as ribs snapped. Shrieks echoed through the house as the bigger man knelt next to her, his huge hand clamping her mouth.

"Tell me where Motson works and I'll leave you alone," he muttered viciously.

"There's no one called Motson living here! Honest to God!"

Chin described Michael Motson. Baxter intervened and gave the whimpering female a rough photo-fit of John Briggs. Norah pleaded ignorance.

"I'll make her talk," said Baxter.

Chin stepped aside, curious to see how the kid would act.

Sandy Baxter pulled out a small knife and ordered his accomplice to hold the victim. He fell to a crouching position, held the woman's ankles with one hand and used the other to remove her slippers. Norah Flannigan managed to lift her horrified head and stare wide-eyed at the leering skinhead. An agonising groan escaped from her clamped mouth and her head shook dementedly from side to side.

"Time for some chiropody treatment!" barked the tormentor. "I'm gonna make those pop eyes even bigger!"

The knife was rammed hard into the soft padding of her foot. The bloody tip of the blade emerged topside looking like a misshapen extra toe. Norah Flannigan jerked uncontrollably as she tried to scream through her clenched, clamped mouth. The excruciating pain made her lose control of her bladder and a strong acidic whiff of urine blanketed the hallway. She began to wail.

Baxter appeared disgusted. He glowered at the frantic, jerking woman before withdrawing the blade.

Sonny Chin removed his hand from Norah's quivering mouth, "I want Michael Motson," he said calmly. "Tell me where he is or I'll let the boy cut you again."

Sandy Baxter ran the blade over the undamaged left foot of the woman leaving a long ugly weal of reddened tissue.

Norah Flannigan screamed hysterically.

Sonny Chin was growing impatient. "Take off her toes!" he growled.

Baxter grabbed at the big toe and began to saw frantically.

"They work near the airport!" cried the terrified landlady. "Three! Jobson, Milson and Briggs … I think that's them."

Baxter relaxed his hold allowing Norah to sit upright.

Sonny Chin nodded and freed her hands. "Don't mess with me grandma," he fumed, "or I'll let the boy loose on you!"

Norah Flannigan squatted on the soiled carpet and tried to hide the urine stains with her skirt. "The boys work at a warehouse in Hayes, near the airport. It's called Metro Store."

"Metro Store?" quizzed Chin, his features as sour as vinegar.

"It's a tyre warehouse in a trading estate," stammered Norah. "That's all I know!"

The words had barely left her mouth when Chin slammed an uppercut into her unprotected chin. The jawbone shattered and dentures flew from her ruined face. Norah Flannigan fell to the floor unconscious.

"Grab her feet," ordered Chin as he grabbed the woman's upper body. "We'll take her upstairs … buy some time!"

"Hey fella," protested Baxter. "How come I get the wrong end of the stick?" Reluctantly putting away the weapon he clamped his fingers around her damp ankles and lifted, "Piss! I'm covered in piss!"

Sonny hoisted the female easily and shuffled towards the staircase, his eyes riveted on the whining youth. Despite the barracking he did not reply.

As the criminals bundled the unconscious landlady up the staircase a small group of Metro Store workers stood wavering in the large outer yard of the warehouse. They were still discussing possible action when, prompt at nine, the two managers arrived. Not a word from Steinbeck or Pickett as they strode past the employees and an awkward-looking Iris and stepped into the lift. Frazier Tubbs arrived next, chauffeuring Griffith Edwards whom he'd picked up at the entrance-gates. When Tubbs saw the female he told Lamont, his second-in-command, that the girl had to leave the premises immediately. Frazier Tubbs then motioned to the coloured workers who followed him into the escalator. The group disappeared inside the building leaving Lenny, Micky and the youngsters alone on the concrete loading bay. Iris was persuaded to leave. Outvoted and outnumbered she drove out of the site and waited impatiently next to the burger-van close to the site entrance.

"What's the plan, Buff?" asked Lenny Jobson.

"If I had one," replied Michael Motson, "I'd tell you."

"Maybe we should leave," said John, looking at his uncle. "Start afresh somewhere else?"

"I've ran enough," replied Michael. "If they can find me here, then they'll find me anywhere." The man looked worried. His forehead creased with a permanent frown as he gazed at the distant entry-gate.

Lenny Jobson glanced at the youngster, "At least we know the car they're driving. Big and maroon?"

John nodded, "It was a French make."

"Citroen or Peugeot?" asked Buff.

"Peugeot."

Motson said quizzically, "Can't understand how the kid who knifed me is now buddy with a Chinese bloke?"

"Simon Baxter," said John.

"Baxter, that's him," replied the bewildered Motson. "Same kid is knocked out and trussed up tight, and then disappears before the police arrive! Magic!"

"Could the link be drugs?" asked John. "Baxter was an addict, used to buy and sell. Parents were low-life. He told me his sister left home as soon as she could. …"

"He had a sister?" interrupted Micky.

"Baxter was always talking about her. Said Dorothy …"

"Dorothy Baxter," cried a triumphant Micky Motson. "That's got to be it!" He started pacing up and down frantically. "Before Ray Robinson done the dirty I would sometimes see him in the nightclubs parading his latest catch. This one was to die for … tall with long black hair practically down to her backside."

John said, "When I was locked up with Baxter I once went to his room. Simon kept her photograph on the wall. She was smart."

"That's Dorothy!" said Motson. "She must be this Baxter's sister! It can't be a coincidence! Last I heard she'd dumped Sugar-Ray for the top man himself, Willy Garcia …" He stopped suddenly, his jaw slack with shock. "I've just remembered, there was a bodyguard as big as a house-end. I saw him once when he was delivering from Leeds. Looked oriental … Sonny Chin!"

"Garcia," asked Lenny, "he a bad boy?"

"He runs most of Yorkshire and Durham," said Micky. "Got his dirty fingers in every pie. The Baxter boy must have run to his sister and blabbed my name. Dorothy must have told Garcia. That's why the Sumo is after me."

"I don't understand?" said John.

"You know why! I was locked up for a ten year stretch thanks to Robinson. He stitched me up good and proper! See this," and he pointed a nicotine-coloured finger across the

245

thick wedge of scar tissue that blazoned above his eyes. "This got me an early release." He took a deep breath, "I whacked Robinson and so Garcia wants his pound of flesh! He's got his reputation to keep …"

"Ma said it was an accident?" said John, interrupting. "Said you never meant to kill Robinson."

Lenny Jobson glanced at the youth and said, "No one on this planet will believe that."

Michael Motson continued, "Police must have searched Robinson's house, trying to nail someone for the damage. All I can think is that stuff has been found … drugs, names, who knows? Maybe Garcia has had his collar felt by the law, maybe he's lost a boatload of money because of me. Whatever, I'll never be on his Christmas list. The Chinaman is going to make sure of that!"

"What will you do?" asked the youngster.

"John, don't think this involves only me. Mr. Samurai has a friend who has a score to settle with you. I'll get *our* coats and *we'll* take a hike from here and go our separate ways until things cool."

Michael Motson hurried up the ramp, crossed the raised walkway and disappeared into the elevator.

*

Iris parked the car opposite the fast-food caravan and waited for the others to join her. She was exhausted, closed her eyes and immediately fell into a deep sleep. As her head slumped forward a maroon-coloured car drove passed the stationary Mini. The Peugeot turned into the trading-estate and followed the signs for Metro-Store. Both occupants knew calamity was looming but only one pleaded for restraint and planning. Surprisingly, it was Simon Baxter who offered a

246

common-sense approach to the problem. He wanted to reconnoitre the area and plot strategy but Chin imagined they could casually drive into the hornet's nest and see how the land lay. Lucidity and reason lost on the bigger man.

An increasingly anxious Baxter tried diplomacy, "Shouldn't we take a peek first," he asked. "Park the car, walk awhile, maybe ask a few questions?" He gestured at the disappeared fast-food stand. "Sonny, let's have something to eat. Fella serving hot-dogs will know everything about the place. Whadya say?"

Baxter didn't want to exacerbate the situation, knew enough of Chin not to force his hand. He brooded knowing they were heading for trouble. It was broad daylight and they were driving into a trading estate with potentially hundreds of witnesses.

He tried again, "Sonny, maybe we should …"

"It's too late!" growled Chin, interrupting. His patience was broken, logic thrown out with the bathwater. The leviathan's slit eyes focussing and assimilating all before him. "I thought Motson would be at the digs. It would have been easy to finish him at the lodging-house. He should have been there! The man's never held a job in his life then decides to change his name and work for a living!"

Baxter said, "Maybe we should have waited for him?"

"Impossible! The place is some kind of bed and breakfast. There must be a dozen men dossing there."

"Can't see the problem," replied the fidgeting Baxter. His mind bulged with the certain knowledge that they were like rats in a sinking ship. "She's tied and gagged. Could have shut the door on her and waited downstairs for Motson to return."

"You're an idiot! The old girl said he was in a group of three so there are others to deal with, and we can't assume they'll return to the lodging-house straight from work?"

247

"Where else would they go?"

"A drink, maybe," said Chin. "That hell-hole of a lodging-house would be the last place they'd want!"

"Rational thought, eh?"

"In my opinion, yes!"

"About as logical as driving here during the day!" whined the ever-more frantic Baxter. "Man, this is so barmy it could qualify for the Guinness Book of Records!" He glowered at his crony, desperate to dissuade him from the suicidal mission, "Sonny," he pleaded, "let's wait awhile!"

A huge back-hand suddenly smashed into Simon Baxter's face. Blood erupted like a geyser and showered the facia and window of the vehicle. Fearful for his life, Baxter somehow found the door-handle and heaved his body sideways. The door shot open and he fell from the moving car, somersaulting like a clown before careering into a perimeter wall. The sound of the impact was sickening. Simon Baxter lay still, gravely injured.

Chin continued and soon reached a large rectangular courtyard. Several articulated wagons waited in an orderly queue. He observed the single fork-lift truck with the youngster squatting inside. Chatting to the teenager was a thin, gaunt, middle-aged man. Sonny Chin decided to ask them if they knew Michael Motson or Milson. He pictured the photograph of Motson with his sister found by Simon Baxter; he was looking for someone below average height with thinning hair tied into a pony-tail. Chin was about to steer the car towards the gossiping pair when a third figure appeared from an opening elevator. The newcomer was carrying a coat. He sported an untidy braid! Michael Motson stepped out on to the raised walkway and froze. He stood staring at Chin, a semblance of a smile filtered over his battered features as he read the situation.

"Buff Motson!" whispered a revitalised Sonny Chin.

The maroon car, windows liberally splattered with Baxter's blood, slowly manoeuvred towards the statuesque, staring figure. So focussed on his intended victim, and with one hand reaching for the pistol hidden in the glove-compartment, Sonny Chin never saw the approaching fork-lift until it was too late. Out of the corner of his eye he observed a blur of yellow, twisted his head and saw the youngster, howling with rage, bearing down on him. Too late to avoid the collision, the gangster closed his eyes, screamed and waited for the impact.

The noise was horrendous as the car was rammed against the small wall. Windows warped, splinted then burst. The Peugeot buckled under the impact, the door bent like putty and wedged around the thick frame of the struggling figure. For seconds there was complete silence before Sonny Chin recovered. He heaved himself upright and aimed a massive fist at the front window. The pane shattered with the first blow.

Michael Motson shouted frantically, told his nephew to use the fork-lift to lift the car. He ran down the ramp towards the mayhem bellowing instructions. John grabbed the small lever but his hands trembled so much he could hardly manipulate the controls. With heart pounding and tears falling he watched the man-mountain grapple and push at the damaged door. Slowly the door was forced open and the blotched and maddened features of the assassin appeared.

"John," shrieked the panic-stricken uncle, "do it now!"

The teenager lifted from the stupor. He rammed the fork-lift into reverse and worked the controls. The metal forks wedged underneath the ruined car were manipulated and the vehicle and its hysterical occupant were lifted skywards. The fork-lift slowly reversed across the big yard, straining and trembling with its abnormal load.

Lenny Jobson screamed, "Give it some revs!"

The machine gathered speed, the boy's mentors either side, directing and instructing. Suddenly the second of the elevator-doors opened and two drivers stepped on to the walkway. They stopped abruptly at the sight of the macabre spectacle, glanced at one another then turned and hurried back into the lift. The elevator-door closed behind them. The works-canteen, even with a consumptive serving refreshments, seemed an altogether safer place.

Michael Motson jumped on to the fork-lift and barked out orders, "Clutch in!" he shouted and rammed the gear-stick forward. "Release it, now!"

The vehicle shuddered, groaned and keeled forward, almost capsizing; Micky manipulated the controls and watched as the steel forks dipped forward. The fork-lift shook like jelly as the load loosened.

The damaged Peugeot scrapped and slipped slowly from the forks.

There was an excruciating noise as the car fell from the fork-lift, hit the concrete yard and rolled on its side. Sonny Chin groaned with pain. He was trapped inside the misshapen cab, the hand-gun out of reach in the warped glove-compartment. Lenny Jobson, jubilant at the outcome, danced round the upturned car. Michael Motson jumped from the fork-lift and ran towards the perimeter fence, grabbed a wooden stave that lay in the dust, leaped on to the overturned vehicle and smashed the pole into the enforcer's bloody face. Sonny Chin was knocked out cold.

Buff Motson knew the net was closing around him. He realised that if criminals could find him then the law wouldn't be so far behind. It was time to disappear.

"John," said Motson, grabbing his jacket, "we'd better go before the police get here. Iris can drive us to the lodgings. We'll grab our gear and split. Take Iris home, okay? When you see your mother, tell her I'll call sometime."

Micky Motson then spoke to his friend, "Lenny, I'll be in touch in a few weeks. Let the heat die down." The pair shook hand and embraced. "Take care, man," he said, "and act like a dodo for the police. Remember … you don't know me."

"Hey," laughed Lenny Jobson, pushing fingers through non-existent hair, "second nature!"

Michael Motson started to walk away, his nephew by his side. "Come on, we'll find Iris," he said.

They walked shoulder to shoulder along the works road, brothers-in-arms. The pair had overcome hurdles and obstacles and survived unscathed, mayhem and murder averted thanks to luck and the illogical irreverent hand of fate.

All of a sudden reality hit Michael Motson, "Sonny Chin was on his own!" he said.

"Baxter!"

"He might be waiting for us at Norah's place," said Micky. "Hong Kong Phooey failed, so maybe Baxter is the reserve?"

"Definitely not!" groaned John.

"You can't be sure!"

"I am," muttered the nervous youth. He gestured ahead, "He's heading towards us!"

Sandy Baxter, suffering massive head trauma, meandered towards the nearing figures. As he closed on them his injured brain started to focus. He recognised the pair. Couldn't remember how he had arrived at the site, forgot all about his

251

missing accomplice and the savage assault, knew only that he had to finish the task in hand. Blood continued to ooze from every orifice in his head. Although delirious, Baxter suddenly remembered the weapon and numb fingers probed through pockets until the knife was found. He began to wave the weapon at the approaching pair.

Michael Motson, always cold and calculated in a crisis, told his nephew to separate in order to make it harder for Baxter.

Simon Baxter was confused. Perspiration ran like rain over his troubled features, reality and fantasy jarring and taunting him. He observed the opposition's spoiling tactics. Made him smile, the strategy was so obvious to him and so easy to counteract. Hallucinations smothered him and made it difficult for him to focus. Baxter's knife hand jerked and twisted so as to unnerve his rivals. He began to shout and taunt his enemies. Images appeared and he became disoriented, he slowed and lowered his body ready to repel the attack but the noise inside his head hurt so much he could not concentrate. He heard a familiar voice calling for him. It was Dottie. His sister was somewhere close, her words filled with compassion. She had sought him out, found him again. Simon Baxter called out for her and forgot about the circling opposition. He began to sway. Knew he had to rest. Dropping the knife he slumped on to the road like a puppet with its strings cut. His legs skewed outwards, his arms pitched forward and fingers sprayed like suction-cups on the surface of the road as he attempted to stay seated.

John stared incomprehensively at the tragic figure. Michael Motson was close enough to overhear the rambling outburst from Baxter. His natural instinct was to attack his adversary no matter the condition of the man. It was always better to be safe now rather than be sorry at a later date. He hesitated and stared at the broken figure, knew enough about street-brawling to understand the lad was seriously hurt. He gestured to his nephew and they continued on the way leaving a drooling Simon Baxter alone in the middle of the works road.

The injured youth sat, staring into nothingness, mute, his features devoid of emotion. One of his eyes was tightly closed.

The pair reached the entry-gates as the police-cars, with sirens howling and lights flashing, skidded into the trading estate. With their heads bowed Motson and Briggs headed away from the trading estate.

John saw the Mini parked close to the hot-dog stand. It looked empty. A flutter of panic ran through his body as he imagined the worst. He ran to the car and saw a prostrate, sleeping Iris. The sight of his slumbering wife brought a smile to his face.

"Thought Baxter had got to her!" gasped John.

Micky opened the door and spoke to Iris. She coughed and stirred and dragged herself upright.

"Iris," said Michael Motson. "We need a lift back to Southall!"

Iris nodded. She was crestfallen and fearing the worst.

"I'm heading for the south coast," said Micky. "I want you to take John home. Okay?"

Iris smiled like she'd won the pools.

**

CHAPTER TWENTY SEVEN

On the same day John and Iris left London on their long drive home a middle-aged woman and her sullen daughter walked into the visitors room at Deerbolt Young Offenders Institution. The two hour bus journey from Shotton to the prison at Barnard Castle in West Durham had been exhausting. The youngster, Donna Turten, had never visited the prison before and had never seen her brother Timmy since his incarceration months earlier. She cared less. It had taken a bribe of a hairdressing appointment from her mother to persuade her to make the trek. Donna now regretted her decision, decided it would be the first and last time she would visit her foolish brother.

The visitors room was a huge spartan place filled to bursting with residents and visitors. Two prison guards lounged near the exit doors. The oppressive heat of the day had made them discard their coats. They propped up the wall; shirts wet with perspiration and gossiped freely, only occasionally glancing across the crowded room when someone guffawed too loudly or an infant wailed too long.

Donna Turten fidgeted with boredom at the stilted conversation between her mother and brother. Sick of the inane chatter, she turned her back on her mother, gazed about the room and began flirting with anyone remotely interesting. That was when she overheard the tittle-tattle. Her mother, Annie Turten, struggling to lift the spirits of her only son and, thinking her daughter was out of earshot, told Tim the news. Cute and devious for one so young, Donna feigned interest at the tattooed youth squatting at the next table. Her ploy worked a treat. As she toyed and teased her admirer - even allowed him the briefest glimpse of her shapely thighs - Donna Turten listened in on her mother. The information was unbelievable.

"I shouldn't have told you, Timothy," whispered Mrs. Turten. "I mean, there's nothing anyone can do about it."

"And it's definite, Mother?" said Timmy, disillusioned at the betrayal.

"From the horse's mouth," whispered Annie Turten. She glanced momentarily at her tempestuous, flirtatious daughter. Thinking she was safe to continue, the woman said in hushed tones, "Tina Holdsworth is a receptionist at Station Road surgery. She has a sister who works for Dr. Porteous in the Peterlee Clinic ... I think she's called Rachel. Anyway, she took the urine sample from Avril Jennings herself!"

Tim Turten could not believe the news about his best friend. The treachery made him grimace. He sighed, shook his head, and tried to imagine the misery felt by Delbert Hancock. It was bad enough being incarcerated, but a whole different ball game wondering if your girl was playing loose and fast. He began to nod absently. He would never know the torment of infidelity because Timmy Turten did not have a girl-friend. *Small mercies,* he mused.

"Are you alright, Timothy?" inquired the woman, puzzling at her son's antics.

"Of course, Mother," he said. "I'm fine."

"She's three months pregnant," whispered the woman.

Delbert Hancock and Timmy Turten had been in jail for three long months. Tim forgot all about the month on remand before the trial.

"So what's the problem?" said Timmy, mentally juggling times and dates.

"My words entirely son, when I was first told," answered Annie Turten. "But there's too many rumours flying about!"

255

She shook her head like an old, wise Methuselah, "No smoke without fire!"

"Bloody hell," gasped Timmy, "Del will butcher her!"

"When he finds out who she's been with," muttered the woman, "there'll be two deaths!"

Timmy Turten waited with bated breath as his mother continued.

"Hard to believe!" whispered the woman, shaking her head from side to side. "When I heard …"

"Mother," whined the youth, "spit it out!"

"Monica Hall told me," said the woman. "She lives opposite Avril Jennings. After you and Delbert were caught, John Briggs called to see Avril about buying the truck. Remember, son?"

"Forget Johnny," said an impatient Timmy, "and tell me who climbed into Avril`s bed."

"I've told you," uttered the mother, "Elsie's son!"

Timmy Turten was aghast. His eyes watered, his jaw sagged and for some moments he couldn't speak. He gestured for his mother to continue.

"Monica Hall knows everyone's business. Got a snout like an ant-eater! Well, she was at the window when John called at Avril's house. She thought it was a bit strange, especially the way the girl was behaving. Anyway, to cut a long story short, Monica was curious so she watched. When Avril invited the lad in and then the bedroom curtains were drawn … well, put two and two together! Monica doesn't like Avril at the best of times, calls her a brazen hussy. I mean, it was the middle of the day, you understand, so she couldn't move from the window. Wanted to know the outcome. Lo and behold, half an hour later John Briggs is adjusting his pants and hurrying away! It gets better! There's Avril as large as life in her bra and pants calling him back for more! Would you believe it?"

"Does Delbert know anything?" asked his partner-in-crime.

"He knows she's pregnant!"

"Might be his, Mother," queried Timmy optimistically. "Between you and me, he's been trying for another kid for a year."

Mrs. Turten was adamant, "Bit of a coincidence, don't you think?"

Timmy glanced at the silent figure of his sister; suddenly realising she might be eavesdropping. He gestured at his mother to assess the situation.

"Donna," asked Annie Turten softly, "you alright, love?"

Although facing away from her mother and brother, Donna could sense the prying attention. She closed her eyes and pretended to sleep. Couldn't believe her good fortune. She smiled wickedly, knew why Delbert had lost to Johnny Briggs in the bedroom stakes. Everyone in Shotton knew about the coalman Casanova.

"It's okay, Timothy," whispered the woman. "She's dozing."

Donna Turten, ever the little vixen, suddenly lifted from the supposed stupor, yawned and stretched and gazed about the visiting-room. She had changed her tune about the tortuous, bone-jarring journey. It had been worth it. The gossip was priceless and she couldn't wait to contact the gorgeous Del Hancock who was residing in Northallerton Prison. Didn't know where Northallerton was and didn't care, only knew she would get information to Delbert. With his head messed he would end the relationship with the pompous Avril Jennings and, fingers crossed, might be persuaded to turn his amorous eyes her way.

Donna shifted her stance and glanced at her Mother. "Ma," she said, "can we go, I'm bored!"

"Talk to Timothy, Donna, we've only just got here."

The youngster sighed, turned away from her family and smiled provocatively at the fawning inmate squatting at the table opposite.

"I don't know why you brought her!" muttered Timmy Turten.

"Donna asked to come, son. She misses you."

The young girl looked first at her brother and then at her mother. "Yeah, Ma, I'm definitely pining!" she said sarcastically.

A week later Delbert's morose mother walked into visitor's room at Northallerton, hurried to her son's side and pressed the hand-written note into the palm of his hand. Minutes later the hysterical Delbert Hancock had to be escorted out of the room by two prison guards.

*

The patient lay prone and exhausted in the side room, his long sinuous frame drained. Delbert's plan had worked enough to get him removed from the prison infirmary and into North Tees Hospital. He had spent two uncomfortable days in the prison hospital because the authorities, purely as a matter of prudence erred on the side of caution while they assessed the complaining patient. They couldn't appear to be too hasty in allowing the prisoner the luxury of outside care but after forty eight hours of careful monitoring worried staff finally acted. Delbert Hancock was transferred to the Teesside Hospital. The criminal's health was deteriorating, and the

258

symptoms were alarming; the young man was suffering from continuous sickness and diarrhoea.

Delbert's physical condition appeared to be failing. He lay prostrate and stiff, his mouth ulcerated and raw with self-inflicted weals and sores, his stomach swollen and pendulous with wind and infection due solely to the repeated poison. He was heartbroken, angry, his head heavy with thoughts of revenge. If the price of freedom meant shitting his pants every hour it was worth it. He had to get back to Durham and sort out his marital problems.

He could not comprehend the news of Avril's adultery but, try as he may, Delbert could not stop the torturous images. The pictures were vile and sordid, the reality unimaginable purgatory. Avril Jennings, his soul-mate for years, the mother of his child, was pregnant with another man's baby? It was beyond belief, Avril so tall and beautiful, having an affair with a man who didn't reach her shoulders. Johnny Briggs was a man with a tainted reputation, jailed for under-aged sex; John was the laughing-stock of the community. The same man had married a whore at sixteen and then seduced his thirteen-year-old babysitter! Johnny Briggs was an undersized, conniving braggart who had overstepped the mark and would pay the price. Delbert would see to it personally, he would make the half-pint realise the error of his ways.

He had months left of his sentence when he heard of the betrayal. Despite his good behaviour it would be ten weeks before he tasted freedom. Delbert could not wait that long, knew he had to tackle the problem immediately or go crazy with grief. He'd known for days about the deceit and already was demented with so many unanswered questions. Was he set-up by Johnny, was the robbery a convenient way of disposing of any opposition that could stall the squalid affair?

Del dismissed such thoughts, reasoned that his sentence was always a temporary affair and he would be free soon enough to seek retribution. The lovers knew about his reputation, everybody in the village knew about Delbert Hancock's temper. No, he reasoned, it had been the fickle hand of fate that had sent John Briggs to Avril's house to buy the wagon. Womanising Johnny alone with feisty, fiery Avril Jennings, it was a nightmare scenario.

All Del wanted was an hour alone with the pair, a brief moment to inflict so much pain that they would never again hurt anyone. He detested Avril, hated her so much for the anguish she had caused. Recalled the lies spilling so readily from her lips, the joy in her face when she told him the wondrous news, *'I'm pregnant, Delbert, now we'll have to get married!'* What a devious, cunning witch she was. Delbert would make her cry.

Del Hancock did nothing by half. Once he had heard the news he thought only of liberty, freedom to put things right. There were obstacles, unforeseen complications, which initially stumped him and hindered his plans. Escape was a non-starter, plausible but deemed too difficult in the short-term so he decided to feign serious illness. Delbert imagined he would be able to secure sufficient medication to warrant a stay in an outside hospital but despite bullying and bargaining, he could not get sufficient tablets to kick-start his plan. A bus-ride to an outside bed appeared to be out of the question.

On the second day he lost it, grabbed his cell-mate, Anton Tibbs, and started choking him. It wasn't until the Scouse crack-addict started rolling his eyes and losing his balance that Delbert gave up the ghost and pushed him aside.

Still retching, the inmate hovered close to the door. He knew his cell-mate was suffering real pain. "Gimme a break, Del," he said.

"Get away!"

"Hey," said Tibbs, "you gotta listen to me, man."

Delbert Hancock slumped on the mattress and put his head in his hands. "Leave me alone," he whispered.

The youth gingerly entered the cell and stopped a safe distance from the volatile kid. "Lemme talk, eh?" There was no opposition so Anton Tibbs sat on his bunk, "Geordie," continued the criminal, "the screws swept the place clean last week. You know that. It'll be a while before the stuff starts to flow again."

"Can't wait!" gasped the newcomer.

Tibbs took a deep breath and told him what he had to do to get out of prison.

Delbert growled, "Stop taking the piss, Scouser!"

"Got it in one,' said the smiling Tibbs. 'Only you have to go a little past the old scrotum!'

The Liverpool low-life told Delbert Hancock to eat his own shit.

*

Elsie Briggs was up and about, mobile at last and driving body and soul with her own steam, the facial injuries mended enough for her to ignore the obvious signs of the earlier assault by the two assailants. The surgery to her nose had been successful, the scarring and the weals the only reminder of the savage beating. The damage to her lower face was ongoing. The jaw showed little outwards sign of the extensive trauma suffered at the hands of Sonny Chin and, once dentures had been fitted, her features would be tolerable.

261

It was early evening and she was enjoying an hour of pleasantries with her youngest son, his wife and their two sons. The summer sun refused to give up the day and radiated warmth and illumination everywhere. The family relaxed in the rear garden in Moore Terrace. The only blemish to the evening - her husband - had safely departed with his tail between his heavy thighs as he sought refuge in the local drinking-den.

"Bit hard on him, Elsie," said Iris, chortling. "You didn't give him the lickings of a dog!"

"You take it for years," replied the woman. "Then one day you've had enough. Man spins more web than a spider on overtime!"

Iris left the boys playing cricket and slumped on to a deck-chair next to her husband and mother-in-law.

"Men," said Iris, chuckling, "they're all the same!"

John smiled but didn't comment. He was having another bad day.

"Frank couldn't leave it be," said Elsie resolutely. She eased back on the seat and sipped at the lemonade. She added sardonically, "The lies he told about fighting those men!"

"Sonny Chin and Sandy Baxter!" said John, trying to lift himself from the growing depression.

Elsie Briggs started mimicking her husband Frank. '*I told you, woman, I managed to subdue the little one! Bang, and down he went like a ton of bricks. Suddenly this big Sumo tackles me from behind, and then the youngun' gets off the floor. Well, Sonny Liston couldn't fight two at once, so that was me finished. Threatened to kill you, Elsie, if I didn't divulge the whereabouts of Buff!*' Elsie started laughing, "Man couldn't fight his way out of a paper-bag and he pretends he's the hero." She shook her head resignedly.

"I reckon the pub crowd are sick of his boasting," said Iris.

The telephone buzzed and Eddie, the eldest boy, flung his cricket-bat in the direction of his brother, "I'll get it! I'll get it!" He ran into the house.

"It's a shame, really," continued Elsie. "If your Dad had kept quiet maybe things might have been so different. I don't think you and our Micky would have ever been found by those men."

"Mother," said John, "if Dad hadn't told them our whereabouts you'd be six feet under!"

"I don't think so," replied the woman.

Eddie shouted from the confines of the house, "Dad, somebody wants to talk to you … hurry!"

The young father moved from the garden and entered the house. He accepted the phone held aloft by his son and listened in stunned silence to the message. His features drained of all colour. He stood moments, bewildered and mute, before replacing the phone.

"Dad," asked his curious son, "what's happened?"

John Briggs walked from the house into the evening sunlight. His son followed.

"Johnny?" said Iris. Her chair was positioned away from the setting sun and facing her husband. "What's the matter?"

Elsie turned in her seat, "Trouble, son?"

"That was Kenny Wilkinson on the phone," he whispered.

"What does he want this time, John?" asked Iris. "He must phone you every day for help!"

John shook his head. "It's not advice he wants." He replied.

Iris sensed disquiet in his voice. "What's happened?" she asked. Her stomach churned with apprehension.

263

"Delbert Hancock escaped last night," said John. "Made it back to Shotton. He went to Avril's house and attacked her! Knocked her through the window."

"She's pregnant!" gasped Iris, her features morbid with disbelief. "What kind of man would do that?"

"Del Hancock!" he whispered.

"Son," asked Elsie Briggs, rising from the chair. She saw the haunted look on her son's face. "Is there something you're not telling us?"

"Half of Shotton has been watching the show," gasped John. "Kenny was one of them. He heard Delbert's threats. That's why he phoned me!"

"I don't understand," said Iris, her voice rising with foreboding. "Why would Kenny need to tell you?"

"I'll have to go," John said.

"Go," gasped Iris, "where?"

"Delbert's on the way to my house," he muttered. "He's after me!"

Iris said, "Why, John, what have you done?"

"I'll tell you later!" he answered.

Iris paled as the realisation hit her, "John, it's about Avril isn't it?"

He stared blankly at her, his features etched in misery.

"Jesus Christ!" muttered Elsie. She shook her head in sad resignation. "Not again!"

John came out of the stupor. Without a word of explanation he hurried across the garden, stepped over the small fence and walked quickly along the rough walkway that paralleled Moore Terrace, stopping only when he had reached the nursing-home. He glanced about the streets. There was no one about. Skirting the gable-end of the building, John eased through a gap in the palings and stood behind a dilapidated garage. He was breathless with fear. A short distance away

264

was the main road. It was deserted. He groaned out loud. He was in a mess, stuck in a small village with a madman after his blood. Searching his pockets he found wagon-keys and some money. He quickly discounted any thoughts of getting the lorry. For all he knew, Del Hancock might be waiting there for him. He would have to escape some other way. He counted the coins. It was a pittance but it might be enough to get him a bus-ride out of the place. Staying in the village was not an option; he had to seek pastures new, at least until Delbert was captured. Taking a deep breath, John left his hiding place and stood next to the bus-stand. He prayed for the speedy arrival of public transport.

Meanwhile, on the northern flank of the village, a lone woman trudged the streets. Despite the beautiful evening, Josephine Brooks wore a heavy three-quarter coat. She was perspiring, and it wasn't only the ample clothing that caused the discomfort. Josephine had walked for miles. Her head ached and she felt light-headed. The daily dose of medication did not help.

Her head was clotted with memories, and none of them pleasant. She had been that way since the unexpected meeting with her long lost lover, Michael Motson. Spent days raging about the incident to her henpecked husband, Maurice; cried buckets about the damage to her beloved car but omitted the truth. Naïve Maurice Brooks believed his hysterical wife when she blamed some local scallywag for the accident. Told him she had parked the motor, spent minutes inside the Co-op before returning to her damaged car.

The car shunt happened weeks earlier and still Josephine fretted. Husband, Maurice, and daughter, Julie, had been relegated to the doghouse as she ranted and raved about anything and everything. After three weeks of unrelenting torture the doctor was called and stronger tablets were prescribed. The medication took effect, the barbed tones lessened and there was peace again in the Brooks' household. An uneasy concord existed.

Josephine did not drive the car again. Couldn't, her head and her heart was at another place. All she could think about was Michael Motson, the father of her only daughter. He was her one true love. She knew that now. When she had met him again after long years apart her heart was torn in two.

Josephine could not confide in anyone. How could she? How could she tell Maurice or Julie how she felt? She kept hold of her memories and fretted. A week after the car accident, Josephine found herself telephoning the Durham hospital inquiring after Michael. She was told no one by that name had been admitted. She tried every hospital in the area and was told the same. The news made her ill. Her condition deteriorated enough for her to be admitted as a day-patient at Cherry Knowle Hospital. She did not tell a soul about her inner torment knowing the staff would delight in her misery.

It was Michael Motson's fault. He had lied again. Josephine realised that. He had seen her and panicked. Done it once and now history was repeating itself. Michael had not been going to any hospital. He wasn't hurt. He was running away again, hence the fabrications about Elsie Briggs' despicable son. It had been a ploy to unnerve her, unbalance her. It had worked because he was gone, and she was alone again.

Josephine reached the centre of the village. It was quiet. The only business open was the fish and chip shop. Two females wearing identical blue uniforms stood propping up the counter. They were too busy gossiping to see the lone walker. A Land Rover trundled past Josephine. It slowed, then stopped and Josephine imagined the occupants were calling at the fast-food premises. She was wrong. When Josephine reached the vehicle the passenger-window was wound down and a thick-set man in his late twenties stuck his head out of the open window.

"Excuse me, love," said Alex Heslop, "I need directions."

Josephine Brooks smiled. The stranger had beautiful manners unlike most of the locals who could barely string a sentence together.

"Ask away, young man," she said. Her words were slurred, soft.

"Moore Terrace?"

Josephine blanched. The name of the council street made her cringe. She was alert for the first time in ages.

"Are you okay, love?" asked the Middlesbrough bouncer.

She recovered, cleared her throat and pointed ahead. "That's Moore Terrace. It's behind the nursing home." Josephine Brooks grimaced. "They're council houses," she added contemptuously.

The female driver looked quizzically at the pedestrian. Dottie Baxter nudged her passenger to enquire further.

Alex Heslop said, "You couldn't help me? I'm looking for someone who lives in the village. His name is Briggs?"

A groan left the open mouth of Josephine Brooks. She seemed captivated by the name. Mesmerised.

Dottie Baxter leaned across the man, "Honey, are you alright?"

Josephine could only glower at the pair.

Dottie and Alex exchanged glances.

"Whadya think, Dorothy?" asked Heslop. "Ask someone else?"

"Put her in the picture, Alex," replied Dottie. She straightened up and wound down her window. She was tired. It had been a long journey.

Alex Heslop tried again, "Johnny Briggs?"

"Thirty one," whispered Josephine Brooks. She was visibly wilting. "I know that for a fact."

A double-decker trundled to a stop on the opposite of the road and half a dozen people began to climb on board. John Briggs stared out of the upstairs window and saw Josephine Brooks in discussion with the occupants of a Land Rover. The nearside window of the vehicle was wound down and the female driver leaned out of the open window and began adjusting the wing-mirror. Her dark tousled mane fell over slim shoulders and jewellery sparkled from her neck and her wrist. She glanced absently at the bus and for the briefest of moments their eyes locked. The woman was beautiful. Suddenly Josephine Brooks started shouting and the female disappeared inside the cab. John pressed his face against the window as the rant continued. He was enthralled.

"Thirty one!" shrieked the demented Josephine. "Thirty one!"

John paled. He knew something was wrong. It was the woman, the driver of the off-road vehicle! He recognised her. He had seen a photograph of her. But where? He suddenly remembered. It was at Medomsley Detention centre. In Simon Baxter's room! The woman was Baxter's sister!

"Thirty one!" screamed Josephine. "He lives at thirty one!"

As the Land Rover screeched away, John scrambled from his seat, ran down the stairs and jumped from the stationery bus. His mind was in turmoil. Baxter's cronies were heading for his parent's home. They were seeking revenge. His mother had been hurt once because of him and it wasn't going to happen again. John Briggs would stop them, or die trying. He sprinted along the street.

As the big car skidded into the side street a tall figure burst on to the scene. It was Delbert Hancock; he had seen

John running for home and was determined to get him. He darted across the road, his deranged mind so intent on revenge he did not see the car until it was too late. Delbert screamed as Dottie Baxter jammed on the brakes. The sound of the impact was nauseating. Delbert Hancock was thrown into the air. He was dead before he hit the road.

Dottie Baxter acted instinctively. Knowing she had to put distance between herself and the accident she rammed the car into reverse and shot into the main road. Both Dottie and Alex Heslop were distracted by the figure that ran at the car. John Briggs was almost abreast of the Land Rover when he spotted the refuse truck bearing down on them. He dived for cover. The occupants of the car were not so fortunate. The vehicle was rammed across the road by the council wagon into the path of a brand new Eddie Stobart juggernaut. The Land Rover was demolished. One of the occupants died within hours, the other was seriously injured.

The carnage brought traffic to a standstill; residents emerged in their droves to aid the wailing, demented victims. In the distance an approaching siren could be heard. News of the pandemonium was spreading fast.

It took minutes for the lives of four people to change forever. Delbert Hancock died immediately. Alex Heslop, gravely injured, lingered for a short time before his broken body succumbed to the horrific wounds. Dottie Baxter was trapped for hours under swathes of twisted metal. Her right foot had been ripped off at the ankle by the force of the impact, her left leg was so badly mangled it had to be amputated below the knee. Johnny Briggs was the lucky one. He survived virtually unscathed. Bedraggled and bruised, he ran from the carnage, his family's safety paramount in his thoughts.

**

CHAPTER TWENTY EIGHT

The small East Durham resort of Seaton Carew was hidden under rolling blankets of gossamer clouds. The air was warm with promise as the hidden sun bore and burned endlessly at the clinging sea-fret. Near to the shore stood the long stretch of shops and outlets catering for tourists; cafés, restaurants and take-away stores, the amusement-arcades, the gift-shops, the miniature theme-park with its roundabouts, slides and side-shows were all jammed packed with joyful visitors. Folks wandered aimlessly between shore and shop with ice-cream, candy-floss and cake enjoying the day. Ice-cream vans played loud, incessant tunes as they plied for trade. Impatient drivers added to the melée and sounded horns as they fought for roadside parking. Day- trippers cranked up transistors ad sightseers shouted and laughed. A garish melody of sounds drifted across golden sands and rolling surf as the make-believe paradise was jarred with the sights and sounds of summer.

The beach was teeming with crowds of holiday-makers, the sea swamped with hordes of excitable children running into the foam, paddling, swimming, running frantically as if the day was their last. There was a feeling of contented, blissful mayhem on a beautiful July day. Suddenly, magically, the clouds fractured and broke open and giant strobes of dazzling sunlight scorched across the sands.

The young couple sat away from the water's edge, close to the esplanade and shaded from the occasional burst of breeze. They lounged on the deck-chairs, sometimes looking towards the ocean at their two boys who frolicked and chased one another, occasionally glancing at one another as if preparing themselves for some waiting calamity. Finally the youth spoke to the girl, his tone humble and soft as he eased forward on the seat.

John Briggs said, "The last time I was here was in the winter. Can you remember all the snow?"

"Do we have to talk about bad times, Johnny?" replied Iris guardedly. She focused on the sea shore feigning vigilance, "Who needs it?"

"Suppose you're right."

"We've a lot to be grateful for," said Iris, determined to concentrate on the present. "I still can't believe Kenny Wilkinson offered to sell back the business."

"He thought it was too much trouble. Customers were always asking for credit. Then the coal-wagon needed repairing. It was nothing, a blocked carburetor, fixed in a minute. Kenny said he didn't like being a boss, would rather work for me than his miserable father."

"Any news on Uncle Buff?"

"Hastings. Ma made a joke about it, said he'd start the next battle."

Iris, never the scholar, gave a quizzical look before moving the conversation smartly along. "I'm pleased about your mother. Her nose is as good as new."

"Ma gets her dentures next week, then she'll look the part."

"The coming court-case, John," said Iris, apprehension written all over her face. "Are you still okay with it?"

"Yes. The police couldn't get me to change my story. I told them I've never seen Uncle Micky in years, and the first time I met Michael Milson was at Norah Flannigan's boarding-house."

"It was pure luck when the police missed the photograph of your mother and Buff when they searched the car."

"Even better when Lenny found it in the yard!"

"At least they found the gun!"

"Did I say Lenny Jobson was sharing lodgings with Buff?"

Iris nodded.

John reminisced, "Simon Baxter dead … Del Hancock too." He shook his head resignedly. "Hard to believe what's happened."

"Any news on that woman, Baxter's sister?"

"Hospital still."

"I think I'd rather be dead than end up like her."

John shrugged his shoulders, "She's alive," he said.

Iris nodded. She closed her eyes and tried to relax. John was edgy and could not settle. The silence bothered him. He stood for a brief moment and reconnoitered the beach-area. The boys were playing close to the shore. The pair looked happy. He squatted on the hired deck-chair and glanced at Iris. She appeared peaceful. John grimaced, his wife looked contented, his sons were in high spirits and he wanted to feel the same. Wondered if he dared approach the subject again. Despite numerous attempts it had always ended in tears and tantrums. The topic was taboo, anathema to Iris. Despite the many rebuffs, John refused to acquiesce. There were still many unanswered questions that needed answers. He wanted closure and the only way to overcome the demons was to face them.

John blurted out, "Can we talk, Iris?"

"Please, Johnny, don't," she replied poignantly. Iris sat up and faced her husband. Her eyes mirrored despair. A faint hue covered her features. "Let it go, please," she whispered.

"Let me talk, Iris."

"I don't want to," she pleaded. "We've said it all before."

Iris rested elbows on the deck-chair and eased her head on to the open cupped palms. She closed her eyes, wanting it over, tired of the inquisition and weary with the denials. There had been weeks, months, of incessant accusations from John and ready-made answers from her. Despite umpteen contradictions and snubs Iris had not stemmed the flow of anguish questions from her husband. *'Ask them, John,'* she had cried in desperation. *'Ask Thelma and Tammy. They'll tell you that Maxi Stubbs was interested, and yes, before you ask, I enjoyed the attention and flattery, who wouldn't? You were locked up for a year! Of course my head was turned when Maxi made his pitch, but I swear I didn't go out with him!'* The stakes were high; her marriage was on the line, so she continued with the make-believe. There was no other way to fight her corner. *'Why don't you go see Maxi Stubbs! He isn't going to lie, he's too frightened of you. Go on, John, ask Maxi! He'll tell you the same rubbish he mouthed at the police-station. It was over, the chasing was over. That's all he said!'*

"You never let me finish, Iris," the man's voice almost a whisper. "It always ends in arguments."

"Always will!"

"Then let *me* talk and you listen" begged the youth. "Don't answer... listen to me!"

"No!"

Silence engulfed the couple as they suddenly looked at one another. The crowded beach, the noise, the frolicking, the laughter, all seemed to dim and disappear as their eyes locked for an instant.

Suddenly, unexpectedly, the woman's resolve cracked. She could not continue with the deceit for a moment longer. Iris looked at her husband, her features red with anticipation, her eyes glazed with fear. She was exhausted. Spent. It was time to open her heart and finish with the ludicrous charade. It was time to speak the truth.

"I'll tell you," she said softly, grudgingly.

The shock registered on John's face.

"What do you want to know?" she said almost inaudibly.

John cleared his throat. He was shaking. His words were hesitant, stammered, from the heart. "The last time I was here it was snowing. We'd had an awful row and I drove the wagon close to the shore. I stayed here for hours. Remember Iris. It was winter. Snowing." He took a deep breath, "I knew then that Frank wasn't mine ..."

"I remember the snow," Iris interrupted. She nodded blankly. "When you came home we stayed up all night and made friends." Her reply was whispered, heart-wrenching.

"All night."

"I made a vow then, John." Iris's voice cracked with emotion and tears welled in her eyes. "I prayed to God... said if he gave me another chance with you ..." Her lips trembled, her head lowered and she began to sob. Moments past before she could continue the confession, "I asked God to give me one more chance to prove that I loved you." Her voice faltered and broke. "I made a mistake, Johnny, the biggest mistake of my life!" Iris began to cry, "I'm sorry, it'll never happen again. I love you! Thought if you found out you'd leave me!" Her head lifted. Her eyes were wet and her nose ran. "Can't live without you, John, that's why I lied! I didn't want to lose you!"

John fought the tide of sentiment but couldn't stem the flow of tears. He stood and instinctively pulled Iris close. His arms wrapped around her as his body shuddered with emotion. The poison of jealousy, the inner rage that had held him back, was suddenly gone. The shawl of love enveloped him and drove away all self-doubt. Overwhelmed with the emotion of intimacy, he kissed Iris, told her how much he cared for her, and begged for forgiveness. In that instant John

Briggs knew he needed Iris, realised he couldn't live without her. Out of the blue, the realization of his own imperfections swamped him with a terrible shame. It was his turn to confess.

He prized himself from Iris.

"It wasn't your fault, Iris," he cried. "I was to blame! All those times I hurt you...."

"Don't John!" she interrupted.

"It's true," he said. "I pushed you away!"

"Stop it, please!"

He was whimpering now. Nothing else mattered. He needed to unburden, to speak the truth, to free the shackles of past lies.

"I've been so bad, let me talk..."

"No, John!" interrupted the girl. "What's done is done!" She pulled at his hair, shaking and gripping it, her fingers prizing and tugging.

The youth stopped crying. He tried to loosen her grip.

"What do you want to do, John?"

Tangled tight in love, souls locked, tears falling, nose to nose her fingers entwined in his sparse locks.

"I'll do anything, John!"

"Would you let go of my hair, Iris!"

"Talk to me!"

"I'd like some hair left, Iris!" He tried to laugh, "There's not much left!"

"Love you if you were bald, Johnny Briggs." She kissed him hard on the lips, bit him with a passion, rocked him, and squeezed him. Suddenly Iris pulled away and stared at him, her voice soft again, "What about Frank, he's my baby!"

He kissed Iris. His hands caressed and held her.

"Forgive me, John, please?"

"I do!"

"And Frank?"

Somehow it didn't matter anymore, Eddie and Frank were brothers. He was their father and he loved them.

"John, talk to me!"

"I have two sons," he whispered. "I love them both. Always have!"

They clung to one another, oblivious to the staring eyes of the people close by. Didn't care about anyone else. They had each other. They had their sons.

Eddie Briggs, his sand-bucket filled with salt water, watched in amazement as his parents locked in another embrace. He nudged his kid brother, "Look, Frank!" he said loudly, "Mum and Dad!"

Young Frank looked disinterested. He smiled grudgingly, more interested in the large sea-shell in his possession.

The oldest lad, intelligent and mature beyond his years, said solemnly, "That's what you do to make babies."

Frank pulled his face, too young to understand. He threw the shell in to the water and looked at his big brother.

"That's the truth! Aimee Tuttle told me," answered the older boy. "And she's eight years old!"

"Eddie," said Frank. There was something more urgent gnawing for attention. "Want a pee!"

"Come on," said Eddie. He waded into the water followed by his brother. Waist deep, he said, "Piss away, Frank. No one will know."

"Where?"

"In the water, stupid!"

"Scared, Eddie!" Frank looked at this brother, "Mom'll shout!"

"Don't be stupid!"

"Got to pee, Eddie!"

"Them do it! Everybody does it in the sea!"

Frank started to fumble with his swimming trunks, desperation overcoming his fear.

Eddie snapped, "Leave your trunks on!"

"Why for?" said a bewildered Frank.

"Just do it!" said Eddie.

"Hold my hand, Eddie!"

"Just piss, Frank!"

The youngest boy sighed anxiously. He crossed his arms, closed his eyes and concentrated. As Frank relaxed a yellow smudge washed about his midriff. He opened his eyes and grinned mischievously.

The oldest boy suddenly bolted to the shore, leaving his brother stranded.

"Ma!" he shouted at the top of his voice. "Our Frank is pissing his pants!"

"Mom!" screamed the distraught youngster. "Dad!" yelled Frank. He scattered from the water, crimson with embarrassment.

**

Hovis Brown

Set in the North East in the early Eighties, Jackie 'Hovis' Brown, a virtual giant of a man, is clinging to the gutter of life. A bully and an enforcer, he was imprisoned for blindly obeying the woman he loved, Anna Belling, then set free to slide into a life of crime, longing to find a true love.

Anna was abused from the age of four and grew up a cold and calculating woman. Manipulating and damaging all who come under her spell. A conniving and cunning vixen who will stop at nothing in her pursuit of personal gain.

Ryan Dimonti – criminal and drug lord. Uses people like Jackie Brown to inflict terror and loyalty in his domain. Cruel and calculating, just like Anna Belling who wins a way into his heart.

The three are thrown together in their daily lives where each one's desires delivers a cruel twist of fate.

ISBN: 978.1.903172.91.9

The Hillbillies

The year is 1990. The collieries are in their final throes. The Hill Family: Adam, Rebecca and son Charlie are all battling their own private demons; surviving – existing – in the wild and wonderful North-East of England.

Adam and Rebecca, both alcoholics, go through the motions of daily life while one still festers over a long-ago broken romance and the other is ready to hit the self-destruct button because of his emotional, erratic spouse.

Charlie Hill, out of control in his final year at school is a bully, a thief and an arsonist who works on a regular basis for a local gangster. Upon leaving school he manages to secure employment at the local colliery like his Dad, even though the industry is dead on its feet.

Some turbulent times lie ahead for the whole family culminating in an unreliable confessional that threatens to destroy all three lives.

ISBN: 978.1.903172.89.6

Street Life

Late fifties, North-East England and chaos in the Connelly Family as womanizing husband, George, abandons wife and children and disappears with his newest love. Vera reluctantly vacates her colliery home and moves to nearby Easington Village, finding shelter with her widowed mother and tries to rebuild her shattered life.

Along the way she becomes involved with the monied Stoker family – Evelyn and Elmore Stoker. One industrious, the other a bounder and a parasite; one an Adonis, the other a stammering, under-sized weakling. On the rebound and manipulated by her devious mother, Vera falls for the tall, gorgeous charmer, Elmore, and starts to learn all about the nefarious Stoker secrets.

Vera's boys: Joe, 11 years old, headstrong, bursting with mettle and grit and Jack, 5 years old, shy, nervous, relying on his brother for survival. Bravely coping with the turmoil and stress of moving home and battle in a different environment: a new school, new friends and without a father's love to support them.

ISBN: 978.1.906542.05.4

Peter Harrison's fourth novel is set in the North-East of England.

Peter has always lived in this area and takes inspiration from the places and people around him.

He spends his time researching and writing novels. He is now working on future novels.